A FURRY FAUX PAW

JESSICA KARA

PAGE STREET
PUBLISHING CO.

PAGE STREET
PUBLISHING CO.

Copyright © 2022 Jessica Kara

First published in 2022 by
Page Street Publishing Co.
27 Congress Street, Suite 1511
Salem, MA 01970
www.pagestreetpublishing.com

Distributed by Macmillan, sales in Canada by The Canadian Manda Group.

26 25 24 23 22   1 2 3 4 5

ISBN-13: 978-1-64567-526-6
ISBN-10: 1-64567-526-2

Library of Congress Control Number: 2021946663

Cover and book design by Laura Benton for Page Street Publishing Co.
Cover texture © Shutterstock

Printed and bound in the United States

Page Street Publishing protects our planet by donating to nonprofits like The Trustees, which focuses on local land conservation.

THIS BOOK IS DEDICATED TO THE
FURRY COMMUNITY

I SLAP THE MAILBOX SHUT.

Empty.

Darn it, darn it. Darn it.

In my head, Mauve's tail twitches. Irritated. I should have an actual tail by now, but it hasn't arrived. I guess it doesn't really matter, though, because I can't wear my tail or ears for graduation. The school was quite clear about that in the pearly note with our instructions.

I drum my fingers along the top of the mailbox painted with tulips and posies and minuscule bluebirds. I remember the day we worked on it, Mom and I, back when we still did stuff together. I shoulder my backpack and stomp my skateboard to flip it up into my hand. Last day of school, check. Graduation is in two days.

Still buzzing from the sugar high from our last-day-of-class party, I step up the short sidewalk to my house, checking the lawn for dandelions. It's cut. Weeds pulled. Good. The kid at the end of the block is keeping up his promise. I have to remember to pay him.

One window is open, and the sour reek of rotting food and mold drifts from inside.

Ugh.

Ugh.

"Mom," I mutter, my chest tightening as my mood sinks. On this day, this launch into adulthood, or at least something new, I should feel a hundred feet tall, shouldn't I?

I'd really been counting on the tail arriving. A little early birthday and graduation present from me to myself. I trudge up the three concrete steps to the porch littered with cigarette butts. Mom isn't allowed to smoke in the house. No, literally—it's not my rule. The fire marshal *suggested* we not have any open flame in the house, and now our insurance backs that up. That was a year ago, the last time the city paid a visit.

At least we've managed to keep the yard in check, which keeps the neighbors from calling in complaints. I scuff the butts off the step with a toe and budge the door open just enough to slide inside.

"Mom!" Easing the door shut causes a waterfall of papers to cascade down from the heap behind the door and flood around my shins. Fresh bundles of free ads slide down. You'd think it would all blend together, but I can always tell what's new.

Mom must have grabbed them off the porch the second someone tossed them there so it looks like people actually live here.

Correction—so it looks like the people who live here actually *care*.

"Mom! Two-foot entryway remember?"

"There's two feet!" Her voice floats back, unconcerned.

"There's . . . nothing," I grunt, shoving boxes and totes and one rogue pile of laundry (unclear if it's dirty or clean, and I don't want to sniff it) as tight to the wall as I can. From the direction of her call, Mom must be in her office. Not surprising. I shove the papers back up into a rough heap, prop my skateboard by the door, and negotiate my way forward.

It takes a bit of oozing to pass the second barricade—a towering wall of bank boxes marked Recycle.

"You got some mail!" Mom calls, "and I left a little something in the kitchen for you."

My heart picks up. She actually ventured outside to get the mail! I hope she didn't get a sunburn.

The sound of typing drifts from her office. *Tickity-tickity-tickity.* She's working. Or whatever. Taking surveys. She thinks she pays the mortgage with a strict schedule of surveys, Google affiliating, ninety-nine cent ebooks on organization, and other things like that. Couponing.

But I have mail. And "a little something" in the kitchen. Oh God, I hope she didn't try to make food in that kitchen. Walls of junk and sticky countertops and mouse poop aside, one rogue flame from the gas stove and that would be it. I take the fire marshal more seriously than Mom does.

Actually, I take most things more seriously than Mom does, except when she's weird and zeroes in on weird things and takes them *very* seriously.

After bending around the maze of totes marked Sort, and clambering through the lake of clothing (Clean & Sort) and a menagerie of lampshades (Sell) in the living room, I reach the kitchen. The mail is stacked with incongruous tidiness on top of a pile of crusty plates that have been there since the last time I had access to the sink. The scent of rotten lettuce washes over me and I swallow hard, resisting the urge to hack up an imaginary hairball. It's not so much the smell of rotten lettuce as knowing that whatever is causing the smell is most likely *not* rotten lettuce.

My practiced solution is to cock my jaw and breathe purposefully through my mouth so the smell is less. Not so for Mauve, who senses rottenness more sharply when we breathe across her scent glands. She retreats, leaving me alone to my dull human senses. I don't blame her.

A single, straining rubber band holds together the wad of mail. A giant, padded manila envelope is squashed against the myriad of catalogs and bills stamped with intimidating red or black letters.

YOU'RE PRE-QUALIFIED!

SECOND NOTICE

FINAL

PAST DUE

Only the manila envelope is addressed to me. The return address, "Haute Creatoure," makes me squeak with excitement. Mauve springs back to life in my heart, poised.

Mom calls from her office. "Wait, wait, I want to see you open it! Bring it in here!"

I freeze, one hand poised to tug the rubber band off the mail. Mauve's tail flicks. Mom doesn't even know about my package or what it should be. Does she?

Then I see the thing. Next to the bundle of mail sits a suspiciously gift-wrapped, squarish item adorned with a crumpled bow, and I realize she's talking about that.

Oh.

Oh.

It's box-shaped, the length of my forearm by ten inches by about three inches deep, and I cannot comprehend what Mom might've gotten me (and spent money on) that she would actually bother to wrap. Eyeing the plaid wrapping paper, my mind zooms through the house. From my mental inventory, I know that she got the bow and the paper from Christmas Box #12, although both are innocuous, not overtly Christmasy, shades of green.

Green. Effing *green.* For my birthday, my graduation, she couldn't even be bothered to find something vaguely pink?

I guess it doesn't matter.

"Mae? Did you find it?"

"Yeah. I'll bring it into the office! Just a sec . . . hey, the water bill's due."

Catlike, I rise to my toes, peering around the kitchen for something sharp to open my package. The bitter irony is that we have fifty pairs of scissors, but what you need never floats to the top.

Mom's voice cracks like a whip. "They know I don't get my check until the fifteenth. They know, don't worry, they won't shut it off. They never do."

"Mmkay."

Rather than wade through the kitchen again, I set my teeth to the paper. Between that and my sharpened, fuchsia nails, the package doesn't have a chance. A quick brush of my hand inside the package rewards me with the touch of cotton-soft fur.

"Eeeeee," I whisper.

You always read the card before you open the gift. Or you should, even though this was a commission and not a gift. That way, you can draw it out, read the note, build your anticipation.

Anyway, there's a note written in impossibly gorgeous calligraphy, and it makes it more like Christmas.

Dearest Mauve—

"Maeve! Bring your present in here!"

"Just a sec!"

So sorry for the delay with your order. We have also included—

"And can you bring my East-West Trading catalog too?"

I let out a slow breath then inhale through my mouth. My therapist always playfully reminded me that breathing is helpful, and I follow an Insta with little exercises.

"Yeah. Just a sec, okay."

a belt clip and string animation attachment—no charge. Happy early birthday!

"Eee!" I purr. Yep, I purr. Not the real way a cat purrs, of course. I don't have the proper biological equipment, but I have perfected a warm, thrumming droll with a hum in my chest and a rolling tongue.

You can see the string if you look for it, but it isn't too obvious in a photo or video (you might 'shop it out) or from a distance. Looking forward to pics and still working on that perfect paw design for you.

All the Best,

Haute Creatoure

PS FURLYMPIA COMING UP PLS COME kthxbye

The elegant calligraphy makes the silly and informal PS extra amazing. It makes me laugh, light, even though I know I won't be able to go to the furcon. It's all everyone's talking about on Twitter. In my chest, Mauve bounces like a kitten.

Mauve is my fursona since forever ago. Okay, ever since I

was thirteen, when I was allowed to get my own online accounts and join the art communities and post my artwork, and I decided to really go as myself—my *real* self. Not short, soft, plain-eyed, plain-haired, lisping Maeve, but the me inside. The smart, quick, brave, spunky me who isn't afraid to rejoice about uncool colors or be nerdy about really amazing animal facts and senses—frankly, superpowers—and wishes I could be a little something extra. So I put myself out there—myself with a little something extra.

And MauveCat was born (color plus animal isn't exactly original, but I was a wee babe).

She's fun, she laughs, she has mystical powers, and she's popular.

She's also an anthropomorphic cat.

(Anthropomorphic: *adjective. 1.* relating to or characterized by anthropomorphism; having human characteristics.)

Well, she's sometimes other things, but almost always a cat, and I'll leave it at that for now because I know it's a lot for some people to take in. Everyone is different about their fursona. Maybe it's just an online personality, or maybe it represents everything they wish they could be, or maybe they just really love birds, or maybe it's closer to them.

For me, it's closer.

Mauve lives under my skin. She's the brighter, more real version of me. Her eyes see everything I see and more in the dark. She hears more than I hear, and she notices different things—like the hindquarters of a dead mouse sticking out from under the fridge just now.

Ugh.

7

So there's me, and there's Mauve, and we're the same being, but since no one else can see her except when I'm online, I have to make the distinction between us so I don't have to see a therapist anymore (although she was helpful about divorce stuff). Thank God my parents finally accepted the online persona—*fursona*—explanation. I pass my classes, I don't drink, I don't smoke, and "the boys" (as Mom calls them as if we live in the '50s) leave me alone and I leave them alone. Actually, I leave everyone alone in that sense. But at this juncture, I don't know if it's because the thought of romance is exhausting or because I'm surrounded by too much stuff and Mom is exhausting, or because . . . well, Jade asked me if I'm ace, once. I've Googled stuff, and maybe? I like looking at people and the idea of having someone to laugh and cuddle with and call. A special someone. Maybe just a friend.

But the furry community is a good place to find people to talk to about that when I have the energy to.

So really, what's Mom got to complain about?

And yes, I know Mauve isn't "real" (except she is), and my parents' divorce didn't cause me to form a separate personality.

If you think about it, everyone has a separate personality. There's public you, smiling, polite, restrained—or funny, loud, and popular. And there's inside you. Realer you. Truer you. Thoughtful—or maybe rude and snarky. Either way, it's the one you hold back. It's the one you only let certain other people see. It's the one that's harder to be because it's *real*, and if someone doesn't like the real you, it hurts. It's painful and dangerous, and we all have that one inside us.

My inside me just happens to be a bipedal, mauve-colored

Scottish Fold who can, if circumstances require, grow pixie wings and become very small and feral and four-legged. And everyone loves her.

Sheer joy washes over me when I slip Haute's creation out of the envelope—a miracle of fluffy, prismatic pink and ghostly lavender fur. The tail hangs just past my knees, perfectly weighted with bouncy, swinging liveliness. I tuck the coiled string away into a brilliant little pouch at the base for now and clip the tail to my jeans.

"Maeve!" Mom's voice has lost its sweetness. Maybe she thinks I'm finally lost in the mercurial quicksand of the kitchen.

"Coming!" As Mauve springs to life again, I scoop up the mail and the present from Mom, feeling optimistic. I'm almost eighteen *and* graduating, so maybe she'll surprise me with something I actually want or need.

That sounds ungrateful, but I know her and this is her thing. She doesn't need an occasion to buy stuff. She buys herself stuff she doesn't need, and she buys me stuff I don't need and don't want and have to secretly cycle out again like a baggage conveyor so my room doesn't end up looking like . . . every other room in the house. There are eight thousand pounds of Stuff in this house, and only about ten pounds of it is mine. But it takes constant vigilance.

So I traverse through the nasty kitchen, mail and gift underarm.

A short hall, made narrow by a gauntlet of broken picture frames (Fix) and boxes of family photos (Frame), leads to Mom's office. Predictably, she's in front of her ancient desktop, clicking away. A sour, rank smell immediately wrinkles my nose and Mauve's, and I almost hiss.

"Were you smoking in here?"

"No. That's all old." Mom waves a hand. "It doesn't go away. I don't even smell it anymore."

"Hey." I edge along the trail between shoulder-high clothes (Try on, Sort) and hip-high boxes (Storage) and hold out the mail. "I thought I'd clean the kitchen today." Absently, my fingers curl in the green bow of my gift.

Mom remains focused on the survey. "What's this weekend? You're not planning to have people over?"

For a moment, I draw a pristine blank. People? Here? Is she joking? "I just thought I'd do some cleaning."

"Just a second sweetie." My mother, tall and gangly with severely short, pale hair, makes me look like I was adopted. Her diet of soda and power bars and sedentary lifestyle has left her wasted, not overweight.

I'm more like my dad—small, comfy and compact, plain hair, plain eyes—and I'm still not convinced Mom and I are related, except we're both crafty.

And yes, I did say *plain hair*. And Dad says my eyes are hazel, but *his* eyes are hazel and mine are really just eye-colored.

But Mauve is a cozy, warm pink and fuchsia striped with shining amethyst eyes—my glitter and magic and joy.

Mom has completed a complicated, timed question, and answers me at last about the cleaning. "Sure, but wait until I can help. There are things I need to save."

Defeat coils in my stomach. Like the smoking, that's a lie. If it's up to her, we would never get any cleaning done. Not with her telling me not to throw away the empty mayonnaise jars and insisting food that expired three years ago is fine to eat. Because of the smoking, she can't smell anymore—the first line of defense in a kitchen like ours.

Mom clicks the last answer on her survey and swivels the creaking office chair to take the bundle of mail. My stomach snarls. Crusty plates, dead mice, and buzzing flies come to mind. Mauve's ears flick back with a brilliant idea. "How about pizza for dinner?"

Mom's face hardens, her pale cheeks starved for sun, turning to stone. "It's not in the budget."

I have no idea what mysterious budget my mother operates off of, except that it prioritizes clearance catalog and thrift store items and ranks things like food and toilet paper at the bottom with the electric bill. "It's still good" is the family motto. *Est Etiam Bonum.*

"My treat." I fidget with the tail, flicking it, rocking to my toes.

Mom's mouth twitches, but now it's the principle of the thing: who's going to win? It's our little game, I guess. Family bonding— it's exhausting. "But pizza, again? You can eat this way now, but keep it up and you'll pack on the freshman fifty, and then you'll look like your father."

One, I already look like my father; and two, it's the freshman fifteen. I don't say that either, of course. But I can change tactics, too. I wave one of the red-stamped envelopes to remind Mom of her precarious sense of judgment. "Do you want me to pay the water bill?"

If I had a real tail, it would be lashing.

Mom levels a look at me that makes *my* look combust into ashes on the floor. "I said I would handle it next week. You don't need to worry about that stuff."

Except I do. The water was cut off once before, and that's when

I discovered that leaving the house early and showering at school was like going to a day spa every morning. No cleaning empty plastic jars and stepladders out of the tub, or just rinsing my pits and crotch in the sink and hoping the mold smell wasn't clinging to my clothes. I learned to stash spare outfits in my locker with a lavender air freshener because smelling weird is better than smelling bad.

"Okay, fine, pay the water bill. But for dinner, I'm just going to order the pizza anyway, and we both know it." But somehow I want her blessing, and somehow she just can't give it.

She points at the tail. "What's that?"

I remove my hand from the tail, and it drops behind my legs again. "It's a tail."

"Thank you for the clarification. Why are you wearing it?"

"It's a costume piece. For my photos." She knows about my Instagram, but I can't tell her the real reason behind the photos is that I would rather be a cat than a person.

"How much was it?"

Now I'm ready to spring from the room. Most people understand the price of hand-made pieces, but I don't want to tell my mother. Any price at all would be too expensive for her to understand. As it was, between the quality of hand-brushed fluff and the custom color airbrushing and hand-painted stripes, this tail ran about $75, plus shipping, and Haute gave me a killer deal on it, taking some of the price off in exchange for some art.

"Don't worry about it, Mom."

Mom stands up as a flush darkens her face again and slams the bundle of mail onto her desk. This triggers an avalanche of papers and half-full soda cans, which I have to spin away from like a weird ballet dancer. But she just ignores it as papers slide to the floor and sludgy soda trickles onto them. "Did your father buy it? Is he buying you more of this pink crap instead of paying support?"

Crap?

"I bought it," I snarl and show her teeth. Sometimes the cat comes out. I can't help it. Mauve's fur bristles. Mom can't even appreciate the artistry of the tail. Just inside my skin, Mauve is hunching and hissing and slashing. I take a deep breath. "I saved up and did commissions and bought it. And Dad does pay support."

But instead of checks to Mom, he has an agreement with the courts that he directly pays half our mortgage, phone, and a grocery stipend redeemable only at the local mart, not cash. The internet is a carrot on a stick for me, entirely dependent on my grades. I don't even think Mom knows that. She probably thinks it's her God-given right. And even though Dad pays for it, she writes it off as a business expense because, somehow, she thinks she's paying for it.

Sometimes I notice the insanity of my life, like, in the corner of my eye. But most of the time, I maneuver around it like the mountains and valleys of junk in the house.

Hostility flickers in Mom's face when I mention Dad paying support, then dies. She's exhausted, probably hungry. I wonder if she's had anything but soda and granola bars to eat today. At least pizza will have some protein and carbs and good old-fashioned grease.

"Sweetie, it's a waste of money. You have college coming up." She reaches forward as if to touch the tail, but I don't move because I know she's not actually close enough. And how awkward would it be to pull away from her right now? She sighs, hand dropping to her lap. "This was fun for you in high school, but that's enough. What are you going to do with this cat stuff then?"

Stuff? My lifeline to my inner self, my friends, my social circle, my art—*stuff*? I clamp down against making that sound she hates, the *ch!* from between my teeth.

She's one to talk about stuff.

"The . . . the same thing I've always done? It's part of me, Mom. It's not just a hobby—it's fun. It inspires my art. It's a community, okay? It's never interfered with grades or work, and it's not going to when I'm twenty or thirty."

This time, I'm smart enough to cap the age and not remind her that there are people in the fandom who are fifty-plus. When I dropped that bomb the first time, she became positive it was exclusively a weird sex fetish and took away my laptop for a month. A *month*. I managed to bring her back around with the Disney argument—talking animals and all. Anthropomorphism is not all that outlandish. People just think you should grow out of it, and I don't know why.

Mickey Mouse is cool, but you draw your own original character and name her Misty Mouse and you're a perv.

But don't get me started.

Her energy shifts. I can feel it—I'm good with stuff like that. You have to be when your folks can go from zero to throwing things in under sixty. Not throwing things at me. It was never like that. But you know—get angry enough to throw something, or break it, or loose a primal scream. That sort of thing. I've seen it all. I'm very sensitive to the weather patterns in this house. We just missed a hurricane.

Mom pats her knees decisively. "Yes. Your art. Open the present."

I accept the offered escape route.

She looks eagerly at the box as if it were her present and not mine. I try to catch up to her emotional state by leaving mine behind. Right—we're happy now. On with the show.

To make Mom laugh, I make a quick show of sniffing the box, tapping it, and shaking gently. Something tiny rattles inside and alarm pricks me. Did I just break something? But she shakes her head—not fragile.

I consider the size of the box and wonder.

"It's for when you go to college," she says. "If you get into that art institute. You always talk about—"

"Oh, Mom, no way . . ." Did she get me a tablet? Was she actually paying attention when I whined about my nonexistent digital art career? I slash the paper (pleased it almost looks like cat claws) and peel it back, heart surging to my throat.

Behind the shredded paper, an illustration of colored pencils, markers, and a drawn vase of flowers greets me. Not a Wacom. Not even a knock-off. Slowing down, I peel the rest of the green wrapping away to reveal an art kit—you know, the kind you get your ten-year-old who's still tracing fan art from their favorite anime.

My throat clamps and my heart quickens to a firm thump. The ridiculous urge to fan myself like a fainting Southern belle swamps me. I can't breathe. And because of an art kit.

But really? This is my eighteenth-slash-graduation present.

Really?

Really.

I think about the surprise party I put together for her fortieth—*I* put together—in a local park, cobbling up guests from her estranged family out east (my family, I guess), from the grocery store, the post office, the guys at the A&W stand. They all came. They came, brought gifts and food. Mom was so thrilled she cried. I think they came more for me than for Mom, but come on. I put in a little effort. I thought it would be a turning point, but I guess not.

"What do you think? You don't already have one, do you?"

No, I don't have one.

I have almost ten. Mom and my out-of-touch aunts in eastern Washington (might as well be Jupiter) keep getting them for my birthday. They're somewhere in the Stuff.

My nose scrunches and I manage a breath. Don't lose it. Don't effing lose it.

My knuckles are whitening around the box. I let Mauve take over, smooth and purring and cool—neutral. Cats don't care; cats don't need anything from anyone. Mauve can play it off as being overwhelmed, but not too much, not over the top. She's perfect.

"Wow, Mom! This'll be great. Really great." I pat the box. "Oh, it even has oil pastels."

Cheap, crumbly, oil pastels. And markers. I haven't used markers in a decade. I'm a colored pencil artist. She doesn't even know that. Really? For twenty dollars she could have found me ten high-quality pencils . . . or one. Warmth pricks my eyes and I close them. One colorless blender would've shown she's been paying two seconds of attention to what I'm all about anymore. I open my eyes to see if she's buying what I'm selling.

Nope. She's reading me, reading my expression. Mauve shrinks back because we're failing.

Crap.

"I'm sorry," she says quietly. "I always see you working with pencils . . ."

God, I'm an ungrateful brat. What does Mom know about my art? Maybe I should've made a list of things I needed.

Mauve knows better.

Prissy, smart Mauve prowls back in forth in agitated circles, knowing my mom is a cheap, thoughtless gift giver. Mauve knows I've been talking about a tablet for two years, dog-earing catalog pages, leaving her browser windows open to cyber sales on the cheapest starter tablets known to man.

I would've rather had the twenty bucks in my pocket than this box of useless crap. I should've just bought one myself. Mom looks genuinely pleased with the gift but hurt and confused as to why I'm not more excited. I can't believe her head is so far in the sand to get me something like this.

Yet I feel like an ungrateful brat.

Days like this are when people who know about everything wonder why I don't leave—and I wonder how they did leave. Because I know Mom's hurt. She's been hurting ever since her own mother died, and I think the mountains of Stuff make her feel safe.

When you know why someone is hurt, why they act the way they do, it makes it harder to give up and walk away.

So I reassure her, pointing out things I like, kind of like you do with a five-year-old, until the pain leaves her face and is replaced by relief.

I'm really good at making Mom feel better. I have to be. I think I'm the only one who tries anymore.

"No, it's great, Mom, it's, yeah, I can definitely use all of this. I could practice with markers again. I like that it's got a couple sketching pencils, erasers, and a sharpener . . ."

"And you'll be able to re-use the box," she points out. As if I'd ever get away with giving anything away. To be fair, the box is the nicest thing about the gift. It's solid aluminum with cool locking clasps. I could put stickers on it. I probably will save it. Saving things is in my DNA, I guess.

"Thanks, Mom." My throat feels like a sudden onset of strep—raw, strained from sounding normal. The family throwing-things gene wells up and lashes through my arm, but I manage to hug the art case instead of hurling it across the room, then ease forward and hug Mom.

For a moment, I start to wonder where the happy-go-lucky me went (Jade tells me that no one says "happy-go-lucky" anymore, but he's one to talk). But that was me. I'm the good girl. No smoking, no drinking, no parties because I have no IRL friends; all my parties are online.

But I was happy—I'm the happy one. I should *be* happy. I have my mauve cat ears and my art and my roleplay and my inside jokes. Who cares about a birthday present that's off the mark?

I guess I do.

"So . . . pizza?" Holding the art case tightly, I start to back out of the room on cat toes to avoid the newly spilled papers and the soda cans and towers of clothes.

Mom shakes her head. "I don't know, sweetie. The budget's

tight right now. Find something in the fridge."

The mysterious budget. Good God. "There's nothing in the fridge, Mom. I swear to God." Weirdly, having evaded a Mom meltdown, I'm feeling better. More optimistic. It's the tail. I feel more like myself, but also itchy, or small, like I need to hide. I just need out of her office. "I'm getting pizza and paying for it."

My phone buzzes in my pocket.

"Maeve—"

"I'll hold anchovies off one side for you!" I blow her a kiss and twirl out of the room.

I THINK THE TAIL HAS increased my agility through sheer happiness. But it takes some maneuvering around and over the piles to make sure it doesn't get snagged.

Mom won't be able to follow or stop me from dialing the pizza place because the hall to my room requires hopping a stepladder to the top of a pile of old coats (Donate) and army-crawling about five feet between the top of the coats and the ceiling until you can slide down the other side along a sheer slope of debris.

Most of it isn't gross, not like the kitchen. It's just junk. It's just stuff; barnacles clinging to the Imperial Frigate Mom. I wonder when the ship will sink, but it hasn't yet. As long as she can prove to the city that she's working on it, and the neighbors don't complain, here we are. Nobody really helps hoarders, not like on those stupid shows. They only care if there are kids. It's part of the reason I stay, I guess, so it feels like people care about her. But it's only me.

I shove myself through the narrow open doorway to my room. I can't open the door all the way because it opens *out* to the hall, for fire safety, but I can't shut it either.

My little eight-by-ten space is mostly clear. I allow Mom two square feet in the corner for a few totes of keepsakes, but only if they have to do with the family. No brochures, no bills, no catalogs, no samples from the companies she surveys for, no porcelain crap bound for eBay someday.

Clothes overflow from my basket, but that's because I haven't yet broken trail to the washer and dryer for the weekend laundry. My desk is bare save for the laptop, my pencils, my lap-desk, and the Styrofoam head form that holds the cat ears that match my new tail. The futon with my beloved and disintegrating Totoro bedspread (custom printed seven years ago) remains in constant up-mode. I prefer stretching out on it couch-style. It feels more independent, as if I'm taking a nap in the middle of the night or that I'm Mauve just curling up on whatever, whenever.

Mini Christmas lights and a single lavender-shaded lamp turn my tiny corner into an oasis of year-round holiday cheer and pink happiness. There's nothing else. Desk, clothes, futon, lights, my closet with the bare minimum of clothing. I don't need anything— not the way Mom does. I eventually draped a tapestry (a gift from Jade) of wild fuchsia and black paisleys over Mom's stack of totes, and put the last remaining plushie from my childhood (Hello Kitty) on top, as a guardian.

Bzzt.

Bzzt.

Slipping my phone out of my pocket, I plop down on the bed to check the messages.

Dad: *Can't make graduation, kitten. Big seminar next week. So sorry. Call me. Should have a check today or tomorrow.*

There are also four or five messages from Jade on Twitter, wondering if I've gotten the tail yet and demanding pictures.

At least someone cares. I'll message him back, but first, pizza.

I call it in, instructing them to the side door where I've cleared enough of a path that anyone who looks in might imagine it's a normal household. Nothing to see here.

Next, Dad.

"Hey, honey!" At the sound of his chipper voice, way too chipper, my throat tightens. "Did you get my text? I have this business retreat—"

"You and Mom don't have to sit together."

"This has been scheduled for six months, honey."

"Graduation's been scheduled for like eighteen years." I hadn't realized how much I'd needed him to attend until now.

"I'm really sorry."

The scent of rain washes in suddenly from my window, almost brushing the mildew and mustiness away.

I try a new tactic on Dad. I hate using guilt, but it's the only thing that works. "Well, maybe I won't walk. Mom barely leaves the house, so she won't care, and they won't let me wear my ears. If you're not there, it's really not worth it."

"You have to walk, Maeve. It's a ritual. It gives you closure."

Dad is all about experiences and building character. Maybe he's afraid I'll end up like Mom, huddled in a room over my computer. "I don't need closure and I don't *have* to do anything. After next weekend I'm a legal adult. I'm practically a home caregiver for another grown-up adult human."

He pauses, the unspoken question tightening the miles between us. But I wait, making him ask it out loud. "How is your mom?"

"Fine. We're really starting to get things organized. And we haven't had a call from the neighbors or the city in a month. Some-one comes and mows the lawn."

I pay the kid from up the block to mow the lawn, but I say it like it just magically happens. I don't tell Dad because he'll get mad at Mom. And I don't tell Mom and she doesn't mention it. Maybe she thinks it's a new service from the city? Or just a nice neighbor? Sometimes I think she knows but can't face what all of it means, so she just accepts it. Like I accept tunneling through twenty years of Stuff to get to the bathroom every night, although sometimes I'm just not up for it and pee out the window instead. The flowers don't do well on this side of the house anyway.

This is me, maneuvering around the insanity.

I see lights from other houses, open windows and no shades drawn, because they don't have to worry about people seeing what's inside. Sometimes I wonder what that feels like.

"That's great honey," Dad finally says. "It's really great of you to help her."

Someone has to. Rain pitter-patters then falls in earnest.

"So, if you aren't coming for graduation, when will I see you?"

"This summer, for sure." He says that every summer. There's a pregnant pause. I stare out the window at the middle distance until he speaks again. "You know you can come to Tacoma any time."

"Yeah." My gaze slides to the door, behind which sits ten-thousand pounds of Stuff, weighing the house down, weighing Mom down, weighing me down, tugging at an invisible chain, anchoring us all. There is only so far I can go. "It's just tough."

"Mae—"

"Where's your business retreat?"

He huffs a sigh and I know where I get that habit from. He silently agrees to the subject change. "Oh, it's great, it's new—" His voice picks up in pitch and animation as he gushes about the Florida Keys, golfing, snorkeling, and finally getting out of Washington for a week. I wonder if he ever considered inviting me as a tagalong. I know he's allowed to. I like golf. Mauve likes golf (little balls flying everywhere). But nope. I have to walk for my graduation. Because *that* will be a more important memory than taking a boat from Islamorada with my Dad to fish for marlin (which he's waxing poetic about now) and trying to get some blondish sun going on my hair-colored hair.

I "mmm" and "wow," then build a pillow nest on the floor, and dig through the laundry for my rainy day hoodie. It has a jaw-dropping fan art of Totoro on it by my idol, an artist who goes by Sunspire. Totoro has a freakishly large grin that is full of both animal innocence and all the knowledge of the world. Next to him is my feral form—Mauve as a plump Scottish Fold with pixie wings.

It makes me happy every time I see it. Jade commissioned it for my 16th birthday to cheer me up after the big Social Services visit meltdown. I wear it every rainy day and plan to be buried in it someday.

Sticking my arms into the warm fleece lining and tugging up the hood is almost like getting a hug.

"I'll make you a deal, Kitten."

Mauve's ears flick back to the phone when Dad finally stops talking about how awesome Florida is (all I hear is how much better it is than attending my graduation).

But I'm game. Dad makes deals for a living. I pick up the phone, switching off the speakerphone. "What deal?"

"If you walk for graduation and I get lots of happy graduate pictures with real smiles and your arms around some teachers and you taking your diploma"—he pauses for effect—"I'll pay for you to go to the fuzzcon in Olympia."

For a minute, I hold really still. Dad doesn't even live here and listens better than Mom. Except, "It's a *fur*con, Dad."

"Hotel and everything."

I can't talk.

His tone sounds like my tone when I try to convince Mom about pizza. "Haven't you wanted to go for a couple years?"

More like six years, since I learned there was such a thing. The anchor line of the house tugs at me, big, dragging chains of Stuff. Can I leave Mom alone? It's just a weekend. "Yeah, I guess."

"Isn't it in June? It's coming up?"

Wow. Maybe I talked about it more than I realized. "Yeah, next weekend."

As I'm pondering, another message notification pops up from Jade. We must have a roleplay date I forgot about because he's never this needy unless he and Athen are fighting.

"Maeve?" Dad presses, his voice brightening. "Did I use the right catnip?"

"Dad." I press my fist to my forehead. "You don't have to appeal to my fursona, it's weird."

"Sorry, didn't mean to cross a boundary."

"It's just that catnip is like a drug, and Mauve doesn't use drugs because it affects her magic." I don't know if he cares, but I take any chance I can to tell him about Mauve. I cross the room again to shut the window. Too much humidity will make things miserable when it warms up again.

"Well?"

I stare at silver rain sliding down the window.

I visualize walking down the proverbial graduation gangplank alongside a group of people with whom I can barely relate and have spoken to only out of necessity for the last four years. People who bullied me about my weight in middle school, my hobbies in high school, my clothes, my smell. Teachers who always asked "how ya doin'," with some trepidation as if I might actually tell them and they would have to do something about it.

With the exception of a couple of standouts from the theater and art kids, I don't know or care about my class much. I'd have to explain Mauve. I tried, once, with one of the theater kids, but I don't think she really got it even though she's an actress and understands characters and stuff. We didn't talk about it again.

Mom doesn't care if I walk for graduation, and I doubt if she'll even go. Without Dad, walking is pointless.

Except now it's not.

Weighing a couple hours of undesirable interaction against a whole glorious weekend of fandom immersion and the chance to meet people I *do* care about.

"Well?" Dad sounds triumphant already.

Haute will be there. Jade. Half of my Twitter friends and followers.

Sunspire will be there.

Oh no.

Sunspire—my art idol, my goddess. She'll be there as the art guest of honor.

Then it hits me. The con is on my birthday weekend. Oh my God.

It would be the best eighteenth birthday ever. My first real birthday since the divorce.

Why am I even wondering? What if Dad changes his mind?

Mauve and I pounce. "Yes. Thanks, Dad. Thank you. That is very awesome. I accept."

"Just remember me when you're a famous animator at Disney."

I shoulder the phone against my ear and flip open my laptop. Time to tell Jade, and tweet it all over. "Animators don't really get famous. And Disney is a corrupt corporate machine with crappy storytelling, pushing a moralist, gay-baiting agenda on—"

"When you start your own progressive animation company, remember me."

"I will," I promise, rolling my eyes with a Cheshire grin.

Dad waxes on. "When you're vacationing in Italy in the summer and on your yacht off the coast of Bermuda in the winter, sipping—"

"Dad."

"Maeve?" The teasing deepens out of his voice. "I'm proud of you. This is a new chapter, whether you realize it now or not. I want pictures from the ceremony."

I melt a little. He means it. "I will get them. I promise."

"Send me information on furcon. I'll get you a room and Paypal you the registration fee."

"Wow, Dad." It's all I can say.

When we hang up, I allow my heart to race, tuck my knuckles against my mouth to hold in a scream, and patter out a little happy dance in the middle of the room. Then I plop down at my desk and open Discord where Jade is prowling across my screen in frustrated messages. We *did* have a roleplay date. Oops.

<JadeSong> *Circles the meadow, searching the ground for a fluffeh kitteh.* All done with high school forever WOOOOO! *Lands and does the graduate dance. Boom.*

<JadeSong> *No kitteh to be seen?*

<JadeSong> *Herrooooow?*

<JadeSong> *Checks the sun for mortal time . . . lands, prowls . . . sniffs?*

<JadeSong> *majestic dragonish pout*

<JadeSong> *Mauvy? Everything okay?*

That must've been when he sent the Twitter message. He knew it would go to my phone. Just like him to wonder, then worry. He's the only friend who knows about the hoarding, so he's well within his right to worry. I send him a dancing cat GIF on Twitter, then drum my fingers on the laptop keys. Let's see . . . the perfect way to tell him about the con . . .

My phone buzzes. Pizza at the door (I told them to text instead of knock, lying that one family member works nights, don't wake them, etc.). Anything to cut down on the disturbance to Mom's life. She hates people coming to the door. To be fair, so do I, but not when they're bearing pizza.

<MauveCat> *Here but BRB! Pizza at the door.*

<JadeSong> *Pounces! Rolls kitteh up into a croquet ball and putts her around while he waits.*

It's raining too hard for small talk with the pizza girl, although I know her. Paige Carson, one of the theater kids, the girl I talked to about being a furry before it got awkward. Tonight she looks like a pretty actress playing the role of a delivery girl in a teen rom-com, her strawberry gold hair braided into two pigtails under the bright green cap of the local pizza place.

"Hi, Maeve! I didn't know you lived here." Her gaze flicks to my tail. "Hey, is that—"

I cannot talk about the tail to her or the fact that I live here. Why should I? Also, it's pouring rain. Maybe she's filling in for the usual guy. But then I recall that her parents manage or own the pizza place. "It's twenty, right?"

She grins. "Yeah."

The rain slashes down and I make a show of shooing her off. "Get out of here, you'll melt!"

She laughs, hands over the box and my iced tea before sprinting back to her car, pausing to call back, "See you at graduation!"

I don't dislike Paige, I just don't know her beyond our brief conversations.

"Mom! Pizza!" Rather than attempt to get the pizza safely to the disgusting kitchen, it's best to leave it in the side entryway on top of the washing machine. Mom can go outside and walk around the house to get it more easily than I can get it out of that room or she can navigate the Stuff, so I just leave it there for her.

I keep a stash of paper plates and picnic-ware in the laundry nook for these occasions. Mom calls a response, and I've done my part—whether she wants any is up to her. I slide the anchovy half of the pizza onto a couple of paper plates, stuff a fistful of napkins and parmesan packets into my pocket, and make the trek back to my room.

Jade has been casting spells and turning me different colors. To be clear, it's all text. It feels as if we're writing a story together. There are a lot of ways to roleplay, but that's how we do.

I decide to savor my news a little—and also wait for any kind of confirmation from Dad that this is actually happening. We play through a bit of our current jewel quest (it's all freeform, respond and react type of stuff, we don't use dice or a certain system). This is my favorite kind of roleplay because it's all about adventure and character development. Some of my favorite art pieces have come from scenarios between Jade and me because he likes the high fantasy stuff like I do.

There are other friends, but Jade and Mauve have been teamed up since his dragon rescued a little changeling kitten from a snowstorm all those years ago in a bigger channel with more people. I realize my backstory was so melodramatic, but how else is a girl supposed to make an entrance? I'm his sometimes-familiar in my feral pixie form, and he's my protector. Jade and Mauve were friends, then *we* became friends out-of-character.

We've never talked on the phone or anything, but we send birthday cards and care packages, like the Totoro hoodie. And no, we're not dating. Even if I had energy for it (I don't), he's 100% gay and in a serious relationship with a wolf who goes by Athen.

We love each other, but Jade is . . . my big brother—my big green dragon brother.

Tonight, we've raided a wyvern's cavern and hauled gems back to Jade's cave. Sometimes we bring other people in on the adventures, but I'm glad it's just us tonight. Sometimes we stay in character, sometimes we blend in real life.

Tonight, I have to blend.

\<MauveCat\> *Picks through the gems for all the pink ones.* Okay. I have news.

\<JadeSong\> *Real news?*

\<MauveCat\> Yeah. *Tosses aside a few peridots and finds some cabochon sapphires.*

\<JadeSong\> Oooooo those are mine! *Steals shiny blue stones, then sniffs around for pizza.* Is this news why you were late?

Rain drums against the walls and the windows. I draw a long, luxurious sip of iced tea and relish my news for a minute, just keeping it close.

\<MauveCat\> Yep.

\<JadeSong\> *Taps Mauve's nose with the tip of his tail.* Dragon wants news and pizza! *toothy grin*

\<MauveCat\> *Pounces the tail!* Pizza's all gone. Dragon's too slow.

\<JadeSong\> *Sulks and droops, then sniffs around for crumbs.*

\<MauveCat\> No! *baps his nose* You are a majestical and noble beast, you do not eat crumbs.

\<JadeSong\> *Eats the box*

\<MauveCat\> CAT FREAKOUT! *Sprints down Jade's back to his tail and flips off the end.*

\<JadeSong\> *Gums the greasy cardboard.* News!

Bzzt.

\<MauveCat\> BRB phone.

\<JadeSong\> What is the news tiny cat?! Smote you for making me wait!

\<MauveCat\> Just a sec.

<JadeSong> *Chews his cardboard quietly.*

The text is from Dad, letting me know the hotel room is booked and that he put the registration fee and a little spending money into my Paypal account. He was not kidding. I wonder if "a little spending money" is just like a subsistence amount or like, "I feel really guilty for not coming to your graduation" amount. I'll check later.

His "I feel guilty" presents are usually pretty great. For a whole year after the Social Services nightmare, he got me a gift card every week for new clothes and music.

I should've asked for a tablet. Oh well, missed opportunities and all that. Back to our chat. Jade is dying for my news. I take a deep breath and type slowly to make sure it's simple and perfect.

<MauveCat> *I'm coming to Furlympia.*

<JadeSong> *~<O___O>~*

<MauveCat> *=^O.O^=*

<JadeSong> *!!!!!!*

<JadeSong> *!!!!!!!!!!!!*

<JadeSong> *AAAAAAaaaaaa!!!*

<MauveCat> *=^.^=*

Before I have a chance to craft a cool announcement, he's dropped the news on Twitter. My phone starts buzzing like a restaurant pager when your table's ready as friends swamp my mentions and DMs.

Furlympian God @AthenMutt

Sweet!! @MauveCat Do you need a ride?

Furlympian Dragon @JadeBeast

@AthenMutt @MauveCat You can't stay in our room though. ;P

Furlympian God @AthenMutt

@MauveCat @JadeBest Don't corrupt her XD.

Mauve Cat @MauveCat

@AthenMutt @JadeBeast Too late. :P A ride would be good though.

Carico Is At Furlympia @Carico

@MauveCat Need a room? You can have our pullout.

Beeping At Furlympia @Lilbeeper

@MauveCat Eeeeeee!!

Your Furlympian Muse @DramaticBat

*@MauveCat OMG Finally!! Maybe we can hang out. ^._.^*

DramaticBat? I pause. What?

DramaticBat is still in high school like me (supposedly), but a total popufur. Mostly with our younger crowd because adults can be weird about interacting with underage furries (I get it, but still, like, we're not the plague), but she's *so* cool. She appeared out of nowhere a couple of years ago, arranges drama panels and skits at cons and late-night coffee meets, and she chats at me sometimes.

Somehow she has tons of money to drop on character art, and her bat 'sona is the cutest thing on the internet. No, it really is. I've done art for her, but hang out? At a con? There are so many people asking the same thing. I respond with a cool, *Would love to!* Then I try to keep up with the rest. It's overwhelming to feel so seen, so valid—wanted.

Apex Is Hungry @ApexPredator

@MauveCat Are you taking commissions at the con?

I Don't Like Fruit Loops @Marlitoo

@ApexPredator @MauveCat Ditto, doing any badges? I want a seahorse toucan. >~~O>

I actually hadn't thought about taking commissions, but how brilliant is that? With Dad paying expenses, I could actually make money at this thing. Or blow it all in the Dealer's Den, who knows. My insides quiver with glee.

I'm going, actually going. I don't have to watch everyone's tweets on my timeline about all the fun things they're doing next week. I'll be there.

MauveCat @MauveCat

@ApexPredator @Marlitoo Absolutely! Use my commission form <link> so I don't lose it in DM tonight, lol.

It's impossible to keep up with the scroll. Twenty new notifications . . . thirty . . . fifty. When am I arriving? Want to do dinner Friday? Lunch? Art jam? Going to the dance? A couple of the Canadians ask if I can bring my favorite American candy.

A stupid grin makes my face ache, wrapped in the excitement of my friends and fans of my art, even though I'm alone in my room. But not really alone. On Discord, Jade asks in earnest if I need a ride, so we chat about that possibility and logistics while I try to keep up with the tweets.

Furlympian God @AthenMutt

@MauveCat Do you want a birthday party?

Beeping At Furlympia @LilBeeper

@AthenMutt @MauveCat OMG yes, on it. PATRAY.

@JadeBeast DMing you.

CaricoIsAtFurlympia @Carico

@ApexMutt @MauveCat @JadeBeast @LilBeeper Yessssss!

BeepingAtFurlympia @Lilbeeper

@ApexMutt @MauveCat @JadeBeast *PARTAY I mean.

For a minute, I have to sit back and press my fingers to my eyes. A birthday party.

A party for me.

They remember. Of course they remember. I haven't had a birthday party since I was a kid. Even then, I had to ask for them and it was just family.

Sunny at Furlympia @SunspireDraws

@MauveCat Awesome, Mauve :)

I stop scrolling.

Sunspire.

In my mentions, her gorgeous lioness avatar gazes at me with all the wisdom and kindness and talent of . . . well, of the sun.

"What." My whisper fills the empty bedroom and, of course, no one answers. I don't even know what I'm saying.

Sweat springs out on my palms, adrenaline slapping my throat as if an armed robber just crashed through the window instead of my art goddess dropping my name on Twitter. As if the sun itself sent down a little ray just for me. The phone tumbles to my lap, then the floor.

Sunspire has followed me for a while and occasionally leaves a nice, short comment on my art, but she does that for a lot of people. She follows most people back, unless they're weird or angry people, because she's amazing and perfect and wonderful.

Before I lose it completely, I scoop my phone back up and thank her. I'm not sweaty and nervous and stammering online. I'm Mauve—pink, chipper, fearless—and no one needs to know that Maeve is anything but.

After thanking her, I start to type *hope to see you* . . . . No, that's too obvious. She's the art guest of honor and she'll have a table. It'll be easy to meet her, so saying "hope" feels redundant.

My heart pounds at the possibility and I start again. *Looking forward to meeting you.* . . . Right, yeah, that sounds like a fifty-year-old sales executive getting hyped for a company barbecue.

Before I can come up with something brilliant and witty, yet casual, she adds:

Sunny at Furlympia @SunspireDraws

@MauveCat I'm doing a panel on "Drawing Cute" on Sunday if you want to join. No pressure, make sure you have lots of con fun. :)

A laugh tickles my throat, then tightens toward tears. Sunspire invited me onto her panel.

To speak. On her art panel.

"Hoooooo." My breath slides out.

Okay. This is worth it. I have to get through graduation, but this very second and all the con-seconds and minutes and hours that will follow are worth it. I vow not to sleep the entire weekend in case I miss something.

"Maeve!" Mom's voice strains down the hall. She's probably having trouble getting to the pizza because it's still pouring rain. I hadn't thought about that. Of course she wouldn't go outside. And most of the side avenues in the house are only big enough for me since I make the room. My subconscious is lashing out over the art kit or something because I don't want to help. Let her struggle as I have.

But not really. I'm not that mean, I don't think, just tired.

"Just a minute!"

"I need your help, now."

"Just a second!" The pizza's been here an hour and she can't wait another second?

"Maeve!"

"Coming." My laptop goes back to the desk.

, I feel invincible, even swipe my cat ears from the head form and place them just so. I peek in the mirror near my closet and, even without my makeup, I can almost see Mauve shining through—bright, determined, unflappable. I show my teeth in a teeny Cheshire look, then slip out of the bedroom to help Mom get some dinner.

I hum lightly as I maneuver through the hall to serve up the pizza. This all feels less real than the other place—the furcon, online, my friends, Mauve. This is just a shadow place.

Mom's carved out a spot to sit on a tote in the living room, waiting for pizza, and I grace her with a peck on the cheek. "Thanks, sweetie." She looks so tired. "I'm sorry I was grouchy, I haven't really eaten today."

"I thought so." Feeling refreshed, I'm able to sit and talk for a minute. After a few bites of pizza, Mom's more normal and asks about the last day of school and graduation, so I tell her.

Not about the furcon. Not yet. She gives my pink ears the stink eye but wisely says nothing. It's a relief because I don't want to tell her Dad's dropping hundreds of dollars on a hotel room and fun money. We stick to graduation. She says she'll come to watch me walk, then asks if I'm going to any parties. I just laugh.

These moments are good, important. They're why I'm still here. Peering at us through the mountains of Stuff is the loss Mom suffered—and that kind of thing can run in families. If I lost her, and didn't do everything I could while she was still here, I'm not sure I wouldn't end up burying myself alive, too.

It's easier now because I know what's in store next week. There's sun on the horizon.

Next week, I will *be* Mauve. Nobody needs to know Maeve, know about this house, the Stuff, the disappointing birthday present, peeing out the window or showering at school, or any of that weird stuff. Jade is the only one who ever knew, and if I have my way, no one else will.

Next week, my real life and real self will begin.

3

"MAEVE FOR HEAVEN'S SAKE, we'll be late!"

Mom's right, and being late to the ceremony is something I do not want. If I'm late, Dad will somehow know and I'm sure he'll revoke his amazing gift.

But looking less like me takes some work, you know? "Just two . . ." I flick a touch of mascara on my left lashes. " . . . seconds." I'm not going full-on Mauve makeup. This just doesn't deserve that. But there will be pictures Dad'll probably print and frame, so I need to look decent. My hair's curling appallingly with the humidity, and I coil it at the nape of my neck to see what it might look like if I chop it all off before the con. The pixie look, right? I might—

"Mae!"

"Coming!" I'm not even annoyed. For the two hours it'll take for me to do this thing, I get a weekend of wonderful.

The last few days, I've gotten everything organized. I've even knocked out a couple of badge commissions that people will pick up at the con. Jade and Athen are picking me up tomorrow morning. They're driving up from Portland, so I'm barely out of their way. We want to hit the registration lines early because there are panels we all want to get to, and I want to scope out Sunspire's table in the Dealer's Den.

I'm still working on what to say. Every time I think about meeting her, my armpits get sweaty. It's awesome.

Dad had to put me in one of the overflow hotels because the main hotel was full months ago, but that's okay. I won't be sleeping much anyway, so there won't be a lot of walking back and forth.

But for now—graduation.

When I look in the mirror and see mostly satisfactory me— pink cheeks, dramatic eyes, glossy lip—I ponder that haircut. To really shed all this. Cut, maybe color . . . but later. I blow a kiss to the mirror and pluck my graduation robe from the hook on my closet door—still wrapped in plastic so it doesn't pick up the aroma of the house.

The day is a picturesque Pacific Northwest morning. Dewy grass, the neighbors' flower gardens bursting with glistening hydrangeas, roses in pink and yellow and blue, and a rainwashed sky.

I skip to the car where Mom is waiting, twirling keys around her index finger. She's dressed up and showered for the occasion, and I even get a whiff of one of the twenty perfumes she's got in the bathroom. A real, true effort to show up for me today.

"Mom, you look great!"

One arm comes around me for a squeeze, and she kisses my cheek. "So do you, sweetie." There's relief, maybe, that I'm not wearing any "fuzzy stuff." But I do have my ears and tail in my satchel for some final photo ops on high school grounds. Have to get some cute pictures for Haute and for my Instagram. Mostly it's art, but I also do Mauve pics. Mauve skateboarding, perched on a wall, in a tree, things like that. It'll be better when I have my paws, but Haute is still working on a design I can wear while drawing.

Mom and I look at each other for a minute. Her eyes brighten and for a horrifying second I think she's going to cry, then she pats me on the hip and we slide into the car.

The neighborhood looks fresh and beautiful, and despite the humidity, I roll the window down for the cooler air. Everything feels better today. The car isn't dirty because Mom barely uses it—just a couple of boxes in the back seat destined for the thrift store. Someday. For now, my graduation robe drapes over them nicely.

"So, no parties or anything?" Mom cants her head toward me but keeps her eyes firmly on the road. Not nervous, but attentive, like a racecar driver.

I should tell her about the furcon, but not yet. Hesitation tightens my voice, so I just shrug and shake my head. "I got a couple of invitations"—ha, ha, ha, ha—"but I have some art things I want to finish."

She nods sagely, lips pursing briefly as if she has wisdom to bestow but then thinks better of it. She has to know. Deep down, she has to know friendship has been impossible. Our town isn't bad, but it's small and pretty straightforward and gives the side-eye to anything weird. Hence, the neighbors calling the city if our trash sits out on the porch too long.

Anyway, I'm not going to tell her about the furcon yet. It's too much to do with Dad, and I want to get some little nugget of the closure and satisfaction I'm supposed to get out of this ceremony. That involves not fighting with Mom beforehand. Right now, the day is good. It's still good.

A line of cars makes it obvious where the drop-off spot is, and a crossing guard directs traffic toward the parking lot with the grave sincerity of a Secret Service agent waving on the President. (To be fair, traffic is flowing and everyone finds a spot.)

"Break a leg! See you after." Mom leans over and wraps an arm around my shoulders, giving me another squeeze.

"Thanks, Mom." There's a pause, and with sincerity, I add, "I'm glad you're here."

She beams and the whole car feels even lighter. I want her to know I see the effort of her dressing up and coming out today. If I do, maybe she'll do it more. Encourage progress, the counselor said.

"Me too." Her eyes brighten again, so I grab the robe quickly and scoot out of the car. "Go get 'em."

"Yep!"

I step back to join the river of classmates meandering toward the gym entrance, and Mom flows into the stream of cars.

"Maeve! Maeve, oh my gosh!" Paige Carson flies up to me but seems to know better than to attempt a hug, my brush-off in the rain last week long forgotten. Or maybe it was never a thing to her.

Her strawberry hair ripples just so in the morning sun, and she's already donned her robe, leaving it open over a cute, tailored sundress printed with blue poppies. She beams at me as if we're closer than we are. I hope the whole day isn't going to be like this—people pretending we're different than we've been over the years. I don't dislike her, she's really nice, but she's really nice to everyone, so I'm not sure if it's put on or if she's just really nice.

"I'm so glad you decided to come!"

"You are?" Cudgeled by her blunt energy and unsure of when I told her I might *not* come (I tweeted about it, but that's all). I feel less like Mauve and more like Maeve, short and drab, even though I picked my blouse to match my lipstick and feel great in a denim skirt and cute and put together. But Paige's legs are tan, and mine are the color of a day-old vanilla milkshake. And my hair's frizzing while she looks like a dryad, like molten honey.

She laughs and her eyes get squinty. "Yeah, of course. Listen, I wanted to talk to you about—"

"Paige!"

Oh God, here come the theater kids. A mob of them, like a flock of birds. Bouncing, quoting musicals, singing, literally piggybacking on each other. I love them—but from a distance, it's like watching wildlife. Up close, it's too much and they touch a lot. I suck a breath and Paige leans in but doesn't touch me—how does she know I hate random touches? Have we been good friends and I didn't notice? Huh.

"It's okay, I'll head them off." She skips backward, finger-gunning at me with nails immaculately manicured in cobalt blue. "Don't disappear afterward. We need to talk about the con."

Before I can examine this statement, she whirls away in a cloud of black gown and blue poppies and rose gold hair and throws herself into the throng of theater geeks to escort each other to the ceremony. I stand there with my mouth gaping like an arctic char.

An announcement crackles over the intercom calling us inside and we all stream to the doors. Mom is in charge of my satchel and I hope she doesn't peek in and see my Mauve stuff. Most of my classmates cluster and walk together. I walk alone, but it's okay.

That's what cats do.

Thinking of Mauve, I straighten and lift my chin and just hang, cool, exactly where I'm supposed to be in line outside the cafeteria. I want this to go quickly and smoothly. I think of Mom sitting there, alone, like I'm alone in the line, waiting to see me. Oh God, I hope she's not talking to people.

Beyond the doors, a hush falls. The warmth of apprehension curls in my stomach like a big acidic question mark as the principal's muffled voice comes through the cinderblock and drywall, welcoming everyone.

Suddenly this feels weird.

I'm graduating. The next months and years unfurl in front of me like butcher block paper, unyielding and blank. A sense of doom inches toward me across the mental horizon.

I force out a breath. It's not blank—it's potential. A blank page. Just like a drawing, I cram images onto the paper—Portland, art school, the furcon, meeting my friends . . . but after that? It just keeps going. The rest of my life unprogrammed. I breathe again. And again.

My classmates fall silent when the principal does, and "Pomp and Circumstance" swells inside the cafeteria. I roll up and down off the balls of my feet, and my gaze darts up the hall until I see a bright pink flyer on a bulletin board and fixate on that.

Pink pink pink. My phone buzzes but to attempt to get it out from under the robe and everything would not end well. I'll assume it's Dad, or Jade, sending me good vibes. I try not to think of Mom in the audience. I wonder if she actually smells good or if I'm nose-blind from the house. I hope the other parents aren't judging her, judging us.

There are only forty-two of us, so it doesn't seem like it should take as long as it does. Finally, the girl ahead of me moves and, for half a second, the music makes this all feel very grand and important.

Rather than glance at the crowd and try to spot my mom, I focus on the girl's cap in front of me. She's sewn beads all along the rim. I let my eyes follow the colors. Red, gray, yellow, teal, and back again. A medicine wheel? I just let my eyes follow the colors around, and it helps.

Principal Knox (or Fort Knox, as we somewhat lovingly refer to him—built like a brick with the same personality) ascends the little stage, but my phone buzzes as he welcomes everyone and I duck my head to check.

Dad: *I know you're in ceremony but WTG! Can't wait to see pictures, hint hint.*

A teeny grin finds its way to my face. Okay, that feels good. He might be off the opposite coast somewhere reeling in dinner, but he's thinking about me.

" . . . one of the most talented classes we've had in years . . ." Light applause floats about. I glance up from my phone, wondering if he says the same thing every year.

A kid two heads over whispers, "Last year he said 'promising.' Guess we're just talented."

Snickers travel through the class and the principal pauses. We all straighten up and fall silent and then he smiles.

A pang hits my chest. I'm not going to miss this place. I'm

really not, but there are a lot of memories. I zone out to the thought of the almost-food-fight I got to observe in this very room and my disappointment that it didn't happen, plays we saw here, my stolen moments alone in the corner at lunch, drawing.

Some of my classmates look genuinely sad, and I wonder what they're thinking. The same sort of things, I suppose. I wonder if this is what Dad meant by closure—taking a minute to acknowledge this chapter.

Ms. Treadwell gives us a second to soak in the speech half of us weren't listening to, then trots up to the podium. "Now, we would like to welcome Class Representative Chance Wooley."

Chance takes the stage. All I know is he's a basketball player and good at chemistry, and I still can't figure out how you have time to be both those things. I'm not going to lie, I zone out during his speech and think about Mom.

He wraps up: ". . . and may we have the serenity to accept the things we can't change, the courage to change what we can, and the wisdom to know the difference. Thank you." He hesitates, then grins at us like we're all best friends. "We did it!"

Ms. Treadwell hugs him and he nearly lifts her off the ground before trotting back to his seat.

"And now . . ." She grins brightly. ". . . our graduates from the Little Tree High School Drama Club will present their . . ." She checks her program. ". . . Graduation Medley."

Paige and three other students slip out of their seats, and my phone buzzes again. I should've turned off Twitter notifications before the ceremony. I take the chance to peek, and it's a long scroll of questions about me coming to the con, lots of well-wishes for graduation, and then jokes about me turning eighteen so I can finally look at NSFW art and maybe draw it? Har har. Back to my ceremony, thanks.

Josiah Scott sits at the piano while Paige and another girl drag the podium away.

Vaguely familiar piano chords bounce through the room. Someone groans. I know the song, thanks to Jade and his obsessions. "Seasons of Love" from *Rent*.

I never watched the whole thing, but this song definitely gets in your head. My foot even starts tapping, and the girl next to me sways and grins, and when a heckler yells, "boooo," Paige blows him a kiss and keeps singing. I'm genuinely impressed. If someone booed me, I would disintegrate on the spot.

The four of them rouse into a surprisingly mighty chorus, then they transition seamlessly (I just don't understand how medleys work, but it's amazing) into "Time of My Life." Paige and River Johnston re-enact some impressively sharp choreography from *Dirty Dancing* that gets all the parents laughing and cheering. One student starts clapping along with the music, and it's downhill from there. It's cheesy, but they're our classmates, they're ours, and they obviously put in a ton of work to make this special, even if it feels like they picked songs our parents would like.

Who wouldn't clap? Even I'm not that jaded. Nobody is. We laugh, and for a few minutes, I feel like an actual part of the group.

From that number, the pianist continues a holding pattern, the intro to a new song. Paige pulls out of the final pose with River and takes center stage, waiting until a hush falls to begin singing "A Million Dreams."

There's some happy muttering. I'm surprised anyone else has even seen the movie it's from, but maybe I don't give them enough credit. As we've established, I don't get out much.

But right now, all eyes are on Paige (who I'm pretty sure is headed straight for Broadway after this). The song is beautiful, she's beautiful, and she means every word. For a second, I wish I could be her. I'm suddenly glad I came, just to see this.

And those stupid, pure lyrics and her yearning voice slap my core, tears clawing out of my eyes. I have a million dreams too. I just have to escape to make them happen.

Somehow.

Suddenly I'm standing up, hand clasped to my chest, but I'm not alone. The rest of the class is standing. Even if we hardly spoke or didn't know each other, for four minutes we're all in agreement that this is awesome. Paige sings, River joins for the second verse with Josiah on the piano, and Tiana harmonizes with them for a final rousing chorus that gets us cheering. For four minutes, our tiny little class in our weird uptight town feels huge and full of possibility.

My phone buzzes and I wrestle it out of my pocket to get some blurry pictures and a little video of the quartet up onstage to send to Dad.

Even the adults stand up for the end, and the cafeteria resounds with applause. The more obnoxious guys try to out wolf-whistle each other until Knox strides up, thanking the actors and hugging them like a benevolent uncle. I glance around and catch sight of my mom a few rows back, but she's not clapping—she's checking her watch.

Wow.

And I thought *I* was the one who didn't want to come. But she looks uncomfortable and I have to sympathize—too many people. Maybe she has the same defenses I do. I wrench my gaze back to the stage as Ms. Treadwell takes over again, clapping and beaming and shooing the actors from the stage.

It's time for student awards, only five, each with a little explanation, and it's hard not to take out my phone again. But I see other kids doing it, and it looks so obnoxious that I resist. I glance around and try to catch Mom again, but I've lost her in the crowd.

Academic excellence, extracurricular achievement (Paige gets that one, surprise), community spirit (what even is that)—I didn't know we were competing for any of these awards. I wonder if they make them up to make the ceremony longer.

" . . . displaying dedication to education and a can-do spirit, this next award shows an understanding of one of life's great lessons for success: the first step is showing up. This year, the award for perfect attendance goes to Maeve Stephens."

I jerk out of reverie. Was that my name? Holy buckets. Sweat springs out over every inch of my skin, heat slides down my face, and people peer around when I don't stand up. Maybe I can pretend I'm not here.

My neighbor nudges me. She doesn't want the ceremony to last any longer than I do, probably. I stand up.

To my horror, my mom's voice snaps across the room. "That's my girl!"

Oh God.

Aren't they obligated to warn you if you're going to get an award? If you're going to have to stand up in front of people?

Temples pounding, I worm through the seats and up the stage. When you can't stand to be in the house, and you can't shower there or eat there, and you need a way out, you go to school. Yeah, I had perfect attendance.

Everyone stares at me and Mom springs out of her seat to take a million pictures as Ms. Treadwell hands me my framed award. She offers a hug as I offer my hand, she laughs and we awkwardly step back so I can hurry away and fumble back to my seat. I guess it's good, for a second, to be seen.

After that, it's a blur. There's not much left. Knox and the superintendents say more words, and then it's time to get our diplomas. I manage not to botch it—I hope Mom gets pictures for Dad.

Then we all march out to the lawn while they blare "Pomp and Circumstance" again, and as the sunlight hits my face— I'm done.

Huh.

High school is done.

Giddy energy rises in the class as Ms. Treadwell shuffles us together. The parents and families all come out, cameras at the ready.

"Families and honored guests," she calls brightly, "your graduates!"

Someone throws their cap up high. Then, of course, everyone else has to throw their hat, so it's a great big shout from us, caps flying through the air. I fake throwing mine and snatch it down again. I don't want to end up grabbing someone else's cap.

Just like that, it's the end of programmed activities, and everything dissolves into happy chaos. People bump and jostle me as they dash to their families and friends, or hug each other, laughing and crying. Ugh. I maneuver out of the cluster to a clear space of lawn.

I did it. I'm done. Checkmark, high school. Next up: life.

And Furlympia.

Genuine happiness bursts up when I remember: I did it! I survived graduation. Now, I can sneak away with Mom, pack, and go to my first con. I tuck my certificate under my arm, checking Twitter quickly, but all the congratulations and sweetness are swept away by the sight of a single direct message.

From Sunspire.

The preview text is all I have time to read.

Hey Mauve, just checking if—

"Good job sweetie!" Mom swoops in and takes another picture just as I'm looking up from my phone.

"Mom!"

"Candid shot."

"You'll send all these to Dad right?"

She waves her hand, motioning for me to pose, which I do with a serious face then a smile. It occurs to me that we used to take pictures together before the divorce. We would go around the town parks and take pictures of flowers, bees, weird close-ups of playground equipment, and things like that, then print out whole Shutterfly albums.

Those books are somewhere, in the mountains of Stuff.

"Maaaaeve!"

Paige swooshes up, strawberry locks gleaming, and with a great big dazzling smile. Her mascara must be waterproof because she looks like she's been crying, but not. "Hi, Maeve's Mom!"

"Picture!" Mom declares without saying "hi" back, and Paige and I, with the obedience of children, scoot close together. Even though we've barely spoken in two years, I resist the urge to give Paige bunny ears. Her sunny energy is infectious, and I'm beginning to think she's genuine, not in-view-of-adults-nice. I don't know what I did to earn it, but I'll take it. We take a couple of cute pictures, and I'm sure seeing myself in proximity with another human will thrill my dad to no end.

"So." Paige grins and I wonder how she gets her teeth so white. I mean, they're like a toothpaste commercial. "Let's talk about the con—"

Con? I flash my eyes wide in the very clear *Please Do Not* expression of distress and warning, and she halts. Her gaze flicks to my mom, who raises her eyebrows, then back to me.

Mom has her phone poised for a photo, then pauses and peers at us. "Talk about the what?"

If Mom hears the word con again, I'm afraid her first thought might be that Paige and I are running a scheme on the side, not a convention. Then she'll get confused and keep asking questions. I talk fast to divert her. "The Conn . . . ers . . . party. Yeah, I'm definitely going. Tomorrow." I look at Mom, who's maybe 72% buying what I'm selling. "A party tomorrow."

Paige squints at me and her mouth gets really small, lips puckered, then pursed inward. For an actress, she's awfully reluctant to lie. "Cool. I will . . . text you?"

"Cool. Thank you. Thanks." That's *thanks for lying for me*. Paige seems to get it.

"I'll just catch you later then?" Her gaze drops and her

expression lights up with delight. I wonder if she sees the pink fur sticking out from my satchel.

"Yeah, later. For sure."

I'm going to tell Mom about Furlympia (I have to) just not in front of people where she's going to get loud and make a scene and ask a truckload of humiliating questions. We can do all of that at home. Paige saunters away to other friends and teachers and there's a brief stab in me, wanting some of that—some of that belonging and groupness. But I isolated myself and with good reason for the last few years. Besides, by tomorrow I'll be surrounded by all the actual friends I could ever ask for.

"Anyone else?"

"Hm?" I about-face to blink at Mom, who lifts her phone hopefully. "Nah. Let's get out of here."

"Agreed." Mom slings an arm around me (she's not subject to the no-touch rule when she's not being weird and hostile), and we escape to the car. The plan is burgers and milkshakes, then she'll drop me at the park so I can take some cute Mauve pics in the tail and ears (she doesn't know that's why she's dropping me at the park, I told her I'd be sketching since it's such a beautiful day), then home to pack.

I'll tell her at home.

That's the plan, anyway.

Our favorite burger shack, the one that used to be our family night dinner spot before the divorce, will be jammed with students (sorry, graduates) as soon as everyone gets out of the parking lot, so it's good we escaped early. I stake out a booth by the window and Mom orders. My order hasn't changed in ten years—chili cheeseburger with curly fries and a strawberry milkshake (not my favorite flavor, it's just pink and makes me happy).

While Mom waits for the food up by the counter, I get the condiment caddy arranged so it's not stressing me out—labels out, sugar packets facing the same way, etcetera. My counselor asked me about that once when I turned the pillows on her couch a certain way, but we came to the idea that I like to make little pockets of order where I can. It helps me feel calm.

Mom plunks down with the tray and there's some quiet ceremony to us unwrapping the burgers and munching the first fry. All in all, the morning has not been as horrifying as I feared, the surprise award aside. I have the perfect way to tell Mom about the con (my art mentor with connections at the art institute in Portland will be there) and I'm feeling pretty confident.

"So tell me about this party?"

I nibble a fry, following the curl, and slide my gaze from the window to Mom's face. "What party?"

Her eye twitches. "Earth to Mae. The Conners party?"

"Oh, that one." The fry lodges in my throat, and attempting to wash it down with strawberry milkshake just results in a coughing fit, my throat seizing and my eyes watering. Mom offers her pop instead, which helps. Finally, I can talk again and clear my throat roughly. "Yeah, um. It's tomorrow afternoon." The energy it takes for me to lie when Mom is staring at me like a kestrel hovering over a grasshopper is exhausting.

My phone buzzes.

"Who all's going to be there?" She munches a fry ever so conversationally.

"Mom, I don't have a guest list. I'm almost eighteen. You don't have to ask all these questions."

"I asked two questions, Maeve." Her eyes narrow at my obvious reluctance, which, in her mind, probably equates to the party being a big, drunken, drugged-up orgy.

That could work to my advantage. Maybe Furlympia will look tame in comparison.

A few families trickle in and the volume of people triples. My pulse jumps. I press a hand to my forehead, then peer at her from under it as if she's too bright to look at. "Can we just talk about it at home?"

She makes a point of sipping her drink slowly as if pondering my fate. "Just tell me now, Maeve. You're overreacting."

Everything around me is normal; the families coming in laugh and snap pictures of each other and order food. But it feels like everything is warped and pressing in on me. Mom's looking at me quietly, but my anxiety leaps to my skin and it feels like my hair is on fire. I know this face of hers. We're not going anywhere until I talk.

I puff out a breath and sit up, smoothing my palms across the cool tabletop. "Dad said if I went to the graduation ceremony, he would pay for me to attend Furlympia this weekend. I want to go. I'm already registered, and a million people I know are going to be there. It's just in Olympia. It's not that far. I even have a ride so you don't have to do anything. My artist mentor is going to be there, and I really want to meet her . . ." I can't stop talking, and Mom's eyebrows climb to her hairline. ". . . and a bunch of others, and my best friend Jade," I add on the off chance she remembers, then suck in a breath and hold it.

Mom stirs her ice cubes, eyebrows all crooked up like I'm funny. I release the breath. For a second, I think she's going to laugh and say, *Of course, sweetie, happy birthday and graduation, I trust you.*

But she says, "*Fur*lympia?"

The sensation of being thirteen again swamps me, of Mom peering over my monitor at furry art and wondering what sort of weirdness I'm getting into. I'm nearly an adult woman with a blossoming art career, friends, invitations to speak on panels with prestigious artists (okay, just one), and I feel like a kid who's done something wrong.

I sit up, square my shoulders, and force my words out, pressing sweaty palms to my unhelpful denim skirt. "Yes. It's the furcon in Olympia. It's the third biggest in the country, and I want to be there for my birthday—for my graduation present."

A few people meander by with trays, side-eyeing us, and I wish we'd taken the food home. Mom stirs her ice cubes. "I don't think so, Maeve."

"What?" My shriek startles Mom, people look, and I suck my lips in and curl my fingers in my lap. "Mom, it's already all done. Jade's picking me up in the morning."

My voice quivers. Oh God, not tears, no, no, no. Drawing a quick breath through my nose, I call upon Mauve, forcing everything to smooth out. Nerves, temper, angry-crying. Mom doesn't say anything and frowns like I'm speaking a foreign language. Maybe I am.

"Please, Mom. This is so, so important to me. It's perfectly safe, there's plenty of under-eighteen events." Her eyes narrow. I realize that was not strategic, so I change tactics, trying to catch her roiling wind. "The artist I mentioned? She's a pro. She does concept art for Maelstrom Games, and she's an alum of the PNW Art Institute. Practically everyone she recommends gets a scholarship. Please, Mom, I need to go. I need to. Please."

She has to see. She has to understand for once in her life that it isn't just "pink cat crap."

She stirs her ice cubes, and once again, keys in on exactly the wrong thing. "Isn't Jade that college boy? Is that his real name?"

"He . . . what? College as in, he's one year older than me and started college last fall? Yes"—wrong move again—"but we're not, he's not—interested in . . ." I don't know what will help or hurt my cause. I thought I knew my Mom, but clearly not. "He's in a serious relationship with someone. It's not like that. And he's literally the nicest, most boring person in the world." My hands jerk up with fidgety energy and patter on the table to make my point. "Mom. This is a big, big deal."

In the silence, my phone buzzes again, traveling a couple inches across the Formica tabletop. But it's not a text, it's a call. Dad's face and mine, at the zoo, gleams from the screen. Mom watches it, then me, expectantly. It buzzes again, scooting toward the edge.

"Are you going to answer him?"

"Mom, please. Please."

She releases a slow breath through her teeth as if all the burdens of the world rest on her weary shoulders.

I get it. I do. All she knows about the fandom is the random stuff that comes on news shows—the big, flashy, wacky, and impressive fursuiters who are the most visible element. Or the occasional write-up in a big magazine or some attention from a celebrity. And then there are all the (not untrue) rumors about it being a sexual fetish. Maybe, yeah, in some ways, because for many LGBTQA+ people, it was one of the first safe spaces for them to explore their identities and express themselves when mainstream media ignored them. It still is.

But that's not all it is. It's like any other fandom. It's whatever you want it to be—whatever you need it to be. We're fans of each other.

I had this out with Dad and he ran out of arguments. He grew up with *The Lion King*—the original Lion King. And he, at least, saw how my art skyrocketed when I started drawing Mauve. When I had some inspiration, and fun, and support, and purpose.

Mom also knows all this—the art, my friends, the element of pretend and escape and self-realization. It's a way to cling to a small, precious part of me that still believes in magic. Anyway, I thought she knew.

She's staring at me, staring at my soul. Her fursona would be a falcon.

"Maeve," her voice is quiet. I know she wants to be the good guy but isn't going to. She wants to be a parent at the wrong moment, in the wrong way. "I don't think so."

I throw my hands up, nearly overturning the fry basket. "Mom! Seriously?"

Heads turn, and I scrunch in. Mauve is nowhere to be found. I'm grasping to be myself in this moment instead of a bratty little girl.

In response, Mom doesn't rise but cools. I wish I could do that. "I said no."

No? Like I'm a kid who wants a box of cookies?

Rage and injustice swamp me. My therapist saw how my emotions overwhelm me and urged me to take a step back and examine when I can, but that sounds like disassociation to me, so I don't often examine. I just let them swamp me and swim through until I can surface again. Mom knows better than to touch me or try to calm me, especially when she's the source of the tide. A battle royale between hurt and anger wages in my throat, and I manage to grind out some words.

"I want to go home."

I don't, really, because home is the opposite of comforting, but it's better than sitting in the burger shack having a meltdown. At least I can bury myself there.

To her credit, Mom rises, sweeps the tray and trash from the table, and makes for the door without a word. She's triumphant—as if my meltdown is the reason I shouldn't be unleashed at the furcon on my own. Eventually, I wrench myself out of the booth, with a death grip on my satchel and hunched forward, every muscle tight so I don't unravel.

In the parking lot, a light breeze playing with my frizzing hair, I halt with my hand on the car door. Mom's already in the car, smoking.

My hand drops from the door as if it's not my hand, just doing its own thing. "I'm going to walk."

"Get in the car, Maeve."

I don't. I don't want my brand-new tail stinking of cigarette smoke. The smell makes me so tense it feels like my neck might snap. Spinning around, I march down the little street that leads to the highway and home. It's a couple miles, and I don't even care. I have a lot to walk off. Maybe I'll head to the park near my house anyway and try to take pictures as promised. Mom starts the car and actually follows me.

Bzzt.

I fumble for my phone, hurrying past buckets overflowing with petunias, enveloped in a cloud of resentment and frustration, with Mom rolling along behind in the car like a creeper. It makes everything impossible. I can't even unlock my phone to see a message from Jade. I give up. Everyone knows it's a busy morning. Mom comes up parallel again and rolls down the passenger window.

"Mae—"

"I'm walking!" I screech at the sidewalk, letting some wrath lash out, which releases my hold on everything. Tears prickle, unbidden, throbbing at my eyes, making everything swim. Worse than sad-crying is rage-crying. It makes me look weak and pathetic when it's just one way all the red gets out. That angry red.

Maybe Mauve turns crimson when she's mad. That would be dramatic. Not nearly as dramatic as me marching down the sidewalk while Mom rolls along beside, imploring me to get in, but dramatic nonetheless. Mauve certainly doesn't cry. Thinking about Mauve is enough to keep the tears at bay for now.

"Maeve."

"I'm walking."

I have to win this one. Short of hauling me bodily into the vehicle, I'm not letting her win this. I was nice about the art kit, and that's all I've got. I know she's trying to be a mom. I just wish it wasn't now, and I can't do anything more today.

"Just let me walk it off, okay? It's my day." I practically spit the last part out.

Mom rolls alongside me for another ten seconds (I know because I'm now trying to count myself down), then, without a word, accelerates and leaves me alone in the sweet spring air.

She said *no*. I don't know what to do. Can she even do that? I'm a high school graduate, and I'll be an adult in two days. She's the one with a fridge full of nearly empty peanut butter jars. Can she really tell me no, anymore? Does it even mean anything?

My phone buzzes again. I swipe it up, roll a noise in my throat, and force myself to perk up.

"Hey, Dad!"

"All done?"

My gaze lifts to make sure the back end of Mom's car is still disappearing down the road. "Yep. Bonafide graduate. Mom took most of the pictures so I'll make sure she sends them to you."

"Are you okay? You sound stuffy."

"Yeah, just . . ." I clear my throat again and slow my pace. "It got to me more than I thought it would." I don't feel like I've ever attempted to lie this much in all my life, but something, maybe Mauve's instinct, warns me against telling him about Mom's reaction to the con. I don't want them to fight, too. I'll figure it out.

Not likely, whispers the knowing voice in the back of my head. Usually, once Mom says no, it's no, just like with the pizza. She's planted her flag, and she'll die on the hill. She's zoned in, and it can get weird and intense when she's zoned in and says *no*. It's as if she has no control over anything but me, and by God, she'll keep it.

Dad's saying something about transition and seems to realize I haven't heard a word. "Maeve?"

"Yeah, sorry. I've been so distracted today."

"You got the money and everything?"

My emotions even out a little, remembering this big deal thing Dad has done for me. "Yeah. Yes, it's all there, and I got the hotel information. Thanks, Dad."

"What did your mother think?"

It's as if he barely knows her and didn't take part in my creation with her. I pause before turning onto the highway. I don't want him to hear cars rushing by, and duck into the shade of a monstrous lilac. "Oh, you know. She's not super excited about it, but she agrees it would be cool if I can meet Sunspire."

"And Sunspire is?" At least he sounds apologetic for not knowing.

A bright laugh finds its way out of my chest. Mauve. She can bluff Dad more easily than Mom. "Just my idol, Dad, no big deal. But she has connections with the art school in Portland. Once I have my residency, she could put in a good word for a scholarship. So, you know." I just end it there because this is taking reserves I don't have.

"See? Perfect, Kitten."

"Yeah, perfect. I'll um . . . call you when I'm safe at the hotel tomorrow?"

"Sure thing. Love you."

"Love you too, Dad. Bye." I sniff. The lilac soothes the frayed edges in my heart, and I count the pale blossoms until my body is sorted enough to walk back to the house.

MOM AND I ARE NOT SPEAKING.

I slam the door to announce my arrival home, but that's it. After navigating through the house to my room and dropping my stuff, it's radio silence. I didn't get any photos in my ears and graduation gown, but I don't even care anymore. The Instagram crowd is different than the friends who will be coming to Furlympia and not really into my graduation stuff.

I have a backlog of messages to catch up on. Feeling defiant, I'd stopped on the way home for a little candle and a lighter. *My* room is clean, so I'll have a candle if I want. I doubt the fire marshal is going to march up to the door the second I light it. Pretty sure Mom's been smoking because the hallway reeks, so I guess we're both rebels today.

So I get my calm on. I light a candle, put on some music, and pack my stuff in between chatting with people. Priorities go first: Art supplies, tail, ears, makeup, at least one cute Mauve outfit, and something to sleep in.

On Discord, Jade checks in about plans for picking me up tomorrow. The thought of telling him about the fight with Mom occurs to me briefly, but I know better. Jade's protective and more of a goodie-two-shoes than I am. If he knows Mom doesn't want me to go, he'll take her side—not because he thinks she's right, but because he's lawful good, that's all.

My thumbs hover over the screen.

<MauveCat> *Actually, gotta pick up a couple things on the way, so you can just pick me up here.*

I give him the address of a Walgreens about a mile from my house and pray it doesn't ping his paladin-like radar as shady.

<JadeSong> *We have road trip food already if that's what you need.*
<MauveCat> *But do you have hair dye. =^o.O^=*
<JadeSong> *Oh yeah. A whole salon in the back. What color? :P*
<MauveCat> *If you can't guess, then we've never been friends.*
<JadeSong> *:O*

Poof. I've successfully smoke-screened the dragon with my nonchalant cat magic. But it's not a lie; I need a serious Mauve makeover. I want to be my full self at the con, which involves more pink than what's happening now.

<JadeSong> *Athy wants to know if we're going to spend lots of time on your grooming because he actually wants to go to opening ceremonies.*

We. I'm going to meet them IRL and actually hang out. I can't help but grin. I've never met any of my online friends. I'm psyched and terrified.

<MauveCat> *Not even a little bit. I'm going to do everything in Olympia so I can make a grand first appearance. Furrrrst appearance.*

<JadeSong> **Dies of a bad case of Pun.**

I maintain a window chatting with him about details and finally open my Twitter DMs. There are nine—*nine*—messages from DramaticBat, and I wonder if I forgot a commission or something.

Your Furlympian Muse @DramaticBat

*You ran away after graduation! ^.___.^*

Hope I didn't get you in trouble

Your mom doesn't like furry?

:/

I'm sorry

Also, I got some graduation money and wonder if you're drawing at the con?

Would love to hang out. It's been a million years!

I'll stop blowing up your messages. @ me okay?

You know this is Paige, right?

My world tips up and over, and a few things I was sure of spill right out.

Paige? Paige Carson?

DramaticBat, aka DeeBee, DB, the Deebs, the cutest, peachiest, friendliest, apparently richest, most popular young fur on Twitter is my classmate? Did she tell me? Did I not know? When I sewed buttons for our junior-year production of *Les Misérables*, was I so far up in myself, hiding my fandom, that I didn't notice? (She was the most heartbreaking Eponine ever, by the way.)

I have a choice: continue my lying streak for the day and say *Jeepers, silly, of course I knew! I was just ignoring you for four years, being discreet, cuz, y'know, morons will talk.*

Or I can be honest and open up and maybe make a real-life friend who lives in the same town (even though I'm out of here as soon as possible) and is also furry.

But Paige? Paige Carson with the penny-gold hair and cerulean eyes and enough endless, effervescent energy to be nice to everyone in the world and bat away bullies with her eyelashes? My palms sweat. Being in imaginary proximity to all these people is amping my anxiety more than usual. There's a prickle of alarm that I might not be able to pull off just-Mauve at the con.

Inside, Mauve flicks her tail and yawns. I'm overthinking this. I don't have to decide this second or at all. Breathe in, breathe out. I can just navigate around it the way I do questions about Mom and the house and why my clothes smell like slightly expired vegetable oil even when freshly clean.

I plop down on my futon, curling around a pillow to answer her and all the others.

Purrrrlympian Pixie @MauveCat

Hey Deebs! Sorry, been swamped today. Mom's cool. But absolutely, let's hang at the con, I'm getting there with Jade & Ath tomorrow. Gotta do some primping before I debut though. ;)

She doesn't answer right away. She probably thinks I'm a flake or that I don't care. I should've just talked to her after the ceremony. In the three-and-a-half minutes or so it apparently takes her to notice my message, I'm afraid I blew it completely.

Your Furlympian Muse @DramaticBat

Oh sweet! Let me know if you need help. I have mad makeup and hair skillz.

Purrrrlympian Pixie @MauveCat

Will do, thx!

Done. I consider asking if she can help with my hair. I can't explain how hard it is to reconcile my twin images, though: class-mate Paige vs. online DramaticBat. I've never met an online friend IRL. The only way I can describe what's happening to my brain is if, like, okay: you're reading a script page, imagining David Tenant, and all of a sudden you look up and it's actually Chris Hemsworth in the role. You form a mental image, a cadence—a whole essence. So it's weird to know that DramaticBat is even more real than I knew (you know what I mean).

I don't know how I come off online, but when I meet people at the con, I want the real me to match as closely to Mauve as possible because a lot of people like her.

My long walk home gave me plenty of time to think about things, life, and Mom. I try to make her happy and show her I care and always be good so I won't draw attention to us—to her—so we can stay together and try to be a family and try to fix things. No one deserves the way we live. I had a chance to think about how most of my life revolves around not losing my mom, trying to find her within the Stuff—to dig out what we used to have, to figure out why she can't see who I am anymore, to figure out why her *no* can hold me at all.

I thought about it with cars rushing by and the smell of June flowers and the dampness of tears on my face.

I came to a decision.

And as I chat with Jade and the others on Twitter and try to hash out plans for dinners and art jams and panels (I still haven't answered Sunspire, and I probably look like a complete flake at this point), it seals the deal.

I'm going to Furlympia whether Mom likes it or not. But I won't know if she likes it or not because I'm not going to ask her about it again.

I'm just going to go.

MOM'S ALWAYS UP EARLY. BUT she won't be doing laundry, so I stashed my little duffel and everything by the side door the night before.

Too nervous to even check Twitter for more messages, I slip into my chosen outfit for the day: my grinning Cheshire Cat shirt that reads "Everything's Funny if You Can Laugh at It," denim capris, my purple Converse that I enhanced with some Sharpie stripes, a couple of sparkly plastic bangles, and the amethyst earrings Dad got me forever ago (Mauve must have sparkle).

You have no idea how long it took me to figure out that outfit last night. Do I go cute, savvy geek, artsy, or nondescript? First impressions are everything, and I want to meet everyone's expectations. I think this is cute-geeky-nondescript. I just want to nab my badge and escape to my hotel room to get my hair dyed before too much happens.

Peering into the mirror reveals a tired Maeve because I barely slept, so I massage my cheekbones and surrender to some lip gloss. The last thing I want to look is tired. It's the last thing I feel. I bounce on my toes and wriggle all over to get the blood flowing.

There's no putting it off; Jade will be at Walgreens within twenty minutes. He messaged to let me know that they're right on schedule.

Butterflies waltz in my stomach as I ease the bedroom door open. A vision of me sprinting down the road with Mom roaring down on me in the car blooms before my mind's eye. It won't happen. It won't happen.

This is any other day. I'm totally calm, cool, and absolutely justified in running away. It's as if all the terrible, selfish, lying, no-good things I've never done will tip the scales back to balance at this moment.

"Mom! I'm going to grab some donuts."

No answer.

"Mom!"

Something falls in the kitchen, followed by a cascade of plastic, tumbling, rattling.

"Mom?"

Is this the end? Succumbed at last to the Stuff?

"That's fine, Sweetie." I can tell she's distracted. "Grab some Pepsi too, okay?"

"Okay." For a second, I wait to feel some guilt or remorse. Nope. "See you later!"

She doesn't answer, and I just squirm my way through the Stuff to the laundry room. I'm not bringing much, just the essentials. My ears and tail are on the dryer, and I pluck up the ears, arranging them just so and giving the headband an extra clip to keep it there, then the beautiful new tail clipped to my jeans. Excitement swells again. I get to meet Haute! I shoulder the duffel, grab my skateboard and let Mom hear the firm smack and roll of wheels on the sidewalk that is my farewell.

There are more options for pink hair at the drugstore than I thought. Crouched on the floor in front of the rows of shiny boxes with my tail coiled around my sneakers, I have five minutes to choose before Jade gets here. There's no mauve shade, per se, so it's a toss between bright pink and a sort of lavender. I wonder if layering them would make a neat effect? Maybe if Paige really can help.

"You need to bleach first."

"Ah!" I jerk away from the unexpected voice and drop one box of dye, staring at a pair of girl's knees. If I were Mauve, I'd be on the ceiling. Where's her super cat hearing when I need it? When I look up, I can only blink, beholding Paige in a blue Walgreens shirt with a Walgreens name tag, offering me a box of hair bleach and a bright smile. Did my thought summon her?

"Yeah, I know." I grab the box again. I didn't actually, but it makes sense. The colors are so soft and light I probably would've ended up with mud-colored hair or even cream-of-mouse instead of pink. Paige's eyes track around the length of my tail and then up to my ears.

"Just making sure."

Embarrassment sweeps my brain, and I blush so hard that I start to sweat. "Um, thanks. So, you're DeeBee."

She bursts out laughing, then covers her mouth and crouches next to me. At graduation, her energy was too much. Now it's like a summer breeze. "You really didn't know?"

That red stays and beats at my face. "No, I didn't. I'm sorry. I just, you know. I wasn't paying attention I guess."

"I guess not." She grins. "I just thought you knew. You're the whole reason I made my fursona."

"I am?"

"Oh yeah." She flips her hair off her shoulder. "After you told me about it, um, in ninth grade?"

"Wow." Yes, I literally say "wow" out loud, and Paige grins, then re-offers me the box of bleach.

"So, I assume you're going pink?"

The red starts to cool from my face, even though my brain is still recalculating the route from ninth grade to here. "Yeah, of course."

Paige pops up to her feet, sets a hand on her hip, and scans the dye boxes. "There's not really a mauve shade, specifically."

I twitch inside. "Um. It's pronounced m-oh-v."

"Huh?" She looks down at me.

"M-oh-v, not m-wah-v."

Her hand drops from her hip. "For real?" Both hands cover her mouth, then she looks up. "I'm so embarrassed!" But instead of spontaneously combusting like I do when I'm embarrassed, she leans over laughing and offers me a hand up. "So it's Mohv-Cat."

"Yes." I grin.

"Hmm. Sort of French. I like it." She regards me with a slow look. "I was thinking you could combine two colors—"

"Paige." A voice floats over the store intercom. "Paige, customer assistance in first aid."

She tsks, waving a box and addressing the ether, then hands

me the box. "Am I not already assisting a customer?"

"It's okay. I'm meeting Jade in a minute. Like, literally."

"I think those two colors will look great. And I can still help if you want." She motions, "call me," before about-facing and heading off.

I trust her judgment and take the colors to pay while the cashier stares at my ears, then head back out, retrieve my skate-board, and wait.

Every car that turns into the parking lot nudges my heart rate up. It's only two minutes, if that, but it feels like a year, stand-ing there on the curb in the soft, diffused light of a Washington morning, the scent of lilacs drifting around, with my duffel and skateboard clutched close. I'm sure I don't look like a runaway at all, and I force myself to relax. Just enjoying the breeze, thanks.

Oh God, what if I told Jade the wrong address? I said Walgreens, not CVS, right? My gaze darts up the road, squinting as if I could see Athen's car in the other pharmacy parking lot up the road. I grab my phone and check. Nope, definitely told him Walgreens. Breathe in, breathe out. Jade would never leave me hanging.

A bunch of cars are lined up at the stoplight. They've gotta be there somewhere.

The light flips green and someone guns their engine. That has to be . . . .

An azure BMW Spectra with the license plate BLU WOLF whips neatly into the parking lot and rolls right up to me with windows down, blaring *Hamilton: The Musical.*

Yep.

My heart starts again. In the corner of my eye, the cashier

peers out the window and looks mildly unsettled. But that doesn't matter.

Jade—my best friend, my big brother, my soulmate—tumbles out of the passenger side, smacks the door shut, and we take each other in, adjusting our mental pictures.

My breath lodges in my chest, and a lump curls into my throat. He's just—beautiful. I mean, he's no supermodel, but he's beautiful to me. We follow each other on Instagram, so I knew he was going to be short and lithe and compact, Latino, and probably wearing green the way I wear pink. All familiar, from his mop of black curls and laughing black eyes to brown skin, clean-shaven with some acne scarring around his cheeks and jaw. Real and here.

Wearing a great big flashy grin, he throws open his arms but doesn't move.

"Mauvy. Hey. Can I hug you?" He's doing that leaning, "come on" pose with his arms wide. Of course *he* can hug me.

"Jade!" I drop the skateboard but not the duffel, and all but fling myself at him. His arms come around me and he smells like vanilla and cinnamon. I burrow my nose right into his shoulder, and he squeezes, lifting me a little with a mighty "urgh," as if he's as happy to see me as I am to see him. Of course he is. There's no weirdness as there was with finding out Paige is DramaticBat. Maybe it's because I was better prepared.

Maybe it's because he's my best friend.

"Hey, little cat." He's laughing with delight and I love it. I've only heard his actual voice on TikTok, and he's usually singing.

"Hey, big dragon." Tears threaten, and I sniff firmly. No. Effing. Way. "Thanks so much. Thanks, this is awesome."

"Right?" He leans back with another grin, then his gaze flits up and around and back to me. "Is your mom here?"

My stomach morphs into a butter churn. "Uh, no. You know she doesn't leave the house much." Oh God, I'm lying to Jade—to his real face. My insides are disintegrating. He grasps my upper arms and offers a reassuring squeeze, so maybe he's racking up the whole thing to excitement and nerves. I manage one more lie. "But she says hi."

"Hey, it's okay." He tips his head down. He's not much taller than me, which is amazing, and holds my gaze steady, drawing a slow breath in as if to encourage me to do the same. I do. We let it out together and smile at the end as if choreographed. "I get it." Then he leans away and draws my attention to his shirt with a swipe of his hand across his chest. "Check this out. I got it just in time for the con."

Rolling my wrist over my eyes (he politely ignores me crying), I take time to appreciate the shirt. It's his dragon character, pale jade (obviously) on glorious emerald green, but wearing sunglasses and disco dancing, and reads "The Real Dragon Con."

"That's awesome. Is that Mereware?"

"Yep. I'm going to have her sign it in person. She's there this year—"

Karoom! The BMW's engine revs once and we both jump.

The guy who can only be Athen leans across the passenger side, peering over the rim of his sunglasses. "Less talking, more getting-to-the-con."

Jade snorks and gallantly opens the back door, then grabs my skateboard and helps me arrange my stuff around their suitcases in the back, except the skateboard, which we determine will not fit and will also mar the pristine gray fabric of Athen's seats, so he takes it to the trunk. Then I scoot in, feeling simultaneously like an adult and a little kid, in the back seat next to the extra suitcases and a cooler.

The car is so *clean*. It's a job just buckling my seatbelt while trying not to touch anything. It's beautiful—the most beautiful car I've ever seen in my short life. It still smells new, nothing else, just new car. There's vaguely knowing someone made gobs of money with an amazing design app at a young age (and has a rich grandmother), and then there's sitting in said person's six-month-old BMW and understanding what money means. I suck another deep breath, trying to levitate so I don't mess up the car.

Athen twists around and I have just a second to assimilate my mental image into the reality of him as he halfway offers a hand but seems unsure if I want to touch. I realize I'm tucked in all close on myself and sitting on my hands. He probably doesn't want to shake my hand now, so I offer a big cheesy Cheshire grin. Even sitting, he is large and tall, like a well-proportioned teddy bear you could just take a nap on. He's sort of your white, preppy geek archetype with short, messy dark hair and sunglasses.

And he's smiling.

"Hey, it's really nice to meet you finally. This means a lot to him." He tips his head back toward Jade, who is stowing my skateboard in the trunk. The shock of realizing Athen is still only twenty-one, as he comes off as a very old soul online, settles me a little. He is an old soul in person, too. He's not douchey because of money, thank God. His energy comes across as someone who's never had to worry about anything in life and just wants to pamper everybody. Jade told me Athen's a Taurus, but I don't know what that means except he just had a birthday. I try to chill.

"It means a lot to me, too." My voice is softer than I meant it to be, and his shoulders twitch forward as if he's going to protect me from something.

"I know. Tell us if you need anything okay?"

There's the faintest whiff of the paternal in that, which makes me feel younger than I want to. He's only three years older than me. I force myself not to feel defensive and nod. These are friends. There will be thousands of people at this event and all kinds of stuff going on. I might need something, and it's good to know someone's there.

Jade shuts my door as he sidles back around, plops into the passenger seat, and then points imperiously toward the windshield. "Onward!"

In the backseat, I shift and withdraw my hands from under my thighs. Now is not the time to scrunch up. I wonder what the Walgreens cashier thinks, seeing me hop in a snazzy car with a couple of clearly not-from-here guys. Or what my mom would think. It's best not to wonder. I dig my phone out of my pocket to execute part two of the lie: letting her know I'm detouring to the park because it's a beautiful morning (my backup plan was the library if it rained).

Jade rummages in a reusable tote printed with jungle flowers and twists around to face me. Palms up as if making a great offering, he displays a cluster of Pixie sticks.

"Eee! How did you know?"

He just grins. Pink and purple striped straws for me. Like an infant, the jangling in my stomach eases a little now that we're driving. Just keep me rolling and I won't fall apart.

Jade has a pocket knife for the straws, and there, at not quite ten in the morning, we get to work on our sugar rush.

Athen eyes this sidelong while Jade and I toast straws. "You sure you have enough sugar to last the drive? I could stop somewhere."

"Lo que sea." Jade tips back his green sugar straw and grins at Athen's snort of disbelief. "Mister Venti Caramel Frap."

He pronounces it care-uh-mel, which I file away as one more thing to love. I don't think I've ever heard anyone say it that way before (just car-mull), and it makes me laugh.

Jade grins. "This was so cool of your dad. And your mom. I'm glad she gets it."

The sugar dries to dust in my throat. Does Jade know? Is he trying to make me crack? I don't flinch, but I dump a bit of sugar into my lap and Athen hisses lightly between his teeth—as if there's a laser sensor for any dirt that might touch his seats. I brush it into my hand, hold it awkwardly, and look at Jade, who tips his head toward the window.

I guess if you can be habitually hoardy, you can be habitually neat, too. I wonder what Athen would think of my house. But it's easy to flick the offending sugar out the window, and being clean is hardly a fault. If I had a car like this, honestly, I would never even drive it. Maybe to the car wash from time to time. Even the tires are clean.

For a second, I think Jade will pursue a line of questions—

why didn't my mom come to meet them, too? Is everything okay? Are you, in fact, a giant, sleazy liar?

But then, he moves on with a chuckle, reaching over to grip Athen's knee and shake it a little in what I think is a silent, *relax big guy*, and tucks himself sideways against the seat so we can converse.

"How was graduation?" His smile is warm, his demeanor eager but not needy or overwhelming. My friend. I wonder why I was ever worried about meeting him. Just like online, he keeps the ball rolling. He knows how to talk, how to make me feel okay.

Something in me clicks on. Usually, when people ask me things, I tighten up and just wait for the conversation to be over. But I want to tell Jade everything.

So I do.

I tell him almost everything, and he doesn't think I'm weird or talking too much. Yes, I ask him stuff too—how he's liking Portland since he moved, his summer plans, and all that. We've said it online, but I like to hear him say stuff with his actual face.

I confess that I didn't know DramaticBat was Paige from my school (they didn't either, so I feel a little justified and wonder if she's coyer than she lets on). I tell him about my Dad's business and fishing trip and how I wanted to go but this is so much better, and . . . well, we don't talk about Mom much. There's a silent agreement. Jade is the only person I've ever told about the hoarding. I don't want Maeve clouding over into Mauve. I don't want to talk about it more than I have to.

We talk about how I might come to Portland, and if I meet Sunspire she might recommend me for a scholarship. In half an hour we cover nearly everything I have to say about real life, then switch to them. Jade confesses he's never been so stressed out as he has been in college, feeling behind and listening to his teachers wax eloquently about old Broadway stars and afraid he doesn't measure up to most of his class. But this summer he's interning at a music camp for kids since his ultimate goal is teaching.

"Even though you could perform," Athen says easily. I admire the perfect balance between supportive and pushy.

"You could," I pile on, leaning forward between them. "I can't believe how many TikTok followers you have."

"I can," Athen says.

"Nah." Jade laughs, buzzed on sugar like me. "That's just for fun. I can sing anywhere for myself."

"The next Lin Manuel Miranda," Athen says loyally.

Jade snorts and rolls his eyes, tipping his head toward me like, *this guy.* "Okay but, like, a Mexican version." He taps his chest.

"Right. The next . . ." Athen's head tips up as he thinks, peering at the road through his shades, and I can see him mentally scrolling through his vast knowledge of Broadway and musical theater, rivaled only by Jade's. His fingers pat the steering wheel in an understated victory tap. "The next Jaime Camil."

Jade bursts out laughing. "He's old."

Athen is unfazed. "Yes, I said the next."

Jade hunkers down in his seat, red touching his cheeks, flattered. "Anyway, I don't want to be the next one, I want to mentor the next one. I want to pass on what music did for me." He finishes off his pixie stick, and I nod once. Music is his salvation from everything else, like art is for me.

"You'll be a great teacher."

Jade ducks his head with a grin.

"Speaking of music . . ." Athen finally begs for a respite from our chatter.

With a flourish, Jade turns *Hamilton* back on, and I'm treated to them flawlessly performing "Aaron Burr, Sir" along with the recording. Then, for our listening pleasure, Jade belts out "Show Yourself" from the second *Frozen* movie, and his soaring tenor fractures and reforms my heart until we roll into Olympia.

It is the singular best car ride I've ever had in my life.

IF YOU'VE NEVER BEEN. Olympia's waterfront is beautiful. Three years ago, they finished construction on the West Bay Convention Center, which is not as huge as it sounds but fits in tidily with the pretty bistros, children's museum, parks, and gardens that run along the west bay of the inlet, along with a string of five hotels. We pass my hotel on the way to the convention center, and I'm so hopped on sugar at this point I blow it a fond kiss and promise to return after registration.

And I see furries! People who are just obviously not from here, with rainbow hair or wearing tails and ears like me, and a few full-on suiters strolling toward the docks on this beautiful day.

"Here's the plan." Athen is very official, and I manage not to giggle when Jade draws up like a soldier coming to attention. Athen is eyes-forward, super serious as if we're part of his software development team. "I'm dropping you guys at the convention center so you can pick up badges, and I'll get us checked in at the hotel. Then, Mauve, I'll bring your stuff back here and take you to your hotel. Okay?"

It's not an invitation for alterations to The Plan, but to acknowledge that we understand. My brain scrambles. Usually, I'm taking care of things, but I realize that I didn't even worry about the next steps during the whole car ride. I nod, and Jade says, "Sir, yes sir."

The convention center avenues and parking lot are a tangle, with little roads leading off to different loading docks, but Athen has been here multiple years and just cruises along. Like a kid, my nose is pressed to the window to see if I can figure out anyone I know or any famous artists or suiters. Athen drops us at the front entry. I thank him quickly for the ride, scramble my sugared-up self out of the car while they have a quick kiss, and then Athen drops his sunglasses back to his nose, revs, and drives off.

The air reeks of car exhaust, flowers from the baskets spilling over around the entry, and the teeniest whisper of the waterfront, cool and fishy. There are people everywhere. Little clumps looking at restaurants on their phones or checking the con schedule or swapping numbers. Suiters pose near the flower baskets, greet cars, and pause for photos while confused humans shuffle along the sidewalk out of the way.

The smallest touch of nerves curl in my belly, and I release a slow breath and focus on all the pink petunias in one basket, counting them slowly.

"Twenty-six," Jade says. He's the one who suggested I focus on pink things when I freak out. My therapist even confirmed this is a thing and actually it works. Jade counting with me so I don't feel weird is just him. He's going to be an amazing teacher.

"Twenty-eight." I point at a couple of blossoms hiding underneath a spray of geranium.

"Twenty-eight!" Jade rectifies, then laughs like the Count

from *Sesame Street.* "Ah! Ah! Ah!"

"You are such a dork."

He grins, teeth flashing. I get a mental image of him as a dragon, and for two seconds, the world is perfect. "I know, and it's why you love me."

"It is. Yes."

"May I?" Jade checks in with a look. I smile, and he slings an arm around my shoulders so we can sashay into the building.

There's a whole other aroma in the building—people. So many people stuffed into a space. It's not bad—yet. And it's not the smell of people not showering—it's the smell of a lot of people on a warm Olympia morning in June. The nerve curls tighter in my stomach, and I resist the urge to sniff my armpit. If anything, I'm covered by Jade's delicious—what is it, aftershave? He smells like a cinnamon roll.

The lobby of the convention center is glorious. Morning light streams through massive windows. Small trees and an array of other plants festoon the entire space, stairs leading to a mezzanine level and conference rooms, a fountain that splashes happily (which a maroon-clad convention center employee is politely requesting people to stay off of and out of, thanks ever so much).

Six-foot banners with the convention mascot, a marmot named Hermes, welcome everyone arriving in the lobby. Smaller signs with arrows point the way to panel rooms, the Dealer's Den, which isn't open yet, and registration. This year's theme is "under the sea," so every sign has adorable corals, bubbles, and sea lions swirling around. A couple of the badges I've done are little mer-versions of people's fursonas, and everyone with a water type 'sona has been going nuts online, proclaiming their steps to world domination.

It's good stuff.

"Come on." Jade laughs and steers me onward. "Badge first, then staring."

"Okay." My phone buzzes and I jump. I turned Twitter back on, so I assume it's someone checking in.

Mom: *Please get something for lunch too. XO*

Breath slides out my nose. That's the only thing my body can do, other than getting sweaty, as I'm reminded of my lie while my innocent friend takes me under his wing. Tell Mom the truth now?

Or later.

Or ever? I could say I'm at Paige's.

No, no. I can't drag more people into the lie.

"Are you okay?" Jade slows down, squeezing my shoulder, then makes a quiet sound because my shoulder is so tense it probably feels like a ball of tungsten.

"Um, yeah, just a sec." Drawing away from him, I hunch over to answer Mom.

Might not be back in time for lunch. Want me to send a pizza?

There's silence, then the typing ellipses goes . . . and goes . . . then stops. My heart throbs as if I've started running, and sweat moistens my armpits. Did I put on deodorant? Ugh. I'll shower at the hotel. The typing signal goes again.

Mom: *No thanks, see you later. XO*

Mom: *Have a fun afternoon.*

For a second, I feel as if I'm made of goo, like the stuff they put inside a Gusher. It's as if I'll just ooze into the floor as some weird, sugary color. The pixie sticks were a mistake. My fingers tremble so badly I have to roll my shoulders and shake one hand to steady it. Keep it simple. Liars elaborate, right?

Thanks! Love you.

PS, get some fresh air. It's really nice out.

I include a wink and kiss and flower emoji. That's good, right? We're all normal here.

Jade steps closer and I click the screen off, then shove the phone back into my pocket. Oh God, he looks so worried. Am I that much of a mess? Being Mauve at the con in the first five minutes? Fail.

"Do you want to sit down for a minute? It's a lot, right?"

"Nah, let's get badges. I don't want to make Athen wait too much, and I want to shower and take care of this." I ruffle my hair because Jade knows the plan.

He squints at me, then shrugs one shoulder. "Mmkay."

From behind us comes a weird, clattering chirp. Jade glances around, then laughs and turns me about to behold a five-foot-something purple toucan wearing a lanyard heavy with badges. For a second, I'm just dazzled by seeing my first suiter up close, then a realization hits me like a splash of sunshine.

I shriek.

She shrieks.

"Marli!"

"Chraw!"

Our screeches fill the entire lobby and I don't even care. We do a little happy dance. Marlitoo chatters and clacks her incredibly crafted golden beak, and shuffles in to envelop me in a fluffy wing hug. The nerve in my stomach whips open and up to my throat. I want to cry again but manage to laugh hysterically instead.

"You look amazing! Oh my God!"

She pulls back and dances in a little circle and then reaches up to touch my pink ears. I twirl so she can admire the new tail, and she leans over to preen at it. I'm dying.

"Oh, Jade—" But he's already got his phone out and flicks his hand to herd us together for posing. I wish I had my makeup and new hair, but this will be for posterity. Meeting my second—well third, Athen counts—furry friend.

"You want these on Twitter? One more. Yeah, that's cute." He laughs when Marlitoo and I come up with a me-fainting-into-her-wings pose with a hand on my forehead.

"No"—I can barely talk for laughing—"don't post them. I really want to get my hair and makeup on first. This is for posterity."

Marlitoo nods enthusiastically, then clacks her beak and inquires, "Chr chr? Chrop?" patting her badges with a wingtip. She never breaks character in-suit, and it's adorable. I really have to keep it together and not cry. Maybe this will get easier as the day goes on.

"Yes, I have it!" I pat both her shoulders. She's asking for the badge she commissioned with her toucan as a sea horse. It sounds wacky, but the design works, I promise. But I realize I have nothing with me. Athen has all my stuff. "Oh, shoot, not with me. I'll bring it later, okay?"

She nods, shimmies her tail, clacks, and carefully preens one of my cat ears. By then, she's attracted more attention, and people are inching in for photos. Jade and I wave her off, and she twirls away to pose near more tropical-looking potted plants.

Some angel has left a box of granola bars on one of the con tables with all the free bookmarks, postcards, flyers, and a few "crisis brochures." Jade and I swipe a couple of granola bars and move down the hall that leads to a great, open arboretum space with more windows and a glass ceiling, registration tables ranged all along the longest wall.

"There's you." Jade leads my attention to the regular lines and last names R–Z. "I'll meet you back in the lobby, okay?"

"Sure thing." We give each other a little squeeze, and I try not to feel bereft when he leaves my side to head toward the sponsor lines. I wouldn't say it's a lonely feeling. I've rarely felt lonely in my life. All my friends are tucked safely in my phone, in my pocket, after all. But it's different being here with people.

Maybe I'm an extrovert after all. Maybe I just have to like the people?

I dunno; Paige is an extrovert because the people don't matter. It doesn't matter who it is. She's nice to everyone. Thinking of her, I slip into place at the back of R–Z and tug out my phone to finalize the details of her helping with my hair when she gets here. I send her my number in a Twitter message so we can weed out our messages from the stream.

"That's a really cool tail."

The girl in front of me has turned around to converse, and I try to remind myself I'm Mauve here—perky and friendly and fun. She's taller than me, a couple of years older, and cute with pale skin made glowy by her purple hair. She's sporting a Charizard shirt and cat ears.

"Thanks." I tuck my phone away. "They're by Haute Creatoure. She'll be at the Dealer's—"

"Oh em geeeeee I love her!" She lights up like a glowstick. "I can tell now. I'm saving up for a pair."

It should be like I've found a kindred spirit, but the cat ears are nondescript black with leopard print on the inside—the kind you buy at Halloween, not from an artist.

Oh my God.

Did I just have my first snobby thought about someone? Am I that person?

I try to think how I want to feel when I meet new people. Sunspire often paints a beautiful little snail character called Sunspot, holding a sign with nice little maxims like: Be the Difference. Being Kind is Free.

"Oh, nice." *Saving up as you did*, I remind my snobby inside self, *you're not more special just because you have better-made stuff.* "Yeah, her stuff is the best."

She gestures around. "Is this your first con?"

I wonder if it's obvious or just a standard question, but when she asks, the excitement I felt when Dad offered this trip bubbles up. "Yeah, actually, it was a graduation present from my dad."

"That's so cool!" She bounces a little, and I let a breath out, trying to relax. "I'm—well, I'm Alexis, but call me Nira."

"Mauve." I offer my hand. I cannot wait until I have paw gloves. Nira, how will I remember that? It's like the Nile. Black cat. Egypt. Nile, Nira, Nile. I have to do stuff like that when I meet new people. It's a trick my mom taught me, of all people.

"Mauve?" She pronounces it carefully. Some people have

peculiar fursona names, and I can tell she's trying to get it right.

I tap my ears. "Like the color?"

"Ah. Oh!" Her whole face brightens again. "Like MauveCat? Are you MauveCat? I love your art!"

Heat rushes my face. The casual happiness I expected to feel when someone recognized my name for the first time doesn't come. Instead, it's a weird, self-conscious feeling and all the cool I would have on Twitter to just say, "thanks, stay cute!" melts away from the heat of my blush. Fortunately, I don't have to say anything because she's still talking.

"Oh my gosh, your stuff is so cute. Are you drawing at the con?"

"Thank you." I can take a compliment; I just didn't expect her enthusiasm. But it's cool; she gets it. "Yeah, I'll probably draw. And Sunspire invited me to do an art panel with her on Sunday." If I say it out loud, maybe I'll be calm by then.

She grins. "That's so cool!"

"Right? I can't believe she invited me." I mime waving to a crowd at a panel. "Hey everyone. Here is world-famous furry artist Sunspire, and . . . small friend. You don't know me, but I'm gonna tell you how to draw."

Nira-Alexis—okay, just Nira—smiles. "I knew who you were."

The sudden sincerity after silliness takes me off guard. I want to be witty, but it turns out it's easier to be witty when you have time to type a response instead of watching another human's face. "Yeah, true. Thanks."

There's a not-completely uncomfortable silence, and she seems to realize I'm feeling awkward, so she smiles a little and turns abortively as if to leave me alone.

"So, come watch me," I add with a little grin. "If you want. Is this your first con?"

"Third," she says, but not in a superior way, and relaxes again. "I went to this one a couple of years ago, and Califur while I was at school last spring."

"Wow." That's my dream: traveling around doing art at cons. I don't tell her that, but maybe she sees it. Or sympathizes, or felt like she was bragging, because she looks compelled to add something.

"Yeah, I like to come. It makes me forget about stress and my family and stuff for a few days." She wraps an arm around her middle, but when she speaks again, it's matter-of-fact. "My dad drinks. It's really hard to be around him, and I don't really like going home on breaks." Another shrug. "I didn't realize how good it felt to not be around it until I wasn't. Last year, I blocked his number for a couple of hours because he kept calling me after he'd been drinking. It was amazing." She grins, but the ache behind it opens an answering pang in my chest.

I want to answer, to empathize, but mostly I'm shocked. We met two minutes ago and she's just telling me this thing. Her dad's an alcoholic. You can just tell people that stuff? Without my consent, my tongue and lips are forming around the words "I know how you feel," but I cannot, will not, must not talk about all the Stuff here. I find the words my counselor has used that help. "That sounds really hard."

"It is." Another shrug. "But I get to see my friends here, and we vent about our weirdness. And that helps, you know? Hey, um . . . maybe we can hang out." She flips both hands up, palms out in a peace/no-pressure way. "I know it's your first con, and you'll be running around and seeing lots of people, but if you want, I usually hang out playing board games."

Jade gave me a heads up that lots of people, especially people who like my art, will give invites. And he said, "you have permission to turn them down." It sounded silly at the time, but now I know why he said it. She's so earnest, and I've rarely had to turn people down (okay, never)—but with her, it's not necessarily that. I just don't know what I'm doing yet. I wouldn't mind chatting with her. I wouldn't mind watching her talk openly about her family business and seeing how other people react.

I dig out my phone. "Yeah, sure. Are you on Twitter?"

"Mmhm. I follow you. Search Lucky Black Cat or just Nira."

I don't recognize either from my list, but I have almost 8,000 followers, so I don't follow everyone back. There's a lot on Twitter, and too much is exhausting. "Cool. I'll be sure to follow you back, and I'll tell you if I camp out somewhere to draw?"

"Awesome." The moment of talking about her alcoholic father has passed, and I'm relieved, but she still seems perky and with it.

My phone buzzes. "Excuse me . . ."

Nira nods and half-turns, peering ahead. Another group of people bustles away from the table, badges in hand, and we inch forward. The message is a text from Paige.

Deebs: *I'll be in Olympia in an hour or so. I'll get my badge and meet you. Is that too late? You can bleach first while you're waiting.*

I laugh and flick my gaze up to Nira, who waves a hand, un-offended. Gracious. I take note. That's how I want to be— touch-and-go with people. I answer Paige.

Shouldn't be too late to make opening ceremonies.

Deebs: *Cool. Send me your hotel info. Make sure you read the instructions. See you later. ;D*

Why is she so nice? Maybe it feels good. It felt good to talk to Nira. Maybe that's how Paige fills up, the way I fill up by drawing. She fills up by being nice. I answer her.

See you! Thanks.

Deebs: *NP :)*

Just like that, I'm relieved. I didn't really want to attempt my hair alone. I can't afford a disaster at this con.

Nira and I chat a little more, and it's about ten minutes till we're at the head of the line. Jade messages to make sure I'm holding up okay, but doesn't come over. Maybe he feels it's his duty to help me branch out. He knows a bunch of people here, so I will try not to be selfish or jealous.

Mom texts again, asking about Lysol, and I assure her we have some. The room is getting hotter, although we finally feel the AC switch on.

At last, we're up. Well, Nira is up. She collects her badge and turns to me. "Thanks for talking to me. Not everyone is as outgoing as you. And, um . . . I really love your art." She twists her blue lanyard and smiles, pointedly meeting my eyes. This time, the bloom of warmth in my cheeks isn't so bad. "I know I said it, but I want you to know in case I don't catch you again. It's a big con." She grins.

I grin back. "It was good talking to you. I'll follow you back on Twitter."

She nods—and she's off. My first casual encounter at the con.

I survived. I watch her go, then hear a chipper, "Good morning!"

I spin around, realizing I'm holding up the line. The volunteer at the table, wearing small antlers, is still bright-eyed and cheerful. He reads my t-shirt before grinning at me. "Last name?"

"Stephens." I roll to my tiptoes, watching as he scrolls down his list. "Mae—"

"Max? No? Maeve? Here you are! Okay, just . . . lets see . . ." He flips through a box of badges and finds mine. It's emblazoned with bubbles and a starfish and reads "MauveCat." A happy thrill wiggles up my chest. My name. Me. Because I'm here. "Blue, green, or purple lanyard?"

"Purple, obviously." I Cheshire-grin. He plucks a purple lanyard from the box with a vigorous nod and a gesture downward, which I assume is to my purple Converse.

"Obviously." He presents the lanyard and my con book. "Have a great con."

"Thanks! You too."

He laughs and waves me on, and I skip back over to Jade who is sunning himself majestically near the window. Standing and observing the room, which is filling fast and getting warm, I'm about ready for fresh air.

"Here, let me." He takes my lanyard, clips the badge to it, and I bow my head with utmost ceremony for him to place it around my neck. "I hereby dub thee Mauve, pixie purveyor of artistic adornments, cheesy puns, and outlandish adventures."

He stands back to frame me with his hands, and I strike a quick pose, then he drops his hands with a grin. "Ready?"

I huff out a breath and look around the jam-packed lobby

before grinning at him. "I think so." Then it occurs to me this is a publishable moment. "Oh, just a sec."

With the badge in the foreground and Hermes the marmot banners and people in the background, I get a picture of the badge, add a couple of dreamy filters and some sparkle, and tweet:

Purrrrlympian Pixie @MauveCat

I am officially under the sea!

7

BY THE TIME JADE AND Athen drop me off at the hotel, Furlympia has taken over West Bay. Bistros, hotel fronts, and sidewalks are all teeming with jubilant furries. I'm itching to get out now that I've met my first stranger, my makeover is nigh, and I'm *here*.

The boys help me schlep my stuff, though there's not that much—skateboard, small duffel, and a satchel for carrying my art stuff to and from the convention center (which I'm learning via Twitter and Discord is usually shortened to WB or Weeby).

Maybe it's because I'm a minor or because Jade has spilled to him about my anxiety, but Athen takes it upon himself to stride to the check-in with me like a massive bodyguard and doesn't back up until I have keycards in hand. The room is in Dad's name, and he informed the hotel I would be eighteen the next day, but Athen's presence and chill-but-no-nonsense attitude helps. Jade once said Athen makes him feel safe. I thought he meant emotionally safe; I didn't know he meant physically safe, but now I get it.

My hotel is smaller, but there's free breakfast, a little coffee kiosk, and a few people also sporting con lanyards. I note them. They note me. I share a nod with a guy who has a *gorgeous* tiger tail draped over the arm of his chair.

"Okay. All set?" Athen moves back to make room for the confused family behind us while the host laughingly explains the furcon.

Jade reaches for my skateboard. "Want help with this stuff?"

"No thanks, I got it. Um, thank you." My throat is tight again. Really? I fiddle with my lanyard. "For the ride and everything."

Jade makes a soft noise, then moves in for a hug and I let him, burrowing briefly. "It's just so good to see you. I'll let you know where we're having lunch, and if your hair's done we'll see you. Otherwise . . ."

I mumble into his shoulder. "Opening ceremonies!"

"Opening ceremonies," he confirms and pulls back, patting both my shoulders firmly. "See you."

And off they go.

Before anyone in the lobby can strike up a conversation, I snatch my stuff and haul it toward the elevator. There are only ten floors on this hotel—actually, all the hotels are under fifteen stories as dictated by the zoning act of the West Bay Beautification Committee. Athen educated us on the two-minute ride from the convention center to the hotel. He grew up with an urban planner for a mom, so he's interested in all that stuff.

Dad put me on the fifth floor, either because it was the only room left or because he knows I like to be high up (cat in a tree). Probably the former, but I'll choose to believe the latter for my well-being. There's a welcoming *click* and the light flashes a go-ahead green from my key card. I press my shoulder to the door.

I pause for half a second, breath suspended. I realize I'm shouldering in as if there will be an obstacle against the door.

But it swings wide.

Noon light pours into the immaculate room, and breath leaves my chest. An acre of bed with about fifty pillows, a crisp white spread, and hospital corners dominates the room. Surfaces gleam. A TV the size of a billboard crowns the wall to my right with the remotes on the dresser aligned at exact right angles to the TV. A little coffee maker sparkles, and there's a mini-fridge and a small table and chair where I can work if I get another commission. There's not a mote of dust or piece of clutter in sight. Even the wastebaskets are clean and empty.

The room smells like . . . nothing. No mildew, no mysterious odor #4. Like clean sheets and . . . okay, there is a soft scent, something warm. Cleaner? Lemon and sunshine? Hope? Is this the smell of hope?

The door creeps shut behind me as I stare. With the click of the lock, I drop duffel and skateboard and fling myself into the bathroom. It's shiny—glistening tile floor, glassed-in shower, an array of lotion and soap products, water glasses, monogrammed towels. I bury my face in a fluffy white towel and breathe deeply in the scent of the clean. Then, I twirl myself out to the room and across the floor to drag open the drapes.

The view looks out over the street—I'll be able to see the lights of the bay at night (if I'm here much), who's walking up and down the street, and the sunset. I wish I could shove open a pair of shutters and sing, but the best I can do is press my hands to the glass and shout at the street below.

"Hello, Furlympians!" The semi-anonymity of shouting from a hotel room window gives me some Mauve energy, even if nobody hears me.

Just walking into the room is like a vacation. I can't imagine what sleeping here will be like (if I sleep).

Next up: belly flop on the bed, then I construct a small pillow fort, and text Dad.

All checked in and safe. The room is amazing! Thank you!

I add a kissy face.

There are no new texts from Mom. Nerves tighten my belly again. Is she mad? Does she know? She's probably just filling out her surveys. I tap our conversation, double-checking. Nothing. I know I need to tell her the truth, but not yet. Realizing I've all but tightened into the fetal position in my pillow fort, I force myself to unfold, text Paige my room info, and toss the phone onto the other half of the bed.

Time to break in that shower.

Bleaching your own hair is not as fun as the movies would have you believe (if they have you believe this, I don't actually know). I'm glad I read the instructions before showering because apparently, the greasier your hair is, the better. The oils protect your hair and so on.

I make use of the shower cap the hotel provided in my goodie basket, which I didn't know was a thing until I saw it in the basket. The shower is an out-of-body experience. Or maybe the best in-body experience. I could make a meme now: "Sure, sex is great, but have you ever had a hot thirty-minute shower without having to move fifty milk cartons and six bins of half-used, expired bath products out of the way?" I've never had sex, but I'm not convinced it's going to be better than this shower.

I haven't had what I would consider a real, private shower since visiting my dad a couple of years ago. But even then, he's a little stingy about the water bill. It's always hard not to compare it to home and think about how much better Mom's life would be if she could just, you know, use the bathroom for its intended purposes.

But the hotel is footing this bill, so I let the steam rise. The soap smells amazing. Verbena, I think. The shampoo and conditioner smell amazing (no, I don't use them, just smell). Even the free little lotions are a knockoff grapefruit that is possibly my new favorite scent. It wells up in me with joy, and to cap it all off, I discover a fluffy white robe in the closet. I fling it over the disintegrating old t-shirt I brought specifically for the hair-dying adventure and get to work on the bleach.

Oh God. It reeks, burns, and my arms ache by the time I'm done. In my future: some freaking exercise.

When Paige knocks, I'm lounged out on that king-sized bed with some junk show about million-dollar homes in the background (a girl can dream) and catching up on Twitter messages with my damp, now-ghostly pale hairs, ready for pink. I try not to be appalled when I look up in the mirror. Platinum is not my color. Hopefully, pink will be.

I flop off the bed, pad across the plush, nonsticky carpet, and check that it's her before opening the door.

"Momo!"

A laugh grabs my chest. "Momo?"

"Mmhm. Mauve. M-oh-v. Momo." She slides her hand

through the air, drawing the obvious conclusion. I'm starting to love her gestures and how it feels to be in the same room with her. Is this friendship? Furry sisterhood? Something else? Maybe I should talk to Jade again about the ace thing and re-evaluate. But not now. I'm just happy to be out of my house and with my people, feeling feelings other than what I feel in the house.

Paige goes on, holding in the doorway. "Now you have to live with it like I live with DeeBee." She grins, and I want to melt. I have a nickname for my nickname, and I don't hate it. "Hey, nice work on the bleach." She takes in my pale hair with a professional nod, then holds up a zippered, compartmented bag plastered with peonies. A memory strikes me of seeing it in the dressing room during *Les Misérables*—all her hair and makeup stuff.

"Thanks! It was painful." Maybe it's her, or maybe it's my hair or the hotel room or knowing she's DramaticBat, but the awkwardness of seeing her delivering pizza and at graduation and Walgreens is more or less gone. Familiarity breeds normalcy, I guess, and I realize that it feels really nice to be around her.

We move into the room and shut the door just as a herd of more con attendees trails off the elevator down the hall.

"Oh wow, what a great room." Paige drops her bag on the TV cabinet-slash-dresser and puts her hands on her hips like Peter Pan, surveying.

"Yeah, Dad felt guilty for not coming to graduation." I laugh, but she just smiles and saunters to the window to peer out.

"Oh hey, look! Look! It's Kyrosa!"

"Oh my God!" Scrambling for my phone, I dash to the window (as if this is the last time we'll ever see this suiter), and there is Kyrosa in the street—a gorgeous (I mean, this suit is nuts) silvery-white and aqua caribou with gleaming silver antlers that flash in the sun and top out at about nine feet tall. The airbrushing and trimming on the suit are flawless. Xe has shining silver hooves, liquidy violet eyes, and the nose looks like a velvety caribou nose. My phone fights against zooming in through the screen while Kyrosa pauses here and there with xyr handler to let people snap photos.

"Eeee!" Paige bumps me as she squeezes in with her phone to try and get a picture. A girl moves in to try and pet Kyrosa's nose, and xe prances back, waving a hoof in a no-touchy way, and xyr handler steps in between them, explaining some etiquette.

"Ugh," Paige mutters, shaking her head. "So rude."

I want to say, "maybe she's new." I mean, if I didn't know etiquette because of years of seeing suiters vent about being touched, hugged, pinched, and groped, I would probably squee and move right in to maul them too. But instead of defending the person, I clam up. Paige and I are getting along, and my habit of talking back to my mom tends to start fights, so I just nod. No point wasting precious reserves defending someone I don't know. It seems to be figured out, anyway. She and the handler are nodding, high five, and the girl slinks back to her friends, face pressed into her hands.

I point it out and smile a little, relieved on the girl's behalf. "Lesson learned."

Kyrosa and handler move on toward the convention center, and Paige scrolls through her pictures. "These are all blurry. I guess we'll probably see everyone two or three times, huh?"

"Hopefully." She finds one good picture, takes a minute to tweet it, then looks to me. "Shall we do a before and after?" Her phone rises and I throw my hands up as if I'm blocking a laser beam.

"Argh! No."

Paige laughs and tilts the phone away as if to assure me she won't snap any sneaky pics. "Come on. I won't share it, but it'll be cool. You'll be happy!"

She's probably right, but I feel squirmy. I'm trying to shed me, not document. Also, the bleached look . . . but I do love a good makeover before and after. Maybe all the Instagrammers I follow felt the same way about their before pic.

"Okay, okay." I draw a breath through my nose and nod, and she ushers me to the bed to sit. Out of habit, I check my phone, scrolling to make sure I didn't miss a message from Mom, but nothing since the earlier stuff.

"Eyes up! Man, I wish I had your neutral expression. You always look mildly interested. I feel like I look constipated."

Laughter bursts right out of my face, and Paige grins, clicking a couple of pictures.

"Yeah, right." I manage to get my face into a normal expression with a teeny smile so later-me looks at the picture and remembers I knew I was about to transform.

"Perfect. I'll send you these. All right, we don't want to miss opening ceremonies." She fiddles on her phone for a second, a song starts softly, then she draws the volume to max and blasts "This One's For Us" by Renata.

"Nice!" We have the same taste in music? For a second, it's easy to almost forget my mom is buried in her house, and I will be too again on Monday. A lump sits in my belly, and I shake my hands to rid myself of it.

The song splashes around us, making the world brighter. I try to focus on the moment. Paige tosses her phone on the bed, strikes her Peter Pan pose again, and flashes a devilish smile. "Let's do this."

Paige's meticulous attention to detail and the setting time means I'll miss lunch with Jade and Athen, but it'll be worth it—I hope. I'm not gonna lie—sitting with tin foil packets stacked in my hair, positive my scalp is melting off, and every olfactory sensor burned to a crisp is not exactly a spa time experience. But at least I have company.

We listen to a few more songs, then Paige flips channels until she finds *Broadway Moms* and glances at me.

"Uh, pass." I can't handle a thing about overbearing moms just now. Or ever. Maybe it's more fun to watch if you don't have to live it.

Paige taps her temple in salute and clicks on. News, sports, music videos, and then the wild colors and familiar voices of one of my all-time favorite cartoons, *Little Gem Dragons*, flashes by. I don't say a word. It's a kids' show. I'm not going to ask witty, sophisticated Paige to watch cartoons with me. She hesitates, though. For a second, I watch her thumb poised over the up arrow.

Neither of us says a word. We just watch for a minute. It's a familiar episode, with the dragons traveling to a legendary valley.

It would be my dream to do concept art for something like this. Also, I know for a fact that Jade based his character off one of the Great Dragons in this show a million years ago, but he won't fess up to it.

Paige cocks a hip and rests her weight, slowly lowering the remote. I drape my tail over my lap and smooth the fur, hand-over-hand, and finally venture, quietly, "I love this show."

Paige flings her hands into the air. "I freaking love this show!"

So that's settled.

A marathon of *Little Gem Dragons* gets us through the dye setting, cutting, and styling. Paige refuses to allow me a glimpse in the mirror. That magical bag of hers is like a salon to-go. She has everything for the dying, even owns hair-cutting scissors.

"Where did you learn how to do this?"

She laughs. Maybe she can see through the question, which is actually, *do you know what you're doing?* Cutting off a few inches is one thing, but giving someone a pixie cut and dye job is another realm.

"Oh, you know." *Snip snip.* Ponder. *Snip snip.*

I watch rainbow-colored dragons cavort across the TV, and then my gaze follows damp, pink locks of hair as they fall onto the towels we've spread out. So far, the color looks amazing. My guts spin into a tight braid from my stomach to my chest. I've never changed my look this drastically in one day.

I realize Paige didn't answer, not in a deflective way, but as if she believes I do know. "Um, I don't know actually."

Snip. "My cousin's a stylist? When she was in beauty school, she practiced on us?" She's not asking me. She's reminding me as if she told me some time ago and is surprised I don't remember.

My ears catch fire. "Oh, right. I forgot." I just fess up. It's exhausting to pretend.

She laughs. "Really? I thought that's why you said I could do this." She brandishes the scissors high like Sweeney Todd. "You let me come at you thinking I was just winging it?"

My throat clamps. She's joking, un-offended, but I feel like a box of litter. "Well, I mean, with theater and stuff . . . ."

She just laughs and touches my jaw to steer my head sideways a little. *Snip.* Thoughtful pause. *Snip.* Hair, weight, and old Maeve fall to the floor, but I feel heavier.

It's the house. It's the Stuff. It's a planet, with its sinking gravitational pull and objects in orbit—mostly me—turned inward and orbiting Mom and the house. I've been so absorbed in fighting the pull that I didn't see anything else, not even this girl who wanted to be my friend.

I manage some words. "I'm sorry."

Her scissors pause and she leans down to peer at me. "For what?"

"For not . . ." I squeeze my tail in both hands. "For not paying attention."

There's no bright laugh this time. "It's okay, Momo. We've all got stuff going on."

The braid of crap inside—nerves, fear, guilt—spins and tightens in my core. Does she know? Is that a subtle invitation to spill my guts? I can't. Sitting in a hotel room on a bright summer morning at a furcon, with another girl doing my freaking hair, is like a fairytale. No way I'm unzipping my baggage and letting it spill out all over this moment.

"Yeah, I guess so." My therapist should've recommended stroking soft objects a long time ago; this tail is doing wonders. I would've loved to have a cat, but not in that house. It would have to be an indoor cat so it didn't destroy all the local fauna, and I would not do that to an innocent creature. Maybe someday. "Thanks for being cool."

"Mmhm." *Snip.*

My mind shifts around the insanity and pounces on a normal topic. "Speaking of stuff going on, how long have you had two jobs?"

"Pfft. Close your eyes."

I obey and she ruffles my hair. A few short strands fall on my face, and the burning scent of the hair dye is still there, despite the rinse.

"It's not really two jobs," she answers. "Walgreens is just in the summer, and I always fill in if Mom and Dad need me to make pizza deliveries. Why, is that weird?" Pausing briefly, her voice pitches lower in amusement. "How do you think I paid for all the DeeBee art?"

"Um."

I can hear her smirk as if it's satisfying to reveal she works her butt off because people assume mommy and daddy pay for everything. "But hey, you're always doing commissions. That's the same thing."

"Not really. I mean, it's work, but I'm in my room with music and snacks, and you're helping old men find their cotton swabs and driving pizza all over Little Tree."

"All over, yeah."

We both snicker. Yeah, there's not that much of Little Tree. The braid in my chest turns and loosens a little. We let a minute of quiet settle in. Quiet and dragons. Before she can ask about my life, I direct us to a solid, safe topic that could see any furry through a few hours of conversation: "So, why a bat?"

Her laugh returns. "Because they're adorable? And a little weird. And nocturnal? Haunting the rafters of the theater?"

Chatter about our 'sonas sees us through the last twenty minutes of the cut. She might be casually trained, but she's not quick. She even styles it with a blow-dry, mousse, and pomade, her fingers picking and twisting and sectioning my hair. All I can do is pet my tail and wait, trying not to jitter and bounce, until she pronounces me done.

When she does, I leap from the chair, sending it back against the bed, and spring to the mirror by the dresser.

"Oh my God." I've gotten used to how I look with long hair and the two styles I know, but this—perfectly soft, shimmering layers of lavender and mauve and pink coifed into rich swirling spikes. Against the soft pink, my eyes look hazel and my round face doesn't look boring. I look like a pixie—a pixie cat. Maeve who? I don't know her. I am Mauve, forever pink, no age, no beginning, and no end. I look how I want to feel.

I look like . . . me.

The braided coil of nerves spins, unravels, and tears slash my eyes. I press the back of my fist to my mouth and sniff firmly, then exhale.

"Paige, this is amazing."

"You look great," she confirms. If she notices how awkwardly emotional I'm getting over a new hairstyle, she breezes right by it.

"Nice color choices. I can't wait to see you in your makeup and everything. I mean, you look great without. Whatever. You know what I mean."

I keep turning my head, touching the perky little swoops of purple-pink hair. *My* hair! "If you weren't going to be a famous actress someday, I would tell you to do hair."

"I thought about styling wigs." She nods in agreement.

"Maybe in-between your scenes." I grin wide. Multitasking Paige, right? "Wouldn't this be, like, a hundred dollars in a salon? I don't know how to repay you."

"Really?" Her voice edges devilishly. "You don't?"

When I glance over, she's miming drawing. "Seriously? You'd trade for art?"

"Uh, yeah." Her ginger brows crook inwards. "But only if you want to. Seriously. I did this for fun, not because I expected art or anything. My little sister is tired of a new hairstyle every three months, so I always need guinea pigs."

"Are you kidding? I would love to draw you something!" For a second, there's a pang in my chest and it feels like regret. I'm not sure where it's coming from. All signs point to this being a good day. Regret has no place here.

Paige bows then lifts her phone and taps it. "Fifteen minutes till opening ceremonies."

"Oh, geez!" I fling myself around the corner to the bathroom to wrap this thing up, meaning my face. My skin's pretty good (drink lots of water seems to be the best advice so far), so it's really a matter of eyes and lips, and I've got that down. "You don't have to wait for me."

Paige is scrolling on her phone. "Don't be silly. I'm not walking in there alone."

I can't figure out if she's serious or joking again. The pang in my chest tightens, then relaxes to understanding. We've all got stuff. Maybe extroverts don't like being alone. "Okay, this will just take a second."

"It takes about six minutes to walk from here to the Weeby. I timed it."

"Excellent."

She comes up behind me to observe my makeup skills. The important part of Mauve is the eye. It draws all the attention from my human face to my eyes, and now my hair. Paige even tucked pink hair over my human ears so my cat ears would stand out and look more real.

"You're so good at eyeliner," Paige observes, with her arms crossed and her hip cocked, as if she's observing planetary movements. Fact: Maeve is good at eyeliner.

"I hope so," I mumble, swiping twice over my right lid and then my left. That's the trick with eyeliner, you gotta go for it. Tiddling with the line will make it wiggly. The key is confidence. They're almost perfectly symmetrical, and I let myself purr. "I've been using it long enough. I'll show you the YouTuber whose tutorials I use."

Then I realize I've purred, freeze, and peek at Paige in the mirror, but she's piling her hair on her head experimentally and didn't seem to notice. This feels weird and also not. I kept to myself in high school, but not because I don't like people. It's because I don't like *most* people. All my friends were online, and if you talk to someone long enough in person, they start to wonder little things such as why they can never come over to your house and why you smell like mildew and cardboard.

Okay, maybe it's not that I don't like people. Maybe I'm afraid of people.

But this feels good, and Paige hasn't asked. Here in the hotel room, almost an adult, knowing a little more about Paige and what she's all about, this feels really good.

Habit ticks my gaze to my phone, but there are no new messages. I guess Mom's holding her own. I hope she got something to eat. I consider ordering a pizza for her, but then she'd have to deal with the delivery person.

"We should get going," Paige touches my shoulder, and I realize I'm just standing there, staring into the mirror.

Maybe that's what cats are doing when they fixate on a random coordinate on the ceiling—worrying about their mom.

"Yep." Lastly, I need lipstick and gloss. I tried a shade of lip that was actually called Mauve, but it wasn't really. The color that works is called Summer's Eve, and I buy Walgreens out every time it's in stock.

"You look awesome." Paige can't contain herself and grabs my shoulders from behind, squeezing warmly.

I flinch. It's just an energy thing, you know? Maybe it's all the Stuff. I'm worried anything touching me is about to fall on me. Or I'm one of the precariously stacked piles in the house. If someone touches me, I might just fall over. Maybe it's Paige. If she touches me, I might collapse into her arms and cry.

I don't know.

Paige retracts when I flinch, hands springing back as if I'm a hot stove. "Sorry, sorry."

"It's okay." It is. I hugged Jade after all. She just caught me off guard. I turn and squeeze her shoulder, and it's a little awkward to randomly touch someone, but she smiles lopsidedly in appreciation. We both decide the moment is just going to be that.

Time for Mauve clothes. I dig in the duffel while Paige bounces anxiously on the balls of her feet. I quickly replace the old t-shirt with a lavender tank, ratty-hemmed shorts, purple fishnets, and little gray boots with almost mauve boot socks with little black buttons. In case it gets chilly later, I knot a pink and black plaid flannel around my waist. Secondhand stores are amazing.

I clip the tail back on, position my ears, and Paige gives me a thumbs up. "I'm ready." I turn to the door, barely remembering to grab my badge from the bed.

"Wait, wait, wait! Picture." Paige points to the bed. Oh yes, my "after" photo.

We pose, arrange—no smiling—and tap the pic, then I cluster close.

Paige is adjusting the lighting in the picture. "Do you have ScrapIt?"

"Yeah, third screen."

Paige turns away to fiddle with the photo, shooing me when I try to see. When she turns back, she's arranged the photos into a before and after with a starry purple background. I know it's me, but it's almost impossible to tell it's the same person. I can't wait for people to see. "It's perfect. You were right."

"I know." And we hustle each other out the door, Paige

leading me since I'm busy uploading the picture to my Instagram.

Mauve Makeover complete.

Usually, I bunch a thick block of hashtags together, but this only gets the one.

#nofilterneeded

PAIGE KNOWS WHERE SHE'S GOING, so I follow her down the hall and up a set of stairs, moving with the traffic toward opening ceremonies. Since she's in the lead, I check the con book. Most of the art panels are in the same room, the Aster, so I try to make note of it on the way. Quickly, it becomes obvious that the breakout rooms in the Weeby are all named after Pacific Northwest flowers.

At last, we arrive at the Rhododendron room, the main ballroom where the opening and closing ceremonies and the largest events like the concert and the Saturday night dance party will take place.

The under the sea theme is prevalent onstage. The house is dim, and animated lights swirl bubbles and fish around the walls. Massive coral structures frame the stage splashed with soothing aquamarine and indigo lighting. Low, atmospheric music suggests we're floating among the corals or on a submarine ride toward the abyss.

For half a second, it arrests my attention before everything snaps back into focus.

At the moment, the room is, almost literally, a zoo.

I suppose we shouldn't have worried about being late. There was no way this was going to start on time. A couple of guys are up futzing with the microphones on the stage, one with a raccoon tail and the other sporting handsome deer antlers. Meanwhile, a sea of furry humanity mills around the floor, shuffling into the rows of chairs, fursuiters booping people or greeting each other with silent, paw-flapping enthusiasm. A constant ripple of camera phone shutters clicks through the air until people start to silence their phones.

I've never seen such a mix of humanity. I guess I don't get out enough. Even if I did, Little Tree is not like this and never could be. The human scent drenches the air, warm and oily, despite propped doors and AC humming. I realize I forgot to re-up my deodorant and just keep my arms close. I'm trying to take in all the people—tall, tiny, big, dorky, devastatingly gorgeous (I nudge Paige to point that one out), and a rainbow of every iteration of Pride pins and patches—a display that's rare to see in my small town and fills my heart with glee. I'm mesmerized by the diversity in the crowd, but try not to stare.

There are so many people, and my brain just stops for a second. I spot a few pink things, but I don't need to count. I don't feel anxious exactly, just saturated. Saturated by movement, color, snippets of conversation, energy, and body heat. It's the way I feel after wandering a museum for six hours. I can't process any more information.

But there's so much more to see.

Fursuiters meander through the crowd—a neon green wolf, a pink one, a naturally painted one—there are a lot of wolf and canine suits. We spot Kyrosa the caribou again, all but cornered near a wall for photos, silver antlers shining as xe angles this way and that near the coral display. A couple of birds and foxes with squeakers (like from a toy) stop and *beep beep beep* at each other until a con volunteer (gold lanyard) asks them to take it to the lobby. They mope away, then flutter out the door, squeaking enthusiastically.

I begin to regret missing lunch. This wonderfulness is going to take some reserves, and my granola bar is long gone.

"Wow." Paige looks around, and her hand comes around my wrist so we don't lose each other as people squeeze by or jostle close. To be honest, I'd forgotten she was there for a second. "I think this is the most attendees I've ever seen. I mean, I've only been twice but . . ."

I can't even say anything. For a second, my breath shorts because of the smell, then the sensation. The familiar, tight sensation of being surrounded whips around me. It feels like being back in my house.

Oh great, is this a thing? I can't do crowds? No way. I wish I had a bottle of water. I force myself to nod to Paige, then cast around for pink things again. There's a t-shirt. One. A lanyard. Two. The inside of someone's bunny ears. Pink boots. Pink leggings—oh, those are cool. A tall person, whip-thin with long auburn hair to their waist, has a beautiful headband of shiny pink fish fins.

I stroke my bangles to hear them click together. This will not be a thing—crowds will not be a thing. I can breathe through this. This is not the house; these are my people.

"Hey," Paige says softly. "Are you okay—"

"Mauve!"

Jade's now-familiar voice, like a rope down a well, pulls me out of the overwhelm. I spin around, bumping a big guy ahead of me clad in blue from head to toe. I mumble, "Sorry!" But I don't think he even noticed, and I peer around. It's easier to spot Athen first, as he's a foot taller than Jade and more of a presence. There's a halo of clear space around them, and Paige and I negotiate our way through the teeming mass.

Speaker feedback cracks through the room with a shriek, and everyone groans.

"Hey, hey!" booms a guy's voice. "Check check. There we go. Please take your seats, everyone. We'll be starting in just a moment."

Jade thrusts out both hands toward me in a look-at-you way. "Hey mamacita, wow! You look unbelievable!" He throws his head back with a laugh and frames me with his hands before moving in for a hug. "Vente pa'ca. You look perfect!" His fingertips brush my perfectly styled hair, and I breathe deep—amidst all the people, he smells good and safe and cinnamony. I can relax. Mauve-mode.

After a hug, I step back to present Paige. "Jade, this is DramaticBat."

"I guessed." He flashes a grin and gestures to her myriad of badges featuring DeeBee's adorable face. "Great to meet you. This looks awesome." Meaning my hair.

Paige flips her hair playfully. "Right? I'm glad she let me."

Athen looms in, hunched as if the number of people is too much for him, but gives me a thumbs up for the hair. He's more contained than Jade, but the stamp of approval feels good. Knowing how I look and that I fit in here, my body relaxes a fraction, and a spark of confidence glimmers on the horizon.

"Athen, DeeBee." They greet each other. Friends meeting friends. A mix of squiggly excitement and nerves coils and uncoils in my stomach.

Jade presses a bottle of water into my hand. "We got you a wrap, too. Want a bite?"

Relief floods me and I want to hug him again. "Yes, please. My hero."

Jade digs out food, but Athen rumbles, "They're starting," which is unnecessary because an exact second after he says so, a voice cracks over the speakers.

"Greetings my fellow Furlympians!"

Everyone cheers and wolf howls overtake the room.

Jade, Paige, and Athen cheer, herding each other toward the back row of chairs. I cheer around a mouthful of a chipotle chicken wrap, waving a hand in the air. Suiters squeak, then fall quiet. The con chair is Monaghan, who's a bustling, hilarious, chubby leopard online. In real life, he's unremarkable in that you'd pass him on the street and think *engineer*, not the head of the largest furcon in the Pacific Northwest.

"Welcome to the ninth annual Furlympia, under the sea!" A ripple of applause and boisterous hollering, and Athen throws back his head with a howl. "We have some fun reminders, some boring yet vitally important reminders, and some introductions. First, I want to thank the con staff."

But before he can, fursuiters invade the stage—a hare, two dogs, a wolf with a shark plush latched to his tail. Monaghan is swarmed and laughter ripples down the audience, skittering out of my chest. It's clearly a skit but still adorable. I'm here.

I'm *here* with my people.

Bzzt.

Air huffs out of me and I slip my phone from my pocket. With

Jade behind me and Paige to my right, I have a buffer against the sea of people, and I almost feel cozy as I read the text from Mom.

Mom: *What time R U coming home? Need to know when to worry & if U can bring something for dinner. :-)*

I'm not sure if Mom's trying to be cool by abbreviating to letters, but the bigger issue is that she does that when her temper is short. Each single capitalized letter taps the panic center in my brain. I wonder if she knows something's up or if I'm being paranoid.

The typing ellipses pulses then stops.

Everything about the room tightens around me again. Sweat beads on my neck and temples. I try to suck in a deep breath, only to gag on the smell of people. Let me be clear: everyone is clean. There are just so many of us. All the action of entering the Rhododendron room has knocked whatever things I told Mom from my mind, and I scramble to remember my story. Library? Conners party?

Monaghan is saying funny and important things and something about the pool and hot tub in the main hotel—elevators, escalators, a panel change. I think I hear the vital words "art contest," and all I can do is stare blankly at my phone. Mom's text might as well be ancient Sanskrit.

Jade touches my shoulder, and Paige nudges her hip against mine, whispering, "You should enter!"

I have zero ideas about what is happening.

A breath comes into my nose. My poor body, taking control of vitals since I'm obviously in systems failure. "Be right back."

Before anyone can ask, I tuck in on myself, face beating hot red, and worm through people toward the door. Someone touches my ears, there's a tug on my tail; ironically, as Monaghan is reminding people about not hugging and touching suiters. Not that I'm a suiter, but Haute's work is highly touchable. I can't even turn to address whomever it is because of the press of people. I just need out.

They begin to introduce the guests of honor, and I whip around to see Sunspire take the stage, her willowy form and short blaze of marigold hair against the aqua backdrop. I could ignore my mom—

Bzzt.

Or not.

"Oh my God," I breathe out. Finally, I reach the propped double doors and ooze out of the room. The door clicks behind me with a soft rush of air.

There's a ripple of laughter and some claps from inside the room. When I look up from my phone, a sense of disorientation swamps me. I'd blithely followed Paige to the Rhododendron room, and now I can't remember which hall leads out. Also, there are stairs? Did we come up stairs? An escalator?

Apparently, staring at suits and squinting at badges looking for people I know has gotten me lost. I suppose it doesn't matter where I go now that I'm out, but I don't want to end up in some forbidden corner of the hall with convention center staff glaring at me.

"Do you need help?" A woman's voice, bright and soft, snaps me out of it, and I zero in on a tiny woman—I'm five foot five inches tall in a solid boot on a good day, and she only comes to my shoulder, *tiny*—who materializes in front of me, meeting my gaze with a smile. Her gold volunteer's lanyard is clustered with a couple of badges of a bright-eyed, red-breasted nuthatch, including one adorable poofy version with hand-lettered words declaring "Beep of Faith."

I notice that one in particular because I drew it a couple of years ago. I can already see what I would improve, but the art is a MauveCat original.

We conclude at the same time: We know each other.

"Wait—Mauve?"

"Beeper?"

She bursts into laughter. Relief floods me. Despite myself, I melt forward a step and all but collapse in to hug this tiny woman. I love that she's there and I know her. She's like a self-appointed cool cousin/auntie to all the furries—warm, supportive, and knowledgeable. She once helped a random new furry on Twitter find an apartment because he had to get out of his house and knew nothing about anything. She's the exact person you want to find you when you're lost in the woods or a brightly lit convention center.

She laughs and gives me a mighty squeeze. "Are you okay? Pretty hot in there, huh? Drink some water."

Bzzt.

I grasp her shoulders, one hand still gripping my phone. "I just need to make a call—I needed some air. I really want to officially meet you, I just . . ."

"Sure, sure." She flicks a hand and I have never seen anyone who fits their 'sona so perfectly. Okay, she's only the fourth furry

I've actually met, but still. Everything about her is birdlike—fine, quick, and graceful.

"How do I get out?" Pressing a hand to my cheek confirms I am red and perspiring.

Beeper doesn't even laugh at me. She gently touches the back of my arm, physically directing my attention to the stairs. "The main lobby and arboretum are down there. Just hang a left, keep going left, and you'll find it." She beams at me. "It is so good to meet you. And you look beautiful!" She mime-ruffles at my hair but doesn't touch it.

"Thanks, you too! I just . . ."

"Go, go go." She shoos me and steps back, and I realize she was manning a table where there's extra con books, maps, and a starfish-covered sign that declares "Ask Me."

I go downstairs, reeling from all the stimulation and meeting another friend.

Not everyone goes to opening ceremonies. Some are meandering or loitering in corners with their phones. A group of girls playing Apples to Apples lounges on the floor around a bench pushed against the wall. I focus on left, left, left, around corners, and down another hall until I see sunlight and emerge into the main lobby.

A few heads turn as I go by, and I wish I was in the look-at-me-I'm-awesome zone instead of the wish-I-were-one-of-the-geometric-dots-on-the-carpet zone. Eyeing a cluster of pink azaleas out the window, I find an empty nook with a bench near one of the tall windows, drop onto it cross-legged, and raise my phone.

Two of the texts are from Dad.

Frustration and relief make my ears pop. I dash off a quick answer to him, show him my makeover before and after, and tell him about Paige. He should know his support and effort are leading to good things, right? Right.

One was a delayed message from Jade informing me that they got me some lunch. I guess reception is weird in the Weeby, or my hotel, or this latitude. I don't know.

The final message is from Mom just now.

Mom: *Call me.*

This is the worst message to send anyone, ever, unless someone is in the hospital.

A few people meander in the lobby or stand in their clusters. I just need air, so I leave my bench, shove through the doors, and almost get taken out by a trio of snow leopards romping down the sidewalk. One throws their paws up and cocks their head, peering at me with enormous, unblinking, purple cartoon eyes. They have nearly a dozen badges of their character hanging on the lanyard and a small sign offering Free Hugs.

Irritation fizzles into a deep desire to boop the soft pink nose. "Sorry."

Snow Leopard waggles a paw over my head. Then I realize they're admiring my ears. I pause, reach up to touch my ears inquiringly, and they nod vigorously and flaps their paws in sneply approval ("snep" meaning snow leopard). I offer a tentative high five, and the snep taps a giant paw against my hand, then twirls around and trots back to the other two with an exaggerated show of glee.

Suiters are effing adorable.

It's like Disneyland, but the characters all belong to individual people. Their performance is free, sweet fun, no strings attached, for themselves and everyone around them. I wonder if my art makes people feel the way the suiters make me feel. I feel a fraction better and resist the urge to ask for a hug.

No.

Maeve wouldn't ask for a hug, but Mauve is in the house. I whirl and trot after them, remembering that I look awesome too.

"Hey! Hey, picture? Please?"

My snep swirls around and immediately strikes a pose, complete with jazz-paws, and I tuck in near the fluffy chest, angling my camera up for a selfie.

The rest of the pack clusters close and we snap few more photos. What is the name for a group of sneps? A flurry? I make note of badge names so I can tag people, then they move along in a flurry of spots and enormous fluffy tails.

It's so silly and magical and I'm *here*, at the con, the con I've seen people tweet about for years and longed to get to. I'm here.

I watch the sneps amble down the walk toward the bay. It makes one thing clear: I need this weekend. I have to let go of the house, of Mom, for a little while. I have to. If I can't get away for one weekend, how will I go to school, go to Portland—grow up?

Sparkles of joy are starting to pierce my nerves at last, and I can't let anything ruin it. I roll my shoulders and stride into the sun to park on a bench down the sidewalk. A peek-a-boo glimpse of the water and a forest of masts in the distance shines between the hotels and bistros.

I breathe in the sweet, moist, salty summer air, let it out, take two bites of my wrap and a drink of water, and tap Mom's face. I have only two favorites in my phone: Mom and Dad. I replaced her old pic from her fortieth birthday party with one from graduation.

She answers after half a ring.

"Maeve?" Her voice is relieved, a little hitched with worry.

Guilt pierces my belly. "Hi! What's up?"

"Where are you?"

My gaze darts left, to the bursts of fuchsia petunias. "At the park, Mom, I told you."

A beat. The grating creak of her ancient office chair tells me exactly where she is and what she looks like. At the computer, ankle-deep in Pepsi cans, no lunch, leaning back and staring at the ceiling discolored from her smoking. I might as well be standing in the room with her. "I thought you would've come back when it started raining."

A pulse slithers faster up my neck. "Oh—?" My voice pitches higher. Higher is liars. I gulp some water. "It's not as bad here." Liars keep it simple. I learned this from Aliwick, a fandom author who posts writing tips online. He writes mystery and . . . anyway, you get the idea—less to remember. Keep it simple, simple, simple.

I guess the truth would be simple too, but the way she answered the phone tells me now is not the time.

"Maeve."

Apparently, she knows all the tips about lying, too. I tuck myself onto the bench, legs crossed, curling over myself.

"Okay, okay." I suck in a breath, counting the masts in the distance. "I lied." Twenty-two masts. Twenty-three. Twenty-four masts. I think of Jade, laughing like the Count. "I'm with Paige."

I press my palm over my eyes. "We cut and dyed my hair, and it's a really dramatic change. I didn't want to tell you because I thought you'd freak out."

Her chair creaks again—*reeeark*—as she slumps forward. I can just feel the typing ellipses pulsing in her head as there is silence over the line. My head throbs. Not with pain, just with, like, Too Much. I start counting petunias again.

Then she laughs.

Crap.

"Really?" She sounds delighted.

That stab of guilt twists in my stomach until I'm sure I'm going to hemorrhage from my cowardice. "Yeah," I mumble. "You're not mad?"

"It's *your* hair, Maeve."

Is it, though? Is anything in my life really mine? My eyes lift from petunias to trace the architecture of the convention center, along the glass windows, sweeping roof, and the sky, which is almost the shade of Paige's eyes, whom I've drawn into my lie without consent.

"I guess. So, um . . ." I press my hand to my throat as if it'll slow my pulse. "I'm going to hang out with her for a while." A bird darts across the sky. For a second, I'm sure it's a hawk, or a raven or swallow, or some mystic harbinger of good things—a guide. It circles down and flutters to land twenty yards away. Just a pigeon. A pigeon of lies.

"That's fine. You could have told me the truth, sweetie."

Could I, though?

"Thanks, Mom. I might . . ." The pigeon struts forward to

peer at me with tiny, judgmental, dinosaur eyes. "I might stay the night."

"Just let me know."

My head hangs and I press fingers to my stinging eyes. My little bench is getting hot, and I stand to air out my thighs, curling an arm back around my stomach. "Thanks. Did you eat? Do you want me to order you some Chinese food or—"

Twenty people burst through the doors and cavort across the sidewalk in front of me, laughing and talking and catcalling each other at full volume. I can't hear what Mom's saying until, "Who's that? Are you still at the park?"

Am I? I don't even know, now. "That—I don't know, a bunch of people just—" Spinning, I stride down the sidewalk, hunched forward. "—a birthday party or something just came in, I don't know—"

"Came in where?"

"The—" My breath shortens as I can't remember what I've told her. Am I at the park or Paige's house? Or somewhere else? "I can't hear you, Mom. I gotta go."

"Mae—"

I hang up.

I thumb the red button to end the madness, draw in a sharp breath, and force my knees to unlock. The group floods around me, still at top volume—a bunch of men's voices Mom would've had a heart attack over, girls shrieking—and then on they go. I feel like I've survived a wildebeest stampede. I watch them bop down the sidewalk, most of them with fluffy tails of indeterminable canine species.

Someone taps my shoulder and I nearly combust. "What!"

The hand firms, gripping me as I jerk forward a step. "Mauve."

It's Jade. When I turn, he's all chivalrous concern, and his gaze drops to the hand clutched around my phone. "Is everything okay?"

"Um." Nope. Not even a little bit. "Just checking in with Mom. Letting her know I'm avoiding the orgies and whatnot, at least until I turn eighteen."

It looks like he wants to laugh. It also looks like he knows I'm lying. And he's hurt that I'm lying to him, brow crinkling after he almost laughs, a frown taking his face.

Crap.

"Mauvy, please tell me."

Air hisses out my throat slowly, like a deflating tire. "Mom doesn't know I'm here."

His hand slides free of my shoulder and drops with a light tap against his thigh. "Dude. You have to tell her."

Alarm and defensiveness fling my hands into the air. "But why? I have Dad's permission. I'm almost eighteen."

His brows crook in, his mouth quirking in sympathy, but I can tell. I can see how the underhandedness bothers him, and he slides both arms around his middle as if my frustration is physically hurting him. "Because you live with her, and it's courteous. Mauvy, she's your mom. She knows you're with me, right?"

I jerk my head to one side. The sensible pleading in his reasonable dark eyes is making me feel like a rat.

Jade gestures. "It'll take her two seconds to figure out where the con is with a quick search, call the hotel or police, and report that you've run off with someone whose badge name says Jade something. I could get in trouble too, Mauvy."

"She . . ." I think, *she wouldn't do that.* But I don't know what she'd do, and Jade's not wrong. I've told him enough about her over the years. If she thinks I'm unsafe, if she's angry I lied, if she's thinking of Jade as "that college boy" running around with her underage daughter—I don't know. "She said I couldn't go. I tried to tell her, and she said no! Like, like . . ." My hands lift and drop, and I nearly drop my phone.

Jade inches forward a step and touches my shoulder. When I don't twitch or move away, he settles his hand firmly as if he's trying to keep me moored on the sidewalk. My throat clamps shut.

"I know, I know," he says sincerely. My big brother. "I know."

He does know. Except, when his parents were horrified by him choosing musical education instead of medical school and refused to support him, he left Illinois and never looked back, as far as I know. I manage a full breath, and he squeezes my shoulder in invitation. I step in for a hug and tuck my face into his shoulder. I thought I would hate hugging more. At the house—where the Stuff is sliding and stacked and looming, where I have no space—the need to maintain an eighteen-inch perimeter around me is strongest. But miles away, here in the sun by the water, wrapped in the hammered silver security of my longest enduring friendship, all I want is hugs and more hugs and hands ruffling my hair, hands on my shoulders, kisses on my cheeks, and understanding.

"I'll tell her." I sniffle against the blazing green of Jade's shirt, pulling back before I get either makeup or dribbles on it. He pulls out a handkerchief—a fricking handkerchief. "You're such a throwback," I whisper and toss my head as if I still have lots of hair, which I don't, so the lack of movement and weight is surprising. And pleasant. I take the hankie and dab my nose, then hold it awkwardly, glancing at his face. Does one give back a snotty hankie?

He takes it, flashing a grin edged with worry. "Promise?"

"Promise. Let me just chill out. She thinks—" I abort, deciding it's best not to tell him I drew Paige into the lie. "She thinks I'm at the park."

"Mauvy—"

"Before dinner. I promise."

The automatic doors whisk open with authority as Athen strides out and down the sidewalk to us. Paige trots behind him. With friends approaching, some of the anxiety trickles away and the colors around me glow with vibrancy.

Athen pops his sunglasses back on, as if the daylight is too much, and surveys us. "Everybody okay out here?"

"Yeah." I check in with myself and nod. "Yeah, I'm fine. Thanks, guys."

Jade meets my eyes in a silent promise not to tell Athen I lied—as long as I tell the truth too. I nod, holding up one pinkie in a silent promise. I realize Athen could get in trouble too.

Athen checks his phone, scrolling, and nudges Jade. "Lulu's music panel is about to start."

Jade eeks and pats my shoulder one last time. "Find you later?"

I hitch the strap to my satchel higher on my shoulder and take a deep breath, catching Jade's eye one last time. "Yeah, go on. I'll find you for dinner?"

Jade grins, and all I see is a green dragon, showing all his teeth. "Definitely."

And they go. Before I can assure Paige I'm not about to disintegrate into the pavement, she makes a little squawk and pivots around so she's standing directly in front of me, gaze dropped to meet my eyes.

"Pretend you're talking to me."

My voice drops in an unconscious mimic of her fierce whisper and I lean in. "I am talking to you."

She laughs at my . . . funny joke? I catch on she's trying to avoid someone, but still, dude, I'm ambushed by this improv.

"Oh my God," she says too loudly, responding to whatever I've apparently said, "that's so true."

My eyes kinda blink and I dig the bottle out of my satchel, chug some water, and offer it to her. She tosses her hair in a fancy *No thanks*. Maybe she has a germ thing the way I have a touching thing. Her eyes flick up and over meaningfully.

I lift my gaze and see a trio heading up the walk from the direction of the bistros and the bay. I try to figure out which one Paige is trying to avoid and have time to register two young guys and a girl our age-ish before she taps my arm.

"Don't look!"

"You—who?"

"Just a couple of people I don't want to deal with right now. They followed me around for the entire con last year." Paige loops her arm in mine and about-faces us back into the convention center. "Let's go, please," she whispers. The doors slide open and we edge around a mixed group of older women heatedly discussing the latest *Dragon Age* game. "Ugh, whew." She fans her face, which is not red, by the way. She's not flustered by anything. Meanwhile, I can barely keep it together if I see a cat fursuit.

"Why don't you just tell them to leave you alone?"

She tsks, and darts a look at me, then checks up and down as if she just can't believe me. "Because. I'm—*me*."

"I don't know what that means," I confess.

She crosses her arms and looks toward the ceiling. It's the first time I've seen her close off. "I'm a networker. I don't want to be bitchy to people on the first day. It's hard to say no, okay?" I must be watching her blankly because she adds with a shrug, "I'm the nice one."

There are so many things I want to say to that, but they all fly away before I can articulate them. Apparently, talking with my mouth is harder than tweeting or typing. "Oh, I mean, I get it." The trio she's avoiding has entered the building. "Dealer's Den?" I offer, though I sure don't know where it is.

"Too obvious." Paige takes off for the escalator, and I trot behind, glancing back once more at one of the girls pointing—at Paige? I catch up and hop the extra step up the escalator below her.

Opening ceremonies are still going, so the halls are relatively quiet. I wave to Beeper from the top of the escalator and give her a thumbs-up, which she returns, then continues pointing out different rooms on the map to a young couple in fox ears.

Paige has her phone and is thumbing through the con app that gives panel times and the room layout. "Oh! I think . . ." She glances over her shoulder. Sure enough, the crew she's trying to

avoid is headed up the escalator. "I'm going to hit this panel on"—
she pauses long enough to randomly pick something—"padding."

"Padding?" I want to laugh, but I don't want to laugh at her.
"Like for fursuits?"

"Yep. Costuming, theater, you know." She brushes wisps of
hair from her cheeks. "Are you okay?"

"Um, yes." I'm okay. I realize that constantly freaking out is
going to make people think I'm fragile. I'm not. I'm so used to
holding it in, there's a little relief to know that if I flee a room in
distress, people will care. I don't have to hold it together for them
the way I do Mom—because Mom is fragile. But still, I don't want
everyone's con to be about taking care of me. Especially when they
have plenty of other stuff going on.

Paige looks genuinely concerned, not patronizing, but I can
see how anxious she is to not be there right now. I get it and nod
again. "Go learn about padding."

She finger-guns me with a tiny grin and a *tck* sound, then
turns and trots off down the hall.

I extract my phone and take the moment to download the
con app, lifting my eyes in time to see the group she's dodging head
down the other hall. Relief swells when I see they're not following
Paige. Is it creepy? I dunno. I hope I'm never in a situation where I
have to flee down a hallway to avoid talking to someone.

What *does* put me in the mood to flee is the prospect of meeting
Sunspire and doing an art panel, so I decide to face that right now.
I would stop in and say thanks again to Beeper, but she's swarmed
by people with questions or pointing at badges. Another time. I've
already missed Sunspire's interview at the opening ceremonies, so

the next step would be to head to the Dealer's Den, where she said she'll be when she doesn't have panels.

I try to draw on Mauve's confidence, and head back down the escalator and follow the map. A kid at the bottom of the escalator stops when she sees me and squeals.

"MauveCat! No way! Can I take a picture with you? I love your art! I love your hair. I just saw it on Instagram!"

Nerves prickle, then a wash of amazement and surprise and joy steals over me in a happy pink wave. Me? My art? She recognizes me? I think of Nira. Two people have recognized me. "Yeah, of course, sure."

Even though I usually do Mauve pictures solo, I fall into that same mode without thinking much—into Mauve. At last. With a stranger calling me by name and asking for a photo, I know how the snow leopard suiter felt and hop down the last couple of steps to meet my fan. She looks maybe fourteen; she's Black and has purple hair and dramatic violet goth attire, in a pretty, fairy way. I can't tell her fursona because her badge twists around before I get a good look. Maybe an angel dragon? Fluffy with spikes and ears.

She flags down her dad-in-tow and opens her camera phone while I draw the string attachment out of the pouch at the top of my tail, buckle the tiny clip to the end of the tail, and the loop around my wrist—and suddenly my tail can twitch and bounce.

Angel Dragon trots back to me and we pose like old friends. In the first one, she tucks in close and we ham for the camera. Then we do more of a character pose to show off the tail and such. Her dad is laughing and offering pose suggestions until she eeks.

"I don't want to miss my panel." She clasps her hands and

wrings them, grinning at me. "Thank you. Thank you so much, I love your art!"

"Thank you." My heart is tight, but not with anxiety. It's nearly the level of joy that struck me when we left Walgreens. "Have a great con."

"You too! Dad, come on!" She flings herself toward the escalator and he follows, offering me a little salute on the way.

It's extremely satisfying to stand there and casually move my tail. People double-take because, yeah, it's awesome. A couple of people take pictures, and one is taking a little video. I don't mind and stroll on tail twitching, Mauve-ing it up. I'm resolved to meet my idol with at least half of the confidence of a fourteen-year-old meeting me. If she can do it, so can I.

MY FIRST STEP INTO THE Dealer's Den is an assault of noise and color as festive as a carnival. Five aisles of vendors sprawl across the expanse with tables lining three of the walls. The fourth wall is all Dealer Operations, the people running the Den.

The staircase above the Den gives me a good view from the top, so I pause to take it all in and get my bearings. Suiters bop down the aisles, pausing to crouch and tilt their heads at the merch; kids tow their parents along, and some people stay midstream, avoiding eye contact with the dealers and walk slow, taking furtive glances to the side and maybe hoping no one says, "Hi how are you?"

My gaze wanders from a plush vendor (there's a *pink* Totoro) in the corner to a few artists whose banners I recognize with a jolt—people I know from online, who might know me, too. There are fursuit makers with premade heads and tails and paws, artists with everything from prints to magnets to pins, tables heavy with sculptures, and three tables smack in the middle dedicated to Actual Penguin Press, one of the biggest furry publishers in the fandom.

Right near the entry at the bottom of the steps are three tables for the guests of honor. One is for Luluella, a musician who's been around forever (furever, haha) with a gorgeous banner of her fursona, a neon green jaguar, belting into a mic. Next to her is a table that's empty except for stickers, postcards, and a pastel rainbow cloth covered in paw prints for a popular fursuiter named Aenix. Through their border collie fursona, they do a lot of work raising awareness for different environmental charities. A lot of this year's con art featured Aenix snorkeling with Hermes the marmot, in various PNW waterways.

I take a couple of slow steps down the stairs, overwhelmed with the possibility of the place.

Sunspire's table is last in the row, adorned with prints, lanyards, stickers, magnets, and buttons. Her partner, Piper, is manning the table, chatting with a couple of people who are picking shyly through the stickers. I vow that won't be me—not shy.

A couple of husky suiters pass me down the steps and I snap out of it, trotting down the rest, tail swinging behind me. The guests of honor will be back once the ceremonies are done, and I want to be there, first in line, in case they're swamped.

Approaching the table quickens my pulse. It's there in my throat again, serpentine and heavy. Pressing damp palms to my hips, which causes my tail to twitch nervously, I all but tiptoe to the table. The shy couple buys three stickers while I marvel at her art in person. I have one Sunspire print, but otherwise, it's all online. One of her characters, Sunspot the Snail, is prominent on the stickers with all her little sayings or single-word inspirations. Three snails in a row proclaim Serenity, Courage, Wisdom. There's a magnet declaring Enjoy All the Things, with Sunspot under a daisy and a raindrop. There are Sunspot lanyards, and lanyards covered with fluffy kittens, songbirds, or fish.

I should get a lanyard. I touch them lightly, letting the clasps click together. Then I remember I'm not the wilting, shy person afraid of showing interest. I have money and interest. If I open my mouth, I'll probably fangirl all over Piper, who, transaction completed, offers me a warm smile. He's wearing a Hawaiian shirt emblazoned with rainbow plumeria flowers that blend with Sunny's happy and colorful artwork, and his badges display his African wild dog 'sona.

Piper never struck me as a particularly dog-ish name, but seeing him with his flowery shirt and chipper, white, hippy millennial grin, it fits.

"Hi! How's it going—oh, hey." He stands up, motioning me up and down in recognition. "Mauve?"

Bzzt.

Really? My phone now? I assume it's Jade. Or Paige sending a picture from her padding panel. I will not look.

"Yeah, it's—yeah, nice to meet you!" My tail swings as I offer my hand over the table. *It's nice to meet you? Really? Wow.* Such wit.

His smile softens. He's maybe in his forties. Everyone after twenty-five looks the same age to me, though. "Sunny's really excited to meet you. She's really proud of you."

My heart arrests then resumes. "Proud of me?"

"Yeah, your artwork has come a long way, and she wants you to keep it up." He winks at me. "We need all the happy art right now. But I'll let her tell you all that when she gets here. Oh, here, she said if you came by, to pick a sticker."

My pulse hammers and the phone keeps buzzing, drawing my focus. Is it just Twitter? Did I turn notifications back on? Piper's words are not processing in order, so I really only hear "proud of you" and "when she gets here" and "pick a thing."

"I can pay for—"

"Pick a sticker." He presses a palm to the table in mock final-ity. "Or I'll get in trouble."

"Um. Thanks. Hm . . ."

Bzzt.

The colors and snails spin in front of me, and, just as when I walked into the Rhododendron room, I'm saturated. I swipe the first sticker that comes into focus, the Wisdom snail, and take a step back from the table.

"Thank you." I probably said that. Pretty sure my sweat is coming through my shirt now, too. I start to make a random excuse about my phone, probably, when a rise of noise floats from the entry. Dozens of voices flow in from the hall as a fresh wave of people pours into the Den.

"Ceremonies must be finished," Piper muses. "So she'll be here any second."

He's right. I glimpse Sunspire's unmistakable marigold head coming our way, but she's thronged by people and chatting ani-matedly. I don't freak out, per se, but the same feeling of having guzzled too much coffee or skipped breakfast makes my hands shaky. I need to meet her—I want to meet her. But I want to feel better when I do.

My phone buzzes again.

I look at Piper as the wave of people streams down into the Den. I've lied enough today, so I feel a little flat as I talk, but there's some relief to just say, "My phone's driving me nuts. Will you tell her I'll come back?"

He looks concerned but smiles in understanding, glancing toward the throng and back to me. "Yeah, sure. Do whatever you need to."

With the Sunspot sticker tucked in one palm, rubbing my thumb against the silky matte finish, I slip back and fall into the stream of people to walk deeper into the Den. After I round the corner to the next aisle, out of sight of Sunspire's table, I tuck in against a display of tails and snatch up my phone.

One text is from Mom, asking if I'm okay because I hung up so fast. The rest are from Dad, one from Paige to apologize for running away, and a message from Jade, checking if their choice for dinner sounds good to me along with a picture of his dorky face at Luluella's music panel, pointing at the famous singer behind him.

I want to fling it across the room. No emergencies. Why can't I react to my phone like a normal person?

My knees bend and I slide down to sit cross-legged right there on the floor, tucked under a bouquet of plush wolf and fox tails. First, Mom.

Yep, call you later.

Then Dad. I assure Paige everything's cool, and then accept Jade's official dinner invitation and offer a "wow" cat face for the Lulu pic.

Dinner can't come soon enough. Maybe I'll strike out on my own later. Right now, I need my people.

"Mauve?"

I'm starting to feel like a celebrity.

I peer around for the voice and see a woman peeking at me through the grid wall display and colorful fur. I realize all these tails are familiar. They look like *my* tail. Surprise and joy surge me to my feet—I'm going to need a nap after this emotional ride.

"Haute, oh my gosh!"

She laughs as I swing around the display wall. She's behind a table, but I fling my hands out and she leans over the table to grasp them, squeezing. "Mauve! You look amazing. I love the hair. I *love* your hair!" Her voice pitches to an octave a canine fur might hear better, but I squeal right back in thanks.

She is just taller than me, magnificently full-figured, and made taller by a beautiful set of velvety doe ears and a dainty crown of silk leaves and berries. They stand out against her creamy white complexion and dyed auburn hair, bringing to mind a forest sprite. How are all my friends so pretty?

"Did you change your fursona?" I indicate the ears and she laughs.

"No, no. These are just new, so I'm showing them off. Emmie says I'll sell more that way." She touches one ear, then tilts her head in so I can see, and touch. Which I do.

"So soft!" I'm amazed. "You're amazing." She laughs, waving a hand. Why do I have all these amazing people in my life? Was I stressed about my mom a second ago? I can't keep up with myself. "These are beautiful."

"Thank you. Let me see the tail!" Haute motions me to twirl. I still have the string attached, so I do a little turn and tail-flick so she can see her work. She laughs and claps.

After my twirl, I'm grinning with reflected happiness. "I love it so much. I can't even tell you." And here's its maker, my maker. The ears and the tail that show my inner self to the world and make me feel whole are both Haute originals, and she's here.

"Let me get a picture. Hey!" She flags down a guy who's lingering with a longing gaze near the tails. He looks up in surprise. "Will you take a picture of us?"

"Uh, yeah. Sure." He steps in to take the phone, and Haute urges me in against the table like a mother bird.

I don't quite sit on the table, but manage a Mauve-ish pose with one hip hiked up, leaning on the table, an arm around Haute's shoulders, and my other wrist flicked up so the tail is coiled into the frame. As Mauve, at least, I know my angles.

"Take a couple," she instructs, and our impromptu photographer obeys.

"Send these to me?" I hop off the table and Haute nods vigorously, thanking the guy. He hovers near the tails another moment, checks a price tag, then moves along, his mouth pursed. Scheming, probably, how he's going to afford one. I know the feeling. I saved up for a Haute piece, and these tails are full price.

"There you go," Haute says. "Sent on Twitter." She looks as if she'll say more, but a couple of men stroll up to the table and one of them clasps his hands happily with a *squee* sound and points out all the beautiful ears to his boyfriend. Haute winks at me, and I slip back a step to let her do her thing.

"I'll see you later. Promise!"

"Oh definitely." She gives me a knowing look, then turns to address the couple. "Hey there, having a fun con?" I wonder what that look was about.

People flow around me as I stand midstream in the aisle. This is ridiculous.

I don't think I'm afraid of meeting Sunspire. I think I'm paranoid and guilty about my Mom, and I know there's only one way to deal with that. My gaze settles on a beautiful, detailed blue owl suiter all but floating down the aisle. The head even swivels, so there's some costuming and some puppetry going on, too. The sight of it is inspiring and soothing, and I slip up near the suiter's handler.

"Can I get a picture?"

"Hoooooo?" The owl swivels and tilts their head at me, and the girl leading them around laughs and helps us pose.

I get some photos and grin. "You look amazing."

"Hoo, hoo." The owl pats my ears and moves along.

Okay. I am fine. I eyeball Sunspire's busy table, but she's mobbed. I know what I need to do to be able to chill out anyway. I nudge the strap of my satchel higher and steer myself through all the people toward the stairs.

I want to plant myself somewhere outside or in the lobby, hand out the badges I made for people, draw, have too much caffeine and watch the show of people go by.

I want to wander down the street to the docks and see the boats. I want to find Paige and see what other panels she's doing. I want to find out if Jade was as psyched to meet Luluella as I am to meet Sunspire.

But I can't do any of that because every time my phone buzzes, my body jumps to critical alert mode, and there's only one solution.

The truth will set me free.

It's time to call Mom.

10

IT FEELS LIKE DAYS SINCE I left my hotel room instead of just over an hour. It smells fresh and amazing. I dump the satchel on my bed, then collect all the hair stuff into the trash since we left in a hurry, and tidy up the bathroom sink from my makeup. I stop to admire myself in the mirror. Happiness rushes me at the sight of my pink pixie head and the ears and tail—a little of my real self showing on the outside.

I refold and stow my few clothes into the drawers because why not? They'll smell nicer coming out of the hotel dresser than being stuffed in my bag all weekend.

I pick up the TV remote, then put it back down. The quiet is good, and voices floating up from outside make a nice ambient noise. So I turn and flop, burying my nose in a crisp, cool pillow.

"Hnnnnng." Mauve knows what I'm doing. I know what I'm doing. It would be easier to find a hundred more things to do in this sparse (comparatively), pretty room than call my mom. I flop over to my back and dig out my phone.

First, a quick check on Insta. My makeover pic has almost one hundred hearts already. I respond to a couple of comments, then swipe over to Twitter. Whoops, so many messages. I tuck a knee up, swinging idly, then stretch out my leg and then the other while I reply to tags and DMs. A few people are asking about their badges, so I set up a definite time I'll be back with the things.

I need to call Mom—like, now.

I stare at the phone so long that it fades to a sleep screen.

Maybe I should stand up for this.

With a grunt, I roll over, shove off the bed, and cross to the window. When I lift the phone, my hand is trembling, but it feels separate. It's as if my core is calm but my hand is taking all the stress. I lean against the wall near the window and tap Mom's face.

There's no going back now.

"Hey, sweetie."

"Hi, Mom."

A pause. "Is everything okay? You don't sound good."

The tremble has crawled up my arm to my throat. "Yeah, no. I mean, I'm fine. I'm really great actually, but I lied to you."

I suck in a breath. It's quiet on the other end, and then her chair creaks back. "Maeve, what is going on?"

A trio of different canine fursuiters romps down the sidewalk. A girl procures a stick from under a dogwood and tosses it. The dogs go nuts, falling over each other to chase it. Freaking adorable.

But it doesn't help me at all.

"I lied to you." I have to say it again, to clear my conscience. "I'm not with Paige—well, she's here, but I'm not in Little Tree. I went to the furcon. I'm in Olympia. Dad has all the hotel information, and it's amazing, Mom, I really—"

"What?"

Hearing shock before anger, I think, throws me off. If I was in the room with her I could see her face, feel the storm clouds, read the weather, so to speak. But now I only have her voice and the dragging, thick tension coiling the miles between us, like a spindle, winding me close, dragging my soul right out of that clean, sunny hotel room and back to the house. My stomach tightens and my knees give out. I slump in the nearest chair by the tidy little table and lamp, waiting for her to say something else.

She doesn't.

I look at the pastoral landscape on the wall—a soothing, boring, neutral piece of artwork.

Still no.

"Mom? I'm okay. I just—it was all paid for. It's totally safe. I had permission from Dad. I'm eighteen tomorrow. I can send you some pictures—"

"I knew it." The sour, wry edge in her voice sucks the life from my body. My lips contort, quivering. More than anger would have, more than fear, more than hurt. Her smug "I knew it" saps the last bit of courage I have.

"Mom," I whisper, trailing one fuchsia nail along a grain on the tabletop. "I'm sorry I lied, I really am."

"Well, I'm glad your father can continue his reign as most popular parent while I have to be the bad guy. You do not have *my* permission, Maeve, and you live under my roof."

And under all your fifty-thousand pounds of crap, too. Anger pops through my sense of defeat and swarming guilt, like too-hot bacon grease. "Well, I'm already here."

That's all the snappy comeback I can muster. Mauve has retreated, and there's just me in pink cat ears and a lot of eyeliner, trying to keep my head above a swelling tide of resentment.

Mom's voice comes through the tide. "I want you on the next bus back. I'm sure your father gave you enough money for that."

To my surprise, and probably Mom's, a hard laugh bursts out of my chest. "No. I'm already here, Mom. I'm trying to tell you how important this is to me."

"It's a convention, sweetie. I promise it's not that important." Her voice eases as if she's imparting wisdom unto me. Heat slaps the back of my neck. The tremble in my hand and arm is changing timbre from guilt and nerves to something else, something red. "It's not appropriate. What are those people *doing* in those weird costumes?"

"Uh, well, at the moment . . ." I drag to my feet and look out the window, settling my weight with an arm over my stomach. "Some people in dog suits are chasing a ball down the sidewalk. And earlier, someone gave me a hug because I asked for one when I was upset. Wild, right?" I suck a deep breath. "It's because I was worried about *you* and this is exactly why. You're paranoid about nothing, and it's insulting to me. Honestly, it hurts. I've told you all the reasons I'm in the fandom, and you don't listen."

"Mae—"

"Actually, all my reasons are none of your business. I tried to tell you. I'm here to meet friends. I have friends here, and mentors, and patrons. People who pay for my—"

"I want you home. Now." Her voice is flat, punctuated, and emotionless. She thinks she has the power, which she does.

Or does she? Does she really have the power when I'm miles away in my sunny hotel room?

Does she?

A breath slicks into my chest. The house's chain on me is taut, hard, links of iron, but it can't pull me, can it? Can she?

"Or what?" My mouth hangs, breathing in deep like I've been running. It's hard to threaten someone if you won't leave the house.

Mom is silent for the exact time it takes me to count five barrels of flowers along the sidewalk. "I want a picture of your bus ticket in twenty minutes, or I'm calling the police and reporting you as a runaway."

Cold breaks over my hot anger and I hold the phone out to stare at it. Is this real? "Are you *serious*?"

"Dead serious, Maeve." She is. She will. I can hear it in her voice the way I hear how she wants to blame the electric company for her bill, or the city for the state of her lawn because they don't spray for dandelions. She absolutely will call the police. This is the hill she's chosen.

What just happened? I think of Jade and sink back into the chair, curling into a ball. For half a second, my impulse is to apologize, to beg her not to. To make peace, to soothe the storm, as I would if I was in the room. Something is digging into my hip and I fling my leg out to fumble in my pocket and pull it out. Sunspire's sticker, all crumpled.

I set bright little Sunspot the Snail on the table and smooth my fingers over it. Wisdom. I should've grabbed the Courage snail.

I muster what I can. If it's silent much longer, Mom will start talking again. And if I hear one more syllable in the sound of her voice, I'm going to flip this table across the room.

I continue stroking the soft sticker as my voice starts talking, and not necessarily with my consent or any control. "Okay. Do that, Mom. That's fine." Betrayal and anger and exhaustion have ironed the tremble out of my voice. "But so you know, they don't consider a person missing until 72 hours has passed." I don't know if that's true, but she knows where I am, so I'm not missing. "And by the time that happens, I'll be home. And eighteen. And you can yell at me in person."

"Maeve—"

End call.

I hang up on my mom for the second time in the same day.

I chuck the phone across the room, lunge from the chair, and grab a pillow, shoving my face into it to loosen a primal scream. Then another. If I don't, I'm going to pass out or stuff the emotion down again and end up doing the same thing. But later, in front of friends, when I least expect it and some stupid thing such as getting the wrong dressing on a salad tips the delicate tower of my sanity into rubble.

I scream it out into the poor, innocent pillow.

When I'm finished, tired and hot, the weight of what I've done sinks in with the wake of her threat. I don't feel it though. I can't. It's like snow melting on soil that's already saturated, so it's just puddles instead. I know what I've done, but I can't add any more emotions to myself right now.

Mom tries to call.

Our picture from graduation grins at me, and I can't for the life of me figure out why the inside can't match the outside. Why can't we just be who we pretend to be when we're outside the house? I let the phone buzz in my hand like an anxious rattlesnake, stare at the picture, then swipe to decline the call.

Air exits my body through both nostrils and I draft up a text to her.

She tries to call again and again. I try to form some cohesive, calm words to her, but it's fractured each time she tries to call.

Swipe.

Swipe.

Decline.

"Stop," I whisper at the phone. "Come on." I shake it, ready to fling it again, but after the third decline, she seems to give up for thirty seconds.

Holding my breath, I finish and send the text.

I melt against the headboard and down into the pillows, buried in the scent of clean linens. If bleach is what makes sheets smell this way, I vow to always own white bedsheets and bleach them.

Unable to will my heart rate down, I try to switch up my attention and do something productive. The brain can really only concentrate on one thing at a time, so I need to do something else, right? Huddled in pillows with the sound of birds outside and voices from below, I open the con app with trembling fingers and start adding in panels. There's one with Sunspire tonight on color. Perfect. I add it and the app will remind me, in case I'm having so much fun at dinner I forget that I want to go see my idol.

I check the progress of the text to Mom, but it hasn't sent yet. Remembering the possibly weird reception, I squirm out from under the pillows and extend my arm toward the window. It's too much to stand up and go over there, at the moment.

The phone buzzes. Never has a buzzing phone given me

anxiety before this day. I don't even want to look, and my stomach tightens as I turn it slowly.

It's Jade. I turned on Discord notifications so I wouldn't miss his messages.

<JadeSong> *Where you at, cat?*

At last, a smile finds its way to my face. Relief that it's not Mom floods my whole being like a gulp of warm chicken soup. Letting out a shaky breath, I'm glad it's a message and not a voice call. He'd hear right through me. Not that we'd call, after years of only messaging. That would be weird.

<MauveCat> *I had to run back to the hotel for commissioned badges.*

<JadeSong> *So busy and important. :O*

<MauveCat> *Yeah, that's me. :P*

Before he can ask, I add:

<MauveCat> *I told Mom*

<JadeSong> *Oh good.*

<JadeSong> *. . . good?*

<MauveCat> *Not really. She's mad, but whatever, it's okay.*

It's okay. If I type it out and put it in text format, it'll be true, and it'll all be okay, right? It's okay.

<JadeSong> *Are you okay?*

A wave of tears threatens. It's not that I think I have to hold everything in (maybe a little, but only because I don't want to spend the whole con crying). It's that I don't want my Mom, miles away, to have so much control over how I feel. I feel the chain, the anchor, the house, the Stuff.

I don't want to lie to Jade. I want to let people in, but I feel like my house sometimes—the door to inside me is closed for everyone's benefit. What if I open the door and people are repulsed by what's inside, or a bunch of junk slides out? It's like Piper said: We need happy art. Happy people. I think of Paige saying *I'm the nice one.*

I'm the happy one.

I'm happy.

I stare at Jade's words, at his simple question. I sniff hard, holding it all in.

I don't want to dump all over Jade and ruin his con because he has to worry about me. We were so excited to have fun together. But shutting him out is almost worse, so I'm as honest as I can be.

<MauveCat> *I'm mad at her. But that's nothing new, right? It'll pass. Don't worry.*

<JadeSong> *I always worry. :)*

<MauveCat> *Stoooooop. *boops nose* I'm bringing badges back and going to sit somewhere and draw. I'll see you at dinner.*

The temptation is to follow him around like Mauve would, riding on her dragon's shoulder, but Jade has a million friends here too. I don't want him feeling like he's babysitting. I need to calm down—I need to be Mauve. I've watched enough Twitter streams of people at cons to know you never get to spend as much time as you want with the people you thought you would, but that's just part of it. There's a lot going on.

We've chatted online so long I can feel him relaxing over the invisible waves between us. He believes I'm okay. And I am.

I'm always okay.

<JadeSong> *Sounds good. And we're gaming at The Reef after!*

<MauveCat> *Yesss!*

I roll out of bed to check the damage, and my screaming-pillow trick has indeed streaked mascara into dramatic black rings under my eyes. New raccoon form for Mauve? My anxious sweating has curled some of my pink hair into a frazzled frame around my real ears and my face. All that, at least, can be fixed. I smile at Jade's message.

Jade doesn't answer, never one to need the last word, but I can't help but check my text to Mom one more time.

All I see is: *Read. 1:15 p.m.*

I wonder if she's staring at her phone, right back at me. Maybe, for a minute, we have a silent stare-down at our phones. The typing ellipses pulses on her end, and the phone trembles in my hand. Rather, my hand trembles around the phone.

Then it fades.

I decide that Mom broke the stare-down first, and yank open my makeup bag to fix my face.

11

THE AFTERNOON WHIRLS AWAY QUICKLY.

A skateboard ride up to the pier and past all the pretty shops, bistros, and flower pots clears my head. Taking in the air and people-watching.

While I love Jade, and now Paige, it's a pleasure to be alone. To have nobody's expectations. To feel all this space around me. To feel like I'm Mauve, out in the world. There is a sense of security and expectation in being surrounded by other furs. My posture changes, lifts. I flaunt the tail for an audience of random onlookers I know will appreciate it. The quick bite and rattle of skateboard wheels down one of the long docks and back shake off the worst of my tension. People point and wave.

Being seen is a feeling I cannot describe. Not seen and laughed at, but seen and loved.

Even the baristas at what will probably be my go-to coffee shop, Tidewater, are eating us up. The girl who takes my order has been looking forward to the con all weekend. Apparently, she worked here last summer and thinks she might want to join the fandom. I extol the virtues of feline-ism to her and think I might have a convert by the time my drink's done. By the end of the weekend,

I bet you she's wearing ears to work.

With a pink "Sea Horse" smoothie in hand that is something coconut, dragon berry, and delicious, specially made to honor the con theme, it's back to the Weeby to hand out badges to anyone who has time to meet me. Paige sent a message reminding me she has a panel with some of the adult furs who are in performing arts, and I'm not sure if she's asking me to attend or just letting me know, like friends do, in case I was worried about her after she ran away. I think the latter. I message back making sure she's recovered after dodging rabid fans, and, because slightly mischievous Mauve is coming out, I tell her I'll be in the lobby if she needs any moral support. I invite her to dinner and gaming after, but she probably has plans. It doesn't hurt to ask, though.

A spot by the fountain with a view of the massive windows and the main entrance is the perfect place for me to settle in. I curl up with my sketchbook, flip to a page, and spread my colored pencils and badges out on the carpet. You can't sell things outside the Artist's Alley or the Dealer's Den, but these are already paid for. I'm just handing them out, so it shouldn't be a violation.

My patrons meander by to collect their badges, compliment my hair, and so on. Apex, in particular, is glad to meet me in person. He has a gorgeous, gritty, punk hyena 'sona, but his guilty pleasure is my chibi drawings of him doing cute things like eating frosted donuts, holding a balloon, or other things that reveal his marshmallow center.

As I hand off the last badge to a painfully shy dude—he doesn't meet my eyes but has a teeny smile that shows he's happy with the badge—my phone buzzes.

And because I've been happy for a couple of hours, I pick up the phone like someone whose life is normal and check it.

Mom: *I don't see a bus ticket.*

My pulse skyrockets. And my skin is, at once, moist. Is sweat my body's natural defense mechanism? If I'm in danger, my body thinks, *I'll become slippery so nothing can catch me*?

It takes everything I have not to hurl the phone again, and mostly I don't just because I'm afraid I'll hit someone. So I shake it instead, and for a second I'm one of those people, making a scene all by myself in public.

"Oh my *God.*"

My exclamation is lost in the general clamor of the enormous, bright room. I drop my phone to the floor, shove all my art supplies back into my satchel, and launch to my feet. My head pulses with a rush that nearly takes my feet from under me.

Mom is officially beginning to ruin my con.

I sling the strap over my shoulder and stare at the text again. My phone is set so that people don't know when I've seen their messages. I don't like that kind of pressure. I could just ignore it for a while to think up the best response. My heart rate isn't going to go down, so that's what I do. I tuck it back in my pocket and head . . . where? I need distraction.

Back to the Dealer's Den. People scurry around me. Nobody moves for you—you just have to navigate through. I clip my tail string on and twitch my wrist to make the end flick, showing irritation.

Maybe it seems too weird or fake to matter, but it feels real to me. It expresses how I feel, and you know what—a girl sees my twitching tail and clears out of the way. It works. Satisfaction blooms in my chest.

Then I feel like a jerk for a second and glance back at her, but she's already moved on. So, down into the depths of the Weeby I go, again. I skirt the guest of honor tables, not ready to face Sunspire yet. My phone buzzes again.

Nope.

It's time to lose myself in a world of art and color and spend a little money. Thanks, Dad. Gotta love that guilt money.

I look for buttons to stick on my satchel strap. A couple of paw prints, some adorable cats, one that says Practically Purrfect, even though I know that's not true. Maybe a con shirt with the "under the sea" logo splashed across the chest. It feels good to see artists perk up when I approach the tables and know that I have money to spend. I know how good it feels when someone buys my stuff, so I'm here for the goodies.

A table with heaps of gorgeous fantasy art catches my eye. Thinking of getting something for Jade, I flick through the prints. Dragons, gryphons, unicorns, all rendered in what I would call a classically epic style. The artist, a slight, androgynous figure clad head to toe in purple and black with a silvery shawl, is chatting with someone else, so I have the artwork to myself to ponder.

I pause on one painting of a Smaug-like dragon coiled around a mountain of books. If only the dragon was green, it could totally be Jade. I start to pull the print for a better look when writing draws my eye. At the bottom is a black frame, like those old motivational posters, and it says:

HOARDING

DOESN'T ALWAYS NEED AN INTERVENTION

I shouldn't feel like someone has punched me in the gut, but I do. My phone buzzes again, which feels like a gut punch followed by a kick to the shins.

It's funny—it should be funny. I get the joke. I don't want to be so fragile that I don't get the joke. But just—not today.

Today, I'm done.

But do I want to be alone?

I halt at the entry to the Den and let people bump into or ooze around me, and then I just start walking. Maybe I'll find a panel to take my mind off it. But if I take my phone out to check the app, I'll see the string of texts.

Maybe I'll go to my room for one more solid scream before dinner.

Bzzt.

I know it's Mom. I know it's not a friend, not Jade, not Dad, not Paige. I just know.

I remember the help table outside the Rhododendron room. Beeper. I will go get a hug from Beeper, and she won't even force me to tell her what's wrong. She'll just give me a hug, make sure I'm hydrated, and tell me she knows I can handle whatever it is.

With a destination in mind, it's easier to move. I stalk down the hall, back upstairs to the escalator, single-mindedly laser pointed to the help table.

The Ask Me sign practically glows—

But Beeper is not there.

It's someone else. Two people, a really young guy (okay, maybe my age) in a wheelchair earnestly helping a group understand the floor plan in the con book, pointing this way and that, and a woman with dazzling blue hair talking to a couple of middle-aged guys in fox tails.

I'm sure they're all nice, but they're not my friend, the person I hoped to see, needed to see. The woman looks like she could be my aunt, and part of me wants to fling myself at the nearest stranger and tell them everything. She looks like she could handle it, but I don't do that.

I slide past the table and down the hall, at random, as if I'm headed toward a panel. I have to keep moving.

A table full of freebies draws me like a magnet, and I whip around to check it out (if only to look like I have a reason for being randomly in the hall).

The table is scattered with postcards for upcoming cons, some in Europe, free stickers, and pamphlets on everything from suicide awareness to safe sex.

One pamphlet practically waves to me because the words are familiar.

Serenity

Courage

Wisdom

The Sunspot the Snail sticker is still in my pocket, and I realize Sunspire got the idea from somewhere. So I pick up the pamphlet. It's for something called Al-anon. I graze the summary. It's for the families of addicts. Huh. A poem called "The Serenity Prayer" is on the back, and now I recognize the lines Chance stole for his graduation speech. I knew it sounded familiar.

Of the questions lining the pamphlet, one stands out.

Are you in crisis?

The Times New Roman type is, like, challenging me. Crisis? Am I? Am I in crisis? I don't think so. I'm in a holding pattern of survival. I put the pamphlet down. I am *not* in crisis. I'm at a furcon, I have friends, I'm free. All I want is to be free. It's not a lot.

Bzzt. Bzzt. Bzzt. Bzzt.

A call, not a text. No, no, no.

Bzzt.

Bzzt.

Bzzt.

Wrenching away from the table as if some force has clamped me to it, I trudge down the hall a few more steps and sink to a crouch near a potted ficus, drawing out my phone and declining Mom's call so I can look at her texts.

Mom: *Answer me, Maeve.*

Mom: *Now.*

Mom: *I'm going to call the hotel.*

Our picture pops up as she tries to call again. I let it buzz in my hand. In a petty way, it feels good to know she's getting angrier and I just don't have to answer.

Breathe in through the nose, out through the mouth. My gaze wanders from the phone and trails along the pattern on the carpet. The vibration of the phone slides up my arm and down my entire body.

I suspect she doesn't care as much about it being a furcon as she does the principle of the thing.

She said no, and I said no back and did what I wanted anyway. She has to win.

The phone keeps buzzing. Two missed calls. Three.

Staring at the opposite wall and the nameplate on the break-out room door (Clover), I wonder, suddenly, if she's even worried or if I'm just one more thing in the house she can't let go of. If I belong to her, like the dirty Ziplock baggies and the lamps she'll never sell and the bags of clothes and totes full of fifteen-year-old paperwork dotted with mouse poop. I wonder if she's panicking the way she panicked when I hauled a bag full of clothes to the thrift store a couple of months ago.

I should probably answer before it seems like I *have* been kidnapped.

But if I open my mouth, I'll cry.

And if I cry now, I might not stop.

She stops calling, and my brain settles like a cloud of dust after a stampede. A concept tiptoes to mind.

You know what? If she wants to escalate this, so can I. If she's going to claim I ran away or was kidnapped, or whatever, I just have to prove I'm not.

Slowly, I stand, back sliding against the solid wall behind me, ficus leaves brushing my arms and cheek. It's a real tree, which makes me happy.

With rattling hands, I manage to compose a text.

I'm not sorry. I know you disagree, but I want to be here. I'm with friends. I'm safe and having fun. Dad has all the details. In twelve hours I'm eighteen. I want to be here.

Keeping it short and simple, I add in a few pictures of suiters, no real faces whom she could accuse of kidnapping or molesting me or whatever. A little paper trail, if you will. She can't say I'm missing if I'm not. She can't say I'm kidnapped or a runaway if my Dad has a receipt for a hotel bill and there are pictures of me surrounded by a hundred people in open daylight.

She can't.

Can she?

She tries to call again. The text hasn't sent yet. Ugh, this effing building. How can her calls get in, but my text can't get out? I want to burst into hysterical giggles. It's like the house. It's like a horror movie: stuff goes in, but it doesn't come out.

With the phone clutched in my hand, I whisk myself back down the hall, down the escalator, outside, and hold up my phone to the sky. After two seconds of standing like Superman, and a couple of people edging around me warily, I drop my arm and look at the screen.

Delivered.

Read. 4:46pm.

She calls. Our faces smile at me from graduation.

Answer? Decline?

My body is drained, like I've been running. I'm hungry again. Dinner with my best friend is in an hour and I don't even remember where we're going because of the chaos. Answer or decline?

I think of Nira and her alcoholic dad. Another option meanders forth, smooth and insidious and promising vast satisfaction. A third option beyond answer or decline. Everything around me hazes until it's the only option.

Block caller.

Pink petunias flicker in my peripheral, and a smile crawls over my mouth. A wide, joyless Cheshire smile. *We're all mad here.*

The phone stops buzzing, at last, but my hand still feels the vibration as I send a final text.

I'll see you on Monday.

I wait until it's sent and read.

Then, holding my breath, I block my mother's number.

Weirdly, I wait for a response from her before remembering she can't. It's quiet.

After a moment of blessed silence, I text Dad.

Please talk to Mom. She's being unreasonable..

He doesn't answer right away, so I assume he's still at work or driving or whatever.

Another moment of quiet, peaceful, nothing passes by.

Con-goers continue milling and laughing down the way. A breeze whispers across the buckets of flowers, and a couple of seagulls ride it back out toward the docks, calling to their friends out on the water. The world isn't stopping. The sky is blue. I'm still standing. My heart's fast, but still going. The hand clenched around my phone tingles, so tense it's probably about to go numb.

Finger by finger I release my phone, dropping it into my satchel. I enjoy a slow breath and let my gaze wander to a line of clouds piling up in the distance, over the ocean.

I stroll back inside, twirling my tail in one hand.

12

"ALL I'M SAYING" JADE BRANDISHES a fork for emphasis. "is the fourth season clearly wasn't planned from the start. They tacked it on after it got popular."

"Opinions, opinions," Paige says airily, finishing off her fries.

"I've never even seen the show," Beeper says, looking back and forth between them. Athen scoots his chair around to catch her up on three seasons of *Triad Star* so she can weigh in.

Dewy evening air holds its breath around the little bistro tables we've pushed together in a trefoil on the patio of Dock 8, the seafood place Jade has been drooling for since we arrived. He always eats here during the con. He raves about it and would probably eat here every meal if Athen didn't have an aversion to shellfish. Not an allergy, just an aversion. But our big blue wolf soldiered through dinner with a catfish po'boy and a couple of beers alongside all our buzzing talk and swapping phones to share our photos from the day.

It's me, Athen and Jade, Paige, Beeper (we saw her leaving the Weeby and kidnapped her to dinner—Athen said so he wouldn't be the oldest person at the table), and an aspiring writer named Tristan who knows Jade and Athen from Twitter. It's unclear if Tristan is his real name or his 'sona name or both, but I feel like I saw it on some of the books in the Dealer's Den? Maybe in an anthology? He's been talking to Paige about theater, as he's from Seattle and wants to break into the playwriting scene.

I'm trying to figure out how to ask if I can draw him without it sounding weird. He has soft brown skin, hazel eyes (actual hazel, not like mine), and a casual flop of bronze locs, and I rarely want to draw humans, but when I do, it's intense. In theory, I need to expand my portfolio from cutesy talking animals, but how do you say that? *Hey, you're a beautiful person, can I draw you?*

Nah.

Maybe I'll get the nerve if I see him again at the con or ask Jade to ask him. As it is, he's quiet and thoughtful, mostly watching everyone, but he lights up when Athen asks him what he's working on now. I wonder if it's possible to draw that—that look.

Anyway. It's good company.

The whole thing is just good and funny. Furries pass on the sidewalk, and this feels like the most family thing I've ever done.

As a kid, we had Thanksgiving with Mom's family, but they're not really my people. Not the people I've chosen, my real family. I mean, they're my real family, but I've barely seen them since the divorce. They don't know about my obsession with Totoro the way Jade does or understand furries the way Paige does or loom like a protective and benevolent overlord like Athen does or even ask about my school plans like Beeper.

I feel like that's what family should be. I'm tucked up in my chair (Mom calls it frog-squatting) with my tail draped over the arm, drinking iced tea with a straw, and nobody's telling me how to sit or not to eat more hush puppies because I might get fat in college later (as if being fat is a bad thing and definitely the thing I should worry about).

I'm just me. With my family.

Out of habit, I check my phone, but the only notifications are from Twitter and people tagging me in pictures across all the different platforms. Dad never answered about Mom, but I'm just gonna let it go.

I tuck in with Beeper and hold up my phone for a picture. She automatically pauses her earnest conversation with Tristan (inquiring about his playwriting hopes and dreams—he's been adopted into her brood now) to cheese it up with me. Jade springs from his chair to photobomb a second shot, dropping to a crouch to peer between our shoulders with wide eyes, like, uwu? It's stupid and hilarious. Has it only been a day, and I'm happier than I've been all year? Or ever?

Our waitress, middle-aged and sporting a fish-fin headband that definitely came from the Dealer's Den, meanders by to check in and collect a few empty plates. Beeper places a delicate hand over the hush puppy basket, which has one left that no one has been brave enough to claim, and the waitress nods sagely.

"Dessert? Coffee?" She seems amused at our group, but not because we're furries, I don't think. I feel like it's because we're all young and a miscellaneous assortment of people. A grab bag of humanity.

"Definitely coffee." I check the time. I've still got half an hour until Sunspire's art panel, and I cannot succumb to a food coma.

Beeper groans. "How can you at this time of night?"

I grin, full-on Mauve. I can't even explain right now. "I've got things to do!"

"Make that two," Jade says, grinning heartily as he flops back into his chair. "Coffees," he clarifies.

The waitress surveys us. "How about a French press to share?"

"Ooh." Paige sits forward. "Me too, then."

Athen peers around as if for a new menu. "What's for dessert?" He leans back, tipping his head up. He's still wearing sunglasses, and now I don't know if it's because he's too cool for school or actually shy. He doesn't talk that much, more like a solid anchor to all our more animated contributions. But a good anchor, not like the house.

The waitress lights up when he asks. Clearly, dessert is her thing. "Oh boy. We have the chef's special, which is a lemon pound cake topped with a local marionberry syrup and fresh whipped cream." Athen sits up and Jade covers a smile while the waitress continues with chocolate offerings and something with nuts and toffee, which sounds about my speed. I slide my sketchbook out of my satchel and start a little sketch of Athen as his wolf 'sona, drooling over marionberries. ". . . and finally our house-made cherry ice cream with hot fudge."

Athen makes a rumbly noise. "I'm gonna need that. And the pound cake thing."

Jade laughs, poking his belly. "Who's the sugar addict now? You're going to pass out."

"Happily." Athen is unphased. "You'll eat half of it anyway."

Tristan snickers and Paige flicks her hand up. "I will also eat half of it."

"Technically, that would be a third, then." I speak without looking up from my drawing, which will be adorable, and another giddy rush bubbles up like there's finally room for happiness without Mom constantly buzzing my pocket.

"Nah, I'll eat half," Paige says. "And Jade can fight me for the rest."

"I would not," Jade declines, mildly, dipping his head. Probably best. Paige has a couple of inches on him.

The waitress hovers, glancing to the rest of us until Athen sits up again and scoots his chair back a little as if to make more room for the food that's coming. "One of everything. We'll share."

"And the coffee!" Beeper pipes up, tossing me a wink.

The waitress beams in approval and turns to take our order inside.

Athen rises and follows her inside, I assume, to find a bathroom, but Jade rolls his eyes. When I lift my eyebrows inquiringly, he just smiles enigmatically.

"They'll be rolling us out of here." Paige props her chin in her hand and leans over to peek at my drawing. "Awwww!"

Then everybody wants to see, so I hand the sketchbook around. Heat slips up my face, and it feels weirdly intimate to see other people's hands on my sketchbook. I twitch when Tristan looks like he'll flip a page to see what's before the Athen sketch, but Beeper takes the book back smoothly and hands it over. She seems to know the deal. You don't scroll photos on someone else's phone, you don't flip pages in an artist's book.

Jade twists around to peer over his shoulder for Athen, then back to me. "Can I buy that from you?"

"No." I roll my eyes. "You can have it."

His dark brows flick up. I know he's going to argue about it, so I just stick out my tongue and tuck tighter in my chair. I'll have to mail it to them, I guess, for Christmas or something.

Paige toys a strand of copper hair around one index finger. "Are you going to draw something for the art contest?"

"Oh, yeah." My pencil pauses on the page, near the corner of Athen's eye. "I missed that at opening ceremonies, what—"

"Oh!" Beeper leans in. "It's for a membership to next year's con! You have to draw Hermes in something to do with this year's theme. They'll feature it in the con book next year and give you a super sponsor package."

"Wow." The thought of coming again, of this being a regular thing, being my life, stops me dead for three heartbeats until Athen strides back out. Jade eyes him suspiciously and Athen just leans over to kiss his cheek before resuming his seat and presiding over the rest of us again. Tristan raises an inquiring brow and Athen winks. I have no idea what's happening.

"So?" Paige nudges me.

"Yeah, I mean, probably. Yeah." All the delicious crab legs I ate seem to be re-animating in my stomach, and I suck down some iced tea just as the waitress returns with our French press and a tray of clear glass mugs. I love clear glass coffee mugs.

I'm swamped now. The thought of coming next year—where I'll be if I actually make it to Portland, if my mom hasn't disowned me, if I can ever quit checking my phone for messages from her. I wonder if this can ever feel normal.

"You're really good." Tristan states this matter-of-factly, and

I rubber-band snap back to the present. "I think you could win."

A silly flattered feeling flutters through my chest, and I offer him a smile I don't have to force. It's not shy or embarrassed or anything. "Thanks. I'll give it a shot."

Beeper grins and starts pouring coffee for everyone. I load up my mug with beautiful bronze lumps of raw sugar first, then let her pour so the cream and everything else blends together without having to stir.

There's a pleasant few minutes of quiet as we all realize how much we've eaten, then our waitress brings out a platter of desserts. An actual platter, piled with beautifully arranged yellow pound cake drizzled with the berry syrup, Athen's cherry-fudge sundae, the toffee cake, chocolate mousse, and a thick brownie with marionberries clumped on top and a dollop of whipped cream with a mint leaf stuck in it like a little flag.

The waitress is pleased with our collective "Ooooh!" She splays a dozen spoons and forks in the middle of the table and leaves us to it. We glance at each other, then everyone dives for their favorite-looking thing and it's a sweets fest for the next fifteen minutes.

Hopped on seven kinds of sugar and rich coffee, I'm ready for the art panel. But the waitress hasn't brought the check. I fidget and check my phone and Tristan and Beeper start to pull out their wallets, but Athen makes a small gesture.

My gaze flicks to Jade, who offers a teeny grin. "He got it."

I'm so stunned—I had money. Everyone had money. I wouldn't have ordered an expensive crab meal if I'd known. I peer at Athen, comfortably enthroned in his little bistro chair, who just inclines his head to me and to Beeper and everyone.

Beeper sets the stage and pointedly tucks her purse away. "Thank you, Athen. This was delicious."

"Thanks, man," Tristan echoes. "That's awesome."

I murmur a thanks, cheeks hot, and Paige just grins. "I wish I'd ordered the salmon and steak."

I laugh and tap my toe against hers under the table (I hope it's hers), and we all offer another thanks. It's not unlike him, although I wish I could do things like that now and then. Well, I might not have that kind of money, but I have other things. I lean into Jade, our shoulders pressing comfortably, and he tips his head in to listen. "Now you're definitely not paying for the drawing."

He laughs, nudging me. "This was a gift."

"So is the drawing."

He sticks his tongue out. I stick my tongue out.

A soft *ding* chimes from Athen's watch, and he looks from Jade to Tristan. "It's almost time for Jonathan's reading. Are we still going?"

Tristan downs whatever's left of his coffee. "You know it."

Jade, fully caffeinated, slaps the table with both hands and stands. "Wouldn't miss it."

"Oh?" Beeper's gaze darts between them. "Is this the new book? The rugby one?"

"Yep." Athen grins then leans forward to see if there's dessert left. Paige's attention has dropped to her phone, probably coordinating Paige things.

The alert for Sunspire's panel chimes from my phone, and I slide my chair back. "I have to go too. See you guys after? Games? Merriment?"

"All the merriment," Jade agrees. "We'll celebrate your last night of being seventeen."

"It's a plan." I give a little Mauve-y bow, flourishing my tail up, a giddy rush frolicking up my chest. It might be caffeine, but it's also emotion. Is this *happy*? I hope so. I hope this is what real life is, out from under the Stuff. I chase away a thought of Mom and stand straight again with a grin.

Beeper stretches an arm toward me, and I lean down to give her a squeeze. Paige blows a kiss, and Tristan and I exchange a nod. I grab my satchel and trudge—yes, trudge, so much food—back up the block to the Weeby to find my panel. And my idol. While I'm staring at her, maybe I'll even absorb something about color theory.

13

THE WEEBY IS BUSIER NOW than I've seen it all day. Furries pack the lobby, clustered around the fountain, benches, tables, and riding up and down the escalator en route to their destinations. Edging around people, energized by a full stomach and coffee just starting to tingle at the edge of my nerves, I wrap myself in the unceasing noise and happily melt into the throng.

A line snakes out of the Rhododendron room, but the doors are still closed, so the noise level increases as I move up. Paige mentioned wanting to go, so I pause to text her about the line and that the doors aren't open yet.

I face the hall. The hall which will lead me to Sunspire. And down I go.

The doors to the room are closed, and I almost don't go in. For a second, my heart rate leaps.

"C'mon." I bounce on the balls of my feet, shake out my hands, then slip inside.

The door is at the back of the room, which is about three-quarters full. A few faces turn to me, and Sunspire—who is booting up a PowerPoint with the help of a staff member—glances up, grins, and lifts a hand in greeting before returning to her task.

Does she wave to everyone like that? Does she know me on sight? She probably waves to everyone.

I've been an absolute disaster today.

Of course, I can't focus on the fact she smiled and personally acknowledged me. I have to focus on all the stuff that went wrong. Ugh.

"You can sit here," says a guy in a fedora two rows up, gesturing to a couple of empty chairs. I was going to sit in the back row, but that's weird when there are closer chairs, right? I'll either look afraid or like I'm trying to be cool.

A color wheel graphic splashes onto the projection screen and a couple of people golf clap. I guess it's been an issue getting set up. As they finish, I ease into the offered seat and dig out my sketchbook to take notes, trying not to stare at Sunspire.

She even looks like an artist. How I picture an artist, anyway. Black boots over black jeans and a fitted black t-shirt, so all my attention is drawn to the peacock blue scarf around her neck and the focal point of her warm face, and that awesome, unnaturally marigold crown of hair. I can't believe I'm sharing air with her. She's sunshine, eternal. Her art is fun and color and life. I breathe deeply.

She thanks the staffer and he slips out, leaving her the room. Everyone shifts, including me, sitting up like the eager gaggle of students we are.

"Hi everyone." She presses her palms together and looks every single one of us in the eye, including me. Instead of breaking out in a nervous sweat or disintegrating in my chair, I find myself offering a quivering smile back. "I'm Sunspire."

I exchange a grin and a glance with the guy to my right—

as if anyone in the room doesn't know who she is?

"I'm excited to talk to you about color tonight." She aims a finger at a girl whose head tips forward as if she might nod off, and I wonder how you can be that tired the first day of the con. "Don't fall asleep. At least, not until after we cover purples and pinks. That's the best part." Sunspire turns a flashing smile on me. Me? I nearly look around like a perfect cliché in a movie. She gestures at me, my attire, perhaps, to indicate my very obvious favorite wedge on the color wheel. "Right, Mauve?"

My throat dries to a crisp.

A few people turn to me and one older, scraggly guy says "Oh yeah," as if he's recognized a C-List celebrity who was in that movie, once, with that guy.

Sunspire is looking at me. She has spoken to me, called me by name. Handed me the spotlight, even. Now is my moment to show her she was wise to invite me to sit on a panel with her in two days. To be my witty online self, to be Mauve, to banter with my idol.

That doesn't happen.

My lips glue themselves together and my eyes widen. The coffee and crab legs and marionberries vie for supremacy in my stomach—and I have, for one brief, dark moment, forgotten the English language.

The room holds its breath around me, expectantly. After two heartbeats, but before it can get awkward, Sunspire realizes I have nothing productive to add. Perhaps my pink ears, tail, and accessories speak for themselves. She winks, turns smartly back to her presentation, and clicks to the first slide, which is a luscious James Gurney painting.

I melt back into my chair, and all the air leaves my body in relief. *Now* the sweat comes. I might have to take a shower before I game with Jade and everyone.

And the panel is—honestly, the best thing I've ever attended regarding art. I had a few shining teachers dotting my career in the public school system, but they had limited resources and time. I would call myself self-taught by YouTube and studying, and this kind of immersion and loving exploration is what I want. Sunspire, who could probably be painting whatever she wanted for important galleries or films or whatever, has dedicated herself to game art and to joyful, sweet characters and color and fun. To her, *that's* what's important.

It comes through in the way she talks about it.

My sketchbook is filling fast with her pithy wisdoms and examples. She's offered to send everyone the PowerPoint for reference, but it doesn't include her off-the-cuff stuff that breathes oxygen against the art ember in my chest.

"So, to avoid what I call the Skittles effect," she says and flicks to a riotous painting of vibrant color. It's like a unicorn vomited all over everything—no balance, no organization, so globbed with color that everyone in the room physically leans back in pain. "Remember to balance your values and hues. You can even desaturate a few and pick the ones you want to stand out. Remember to work with complements and light."

She clicks through several versions of the same painting, which I realize she has made, and purposefully painted several variations just for this presentation. That's a lot of work. I think we all realize it at the same time and sit forward a little to pay proper attention, even the girl who was nodding off.

"And remember the cultural meanings of colors, too." Sunspire clicks to a slide with rows of colors and various meanings. "Keep your audience in mind, and do some research because the color red, for instance, can mean blood, or power, or nobility, or evil, depending on where you are. Know what you're putting in a painting. Do everything on purpose."

After scrawling *do everything on purpose* in shorthand, my attention falls on the row of pinks. Underneath are the words *love, beauty, sweetness, healing, sensitivity, romance,* and *sass.* And beneath purple reads *luxury, spirituality,* and *royalty.*

Sunspire pauses as we all read the notes on each color. "You can play with subtly influencing the emotions of the viewer if you use the *emotions* of color."

I scribble *emotions of color* in my book, my heart beating faster as I think about how to incorporate all these ideas into my work. Is this what art school will be like? I hope so. God, I hope so. Maybe I can follow Sunspire around for a few years, watch her work, and paint in the corners like a Renaissance apprentice.

She moves on to mood and quizzes us on several images—do we feel forlorn? Hopeful? Tense? Do we feel the artist succeeded? Would we paint anything differently?

I wish I could come alive and start shouting answers and offering input and display some of my knowledge, but I'm speechless. It's not a bad speechless, though. It's elated saturation. Energy and happiness buzz against my skin, and by the end, I've tucked into my chair with my sketchbook against my thighs as I write shorthand I hope makes sense later. She's tried to pack a semester of color theory into an hour, and my brain is pulsing with inspiration.

"In conclusion . . ." Sunspire ends the slideshow with one of her own paintings, a favorite of mine with a little fish and bird saying hello. "I won't be one of those people who says, 'learn the rules before you break them,' but"—she grins wide—"you will probably have better results if you know what you're doing. So study, study, observe, and never stop learning. Thanks, guys."

Someone applauds—we applaud for panels? I drop my pencil and join, grinning. Then people flock to her with questions. Slowly, I tuck my sketchbook away, moving only to let people out of the row, and shoulder my satchel. I should go say hello. Really, I should introduce myself officially. I shake my hands again, draw a breath—

Bzzt.

For real? Nerves zing up my spine—but it can't possibly be Mom. Easing back against the wall to let people pass, I draw out my phone.

Deebs: *SOS concert please.*

What? SOS? Stars prickle my vision. SOS means emergency, right? A quick look shows a staffer coming in to collect Sunspire, and a trail of people follow her as if she's the fiery ball of a comet and they're her tail. Whatever I was going to say is lost in Paige's emergency and I whip around, out the rear door of the room and down the hall, ducking a little, and rush by Sunny and her entourage.

"Hey, Mauve!"

It's Sunspire.

I halt, compose myself, and turn. I lift a hand and she waves back, motioning me to her. It's not demanding, though—more like a friendly *hey, I won't bite*. I raise my phone as if it's an explanation. "I—I'm sorry, my—friend, I have to . . ."

Her face flashes understanding. "Message me about our panel okay?"

Our panel. "Yeah, for sure. I will. That was amazing. Thank you, too." I motion down the hall. "For the panel I mean."

She grins and motions me on, backing away a step.

My phone doesn't buzz again, but I have visions of Paige collapsed in the middle of the concert hall or trying to fend off creepers, so I turn and speed-walk back through the hall to the Rhododendron room. Bass thrums the floor, pierced with high notes and a cymbal crash from within. There's a cheer. I flash my con badge to the green-haired, cat-tailed guy manning the door, and he opens it with a flourish to let me in.

Cerulean strobe lights flash to magenta, then aqua, and bubbles spin around the wall. For a moment, I only see the brightly lit stage and the band, then silhouettes of a hundred heads. There are chairs for about ten rows, then it's standing room only for the back half of the room so people can move around if they want, I guess.

There's no way I will find Paige in this. Hoping the reception is on my side for a minute, I lift my phone to text her, asking for some kind of coordinates. The message bar slides then stops.

Onstage, the lead singer kicks off another number and her voice soars across the room, broken by a cheer and applause. Cat-guy looks inquiringly at me and I wave a hand, stepping away until I hear from Paige. He slowly closes the door again.

Deebs: *In the bathroom sry.*

I stand still for a second, reeling as the muffled buzz of the lobby and hallways fills the space where the wailing guitar and drums had been.

"Momo!" Paige strides down the hall. "Oh my God, thanks for coming."

I sweep a look over her. She is artful in a cute dress with high button-up boots, her hair coiled up on her head, and some false eyelashes that make her look like a model. She does not appear to be in any kind of distress at all.

"What happened? What's wrong?"

Cat-guy manning the door watches us with interest, so Paige escorts me away a few steps, voice low. "I can't go in there alone."

Disbelief and irritation sizzle under my skin. This? She pulled me from Sunspire for this? "What? Why not?"

She toys a copper strand of hair around her finger, pleading. "I know. I know it seems silly. I just can't. Please? You don't have to stay long. Just—walk in with me until I find some people I know? I can't—"

"It's fine." I cut her off, and take a short breath through my nose. It's not like I'm a hundred percent together this weekend, but Paige? "I just can't stay long, okay? It gives me a headache."

She squeezes my shoulders, and I don't mind because she looks so happy and relieved. Maybe someday she'll tell me about why she can't go places alone, but not now. Her relief swamps me and I feel weirdly protective, so I offer my arm and we link up and head toward the doors.

Cat-guy opens it for us again, and Paige gives him a finger-gun as drums crack the air around us.

It takes a second to orient, fingers pressed to my temples. For a moment, I'm envious, then amused, that Paige is having a completely different con than I am if her biggest problem is not wanting to show up to any events alone. Maybe she likes to maintain her extrovert thing, or she needs a push from the dock, like a little boat.

The strobes and colors and bodies swarm around me and all I have is Paige, taller and suddenly confident, and her arm in mine. My coffee rush from dinner is completely gone. The art panel saturated me, and now the music and people and smell vibrates against my core. This concert might be what does me in, not Mom, after all. I shut my eyes.

"Oh!" Paige pats my arm. "I see some people, come on!"

Revving up for a few seconds of interaction, we weave forward to a clump of people who look like all the other people. I wonder why she needed me for this. But I will *not* be resentful. Paige did my hair, hung out at dinner, and we're making friends. She's not Mom. She's not taking without giving. She gives and replenishes, and she needs me.

"Hi!" Paige bellows over the music, receiving some glares from the back row. The younger folks she's shouting at turn around and swell forward to engulf us. Nope, nope, nope.

"Okay, gotta go!" I wrench free before I'm drowned in the people. Paige thrusts herself between the others and me and twists to finger-gun at me.

"Thank you so much! Catch you later!"

"Yeah!"

I wave paw-hands to Paige's buddies and trot backward, nearly tangling in my own tail to escape the splitting drums and people.

Once I'm free, I suck a breath of clear air and orient myself.

Okay. I did a good thing. A good friend thing. I can relax now.

There's probably no tracking down Sunspire at this point. She's probably either with personal friends (and no way I'm trying to crash that) or doing guest of honor things, or sleeping, even though it's barely past eight o'clock.

Anyway, it's fine. I have a date.

On the same level as the Dealer's Den, there are a couple more large breakout rooms with less creative names like Ballroom 1, 2, or 3. For our purposes, Ballroom 3 is now called The Reef, and it's scattered with tables, chairs, a couple of sofas, and a handful of giant beanbags for hanging out. Along the far wall from the entrance, there are three TVs hooked up and clusters of people gaming.

Just like the Dealer's Den, I hold on at the top step of the staircase, peering around for Jade. I spot his emerald shirt before anything else. He glances up as if his dragon sense is tingling, spies me, and waves me down with a grin. My heart lifts. Okay, yes, I consider him my best friend, but I don't know if he considers me his best friend. He's here with Athen, and there's a couple of people I don't know at the table, and sometimes, I worry that he's just being nice and I'm intruding or . . . whatever.

But he's grinning and motions me down. I hit the first step and—

Bzzt.

My pulse lurches. I grab the handrail and . . . wow. For a second, my mind blurs around the fact that my Pavlovian response to a text message is now stress because it might be Mom. But it won't be Mom. It *can't* be Mom. I've taken control of my life, thanks.

And yet.

There's nothing pink in the room for me to count. Really? Nothing at all? My amazement is enough to bring me down from the brink and look at the phone.

It's from Paige.

Of course it's from Paige. I swipe to open the message, and it's a selfie of her and her groupies at the concert with a cute puppy dog ears filter.

Awww! Have fun! We're playing in the reef if you want to stop by later.

Deebs: *Thx! And thanks for the help. LOL I'm such a dork.*

Yeah you are. Catch you later maybe.

Deebs: *Sounds good!!*

She adds a bunch of flower and heart emojis.

After stashing the phone, I skip down to meet Jade, who stands to hug me and pull out a chair (he's all chivalrous like that), introduces me to the rest of the group, and shows me a little cooler they brought with pops and snacks (in case any of the dinner ever wears off, whew).

At last, we sit again to get down to business, and it's the second-best thing I've done in my life since dinner that evening. When I get bored of playing Settlers of Catan, I tug out my sketchbook and start doodling ideas for the art contest, taking ideas from everyone at the gathering. No cares that I'm drawing while they game. It is accepted, even encouraged.

Take that, Mom.

Everyone's happy, and there's not a thing she can do about it.

14

THE BREAKFAST BAR AT MY hotel is a weird mix of normies in khakis or golf clothes or business suits and others who are obviously furries. Trust me, you can tell. If they're not wearing their con lanyard like me, they're wearing ears or t-shirts with niche references or various knock-offs of three wolf moon.

For my part, I am adorable, thanks. I took one look at my mashed-on-the-left pixie bedhead this morning, squished my cat ears on top, and headed down for free pancakes in my nightshirt and Hello Kitty flannel pants. I'm barely awake, but I can do that because I'm an adult now. Officially.

We toasted my 18-ness at midnight, they kicked us out of The Reef at one o'clock, and then we all congregated in someone else's room in another overflow hotel (maybe Tristan's, I was unclear) playing *Smash X2* until Athen passed out and Jade walked me back to my hotel.

The plan now is pancakes, sausage, OJ, and then chilling until Jade calls. In theory, he's going to the farmers' market a few blocks away for some out-of-this-world breakfast burrito he's been talking about since March. Maybe. I have my doubts they'll be conscious before noon.

I don't know if there's such thing as a sugar-and-salty-snacks hangover, but if there is, I have one. I'm pretty sure pancakes are the cure, too. I curl myself up at a table with a heaping plate of pancakes, sausage, hash browns, and passable scrambled eggs all drenched in syrup.

I open Twitter, and it's like someone lobbed a birthday cake at my face.

Balloons and confetti float up on my profile screen, and about a hundred happy birthday messages to scroll through. A couple of people have even drawn Mauve holding cupcakes or balloons, and I'm about to die at breakfast because it's so adorable. Then, there are more practical people.

Carico Is At Furlympia @Carico

Now you can vote! Happy happy day, Mauve. See you later. :)

Not sure what he means by "see you later," but he probably just meant around. I answer a couple more tweets, but there are just too many, and most people aren't responding to my replies anyway. Not everyone is as dedicated to free breakfast as I am and are sleeping. Paige didn't join us for games, so I don't know how the rest of her evening went. After a moment's hesitation, I send her a text that I'm heading to the farmers' market in a bit, just in case.

A text comes in from Dad with about fifty balloon and cupcake emojis—he never responded about me asking him to talk to Mom. I mean, would you? Maybe he's perfected the art of ignoring her. I send him a picture of my pancakes, then open the con app to plan my day.

My birthday—which will be better than yesterday *because* it's my birthday, and also because I won't be fending off Mom the whole time.

There are a couple of early panels, and I ponder hitting one before tracking down Jade to go to the farmers' market—or there are Saturday morning cartoons in The Reef! But first, coffee.

"Done," I agree with myself, finish up breakfast, tweet that I'm going to watch cartoons if anyone wants to wish me a happy birthday, and head upstairs to groom.

The street leading to the Weeby is not as quiet as I would've thought, but maybe everyone is like me—so happy to be here, they're up and about and ready to play. It's a gusty morning with a wind off Puget Sound and clouds stacking on the horizon. I lean into it, rolling toward Tidewater.

Birds chirp and a couple of random furries wave to me. I've got the tail clip on so my tail swings behind me as I ride, and every time someone whips out a phone to take a picture, a little bubble of elation fills in my chest.

I hop off at Tidewater, stomp the board and lean it on the side of the building, pausing to admire the new stickers I applied from the Dealer's Den. The baristas recognize me from Instagram, and when I inform them it's my birthday, they treat me to a magical chocolate and raspberry frappe concoction that is exactly what I didn't know I needed to kickstart my day. While I'm digging out a tip, a message comes in from Jade.

Jade: *Wakey wakey. Heading to the farmers' market for a breakfast burrito. Meet at Bay and Front St?*

Rolling a few blocks takes me away from furry central, though plenty of people are heading the same way. The crowd thickens ahead, and I spot the looming green park and Jade. He's wearing his con lanyard and a bright red tee with furry *Star Wars* characters with the words "May the Furs Be With You."

I hop off my board and move in for a hug, then pause. His curls are unkempt and he is slumped as if defeated, wearing Athen's sunglasses.

"Uh, are you okay? Are you sick? Stay away!" I step back dramatically and wave a hand at him, but he just flashes a weary grin.

"No way. This is what staying up until four looks like."

It's hard not to laugh because Jade is usually in bed by ten o'clock, but it never really registered until now. "Poor old man. What's the cure?"

He peers toward the market. "Lots of food. And caffeine."

"Mission accepted," I state, looping my arm in his, and offer some of my birthday frappuccino.

Two massive rhododendrons mark the entrance to the park and the market, heavy with vivid blossoms. I don't notice when Jade plucks one from a low branch, but I do when he tugs me to a stop to tuck it next to my cat ear, using the headband to secure it. It's the sweetest thing anyone has ever done. My lip quivers.

"Happy birthday, little cat," he says quietly and kisses my cheek. "I'm glad you're here."

"Me too." My arm tightens on his, and I curl in for another hug.

He takes a breath as if to say something else, but then a child's voice squeals.

"Ki-cat keee-cat!"

It has to be aimed at me, right? I turn and the little human is pointing in delight at my tail.

Her mother looks skeptical but amused, and when I offer a friendly paw wave and meow, the child shrieks and clings to her leg. The mom pats her head. "Okay, thank you! Let's go, Dany."

Jade snorks and taps the back of his hand against my arm. "You're scaring the children."

"*You're* scaring the children with bad Star Wars puns."

He flashes a grin.

In comfortable silence, we both let the market atmosphere infuse us. Jade is also a people-watcher, comforted by being in public alone. He's an introvert, but he fakes extrovert pretty well. We wander the path, pausing at stalls, nodding to others with con lanyards, and pausing to let people take a photo of me. Occasionally, he nudges my ribs and nods toward an interesting (or attractive) person he thinks I should notice.

We find his breakfast place, but I'm still stuffed, so I hang back to check Twitter.

It's full of messages of people asking where I am because I said I was going to watch cartoons. Crap. A little flush hits my face. The morning is heating up, and humidity is starting to threaten my perfect pink locks toward frizzing. Huffing a sigh, I respond with my change-of-plans, stifling guilt.

Jade strolls up with his breakfast burrito and shoves nearly half of it into his face while I'm answering messages. He peers around my shoulder, and after some prolonged chewing, he advises, "Don't sweat it. Nobody expects anyone to stick to a plan here."

"Yeah, I know. I mean, I guess." I answer a couple of DMs about birthday things but keep it vague because I don't know. Like, if I had a dinner every night like the one last night, that would be gold. It would be all I need for the rest of my life, probably. I look up and form a pout. "I was going to buy your breakfast."

Jade grins and I want to tell him about the spinach in his teeth, but also not. "Don't do that. You know I'm fine."

"I know, but it's a gesture." I tap him with the end of my tail, then offer more of my whipped dark chocolate and raspberry miracle. "Have more caffeine. Besides, it's not my money. It's Dad's guilt money for not coming to graduation."

Jade's brows crook in and his gaze drops, and either he's intensely into the chocolate raspberry frappuccino, or he disapproves of me calling Dad's gift "guilt money." I can't handle Jade's disapproval.

"Okay, I know it's probably not healthy or whatever for our relationship. I get it. But it was a gift. And sometimes I'm still angry about him tattling on Mom to Social Services." I need Jade to understand. He's the only one who knows about the hoarding, the city regulations, and the weird things I have to do, like showering at school and crawling out my bedroom window so I don't have to go through the gauntlet.

But he's not looking at me. My heart picks up the pace, but at least I don't start sweating. Is it too weird in person? Like, chatting is okay, where he doesn't have to look at me and think about it. But, in person, is it too much?

I can't lose Jade. I can't. He can't think I'm weird or my life is too weird. "You know?" I prompt, my voice pathetically quivery.

"Yeah." He meets my eyes briefly and meticulously rolls back the foil wrap around his burrito so as not to tear it. I want to grab it out of his hands and strip it bare. "Listen, Mauvy." He glances up and takes a deep breath. "There's something I want to talk to you about while we're here in person. Last night wasn't good because we were having so much fun, and I didn't want to start confessing things around our friends, in case—"

"Confessing?" I peer at him. What the actual—anyway. My heart should be going faster, but it feels sluggish. People nudge around us, and Jade touches my elbow to escort me from the sidewalk toward a bench and some baskets exploding with flowers. "Okay."

He sits me down like he's about to tell me someone died. His hands are shaking, and now I'm really scared. I can't think what Jade, my brother, my dragon, could possibly have done that requires confessing.

The same feeling as when Mom wouldn't stop calling crawls up the muscles of my back, tapping at my nerves. But my skin feels cool. Maybe I only sweat when I'm angry or anxious.

This is neither of those things. I'm afraid of whatever Jade needs to tell me.

He clears his throat, looking at his hands wrapped neatly around the second half of his burrito. "So . . . remember that—"

"Heyyyy guys!"

Paige's mellifluous voice slices through Jade's confession, and she swoops down from behind the bench, throwing her arms around our shoulders and squeezing. I wrench around and nearly slap her, I swear to God. Jade jumps. Paige laughs.

"Found ya!" She seems proud that I didn't manage to throw her off the trail.

"Hey," Jade says easily, "this isn't really a good—"

I cut him off. Me, not Paige. "How was last night?" I force myself to settle, stretching my back, leaning against the bench and into Paige's arm. Jade frowns, but I don't look at him. It's my birthday. I don't want potentially bad news on my birthday. He can tell me Sunday. Or Monday, at the end of the car ride home, or online, so if it's as bad as his tight expression tells me it might be, I can go hide under all the Stuff again.

"Oh my gosh." Paige eeks and drapes forward against the bench. "The concert was amazing." She holds up both hands, shaking them dramatically. "Like, I'm still vibrating. We almost moshed, but they stopped us."

I offer Paige a sip of my frappuccino and she waves a polite no at the same time I remember she didn't want to share a water bottle. Jade tilts his head to catch my eye, but I'm finding the rhododendrons fascinating. He squeezes my shoulder and I don't pull away. I'm not mad, just scared. While Paige continues her tale about meeting the drummer and the band and someone named Brionwyn who works for Seattle Children's Theatre, Jade turns away, hunching slightly to finish his breakfast. If he was his dragon, his wings would be cocooned around himself, I can see it.

"So Brionwyn promised to give my name to the education director at the theater. I just can't believe she's furry and I got to meet her." Paige sighs wistfully, brushing some wayward strands of copper hair from her cheek. A bit of her happiness dusts off on me, and I smile genuinely, watching her face.

"Well, you're furry," Jade points out.

Paige picks at some peeling blue paint on the bench. "What do you mean?"

"I mean, you can't believe she's furry, but you're furry. Small world," he murmurs into his eggs and chorizo with some strained mischief. I offer a soft elbow.

"True, very true. Maybe all the best people are." Paige taps his shoulder. "So we're meeting for coffee in a little bit, and she said she'd look at my resume." She nudges me with her shoulder and her voice drops, less dreamy. "Thanks again."

"I'm super happy for you." I am. Paige meeting someone who might help her connections is inspiring. It reminds me that I need to get it together and talk to Sunspire.

Sugar rushes my veins, but I manage to get a hold of myself, listening to her story and convincing myself Jade's confession won't be the end of the world. He was about to tell me out in open daylight around other people, instead of taking me to a quiet room alone like my parents did when they decided on the divorce.

Or like Dad did after he called Social Services on us, saying I could come live with him if I wanted. Authorities wouldn't force it because I wasn't abused, and my room was clean, and because Mom promised to clean. And we did a few times. But I could leave if I wanted—if I wanted to abandon Mom like everyone else.

I can still hear Mom in the background, crying and apologizing and promising, *This is it, I'll change.*

"Where did you get that?" Paige points at Jade's burrito, and I shake my head as if it'll scatter all the unproductive memories.

"Just over there." Jade lifts his chin. "We'll show you."

He stands and offers me a hand up, which I take absently. He seems relieved, as if I wouldn't take his hand or something. Guilt flickers again and I meet his eyes with a teeny smile, wondering how much it must show when I'm upset. Paige doesn't notice. Or if she does, she doesn't draw attention to our awkward moment.

So we leave it at that and go to get our ambitious redhead some breakfast.

The rest of the farmers' market is just fine, honestly. Jade doesn't seem stressed that he didn't get to say whatever he was going to say, so I'm able to let it go for a while too. It doesn't stop him from cracking terrible jokes or buying me a pink peony or teasing Paige about how maybe all her theater heroes are furry before she leaves to get coffee.

Jade and I meander toward the docks. The wind picks up and rain is in the air. People have clustered inside the cafes and shops, but we walk out toward the water to take it all in.

Bzzt.

It's a text from Dad, but honestly, I'm not feeling it now. Maybe he's actually responding about Mom, but I'm kinda frustrated with everything that isn't the con or my friends. I know Dad paid for this, but the whole experience with Mom has me soured on parents, and he didn't intervene with her when I needed him to. So I just don't look, and it's nice. I keep expecting a text or call from Mom before I remember, happily, she cannot. Jade and I head to the end of the dock to watch the boats coming in to escape the wind and the steel-dark line of clouds over the sound.

Dad tries to call and Jade glances at me. "Gonna get that?"

"Nah." I scuff a toe against the dock. Jade glances at my

buzzing satchel, then ducks his head with a smile and a shrug. I realize we're alone, and he might try to tell me the thing again, so I keep on talking. "Just Dad saying happy birthday. But hey, I have a panel in a few minutes. I'll see you later?"

"Oh." He glances at his phone, maybe to see if Athen's up now that it's nearly noon. "Yeah, sure thing. Hey." He touches my shoulder and I tense, but he only draws me into a hug. "Happy birthday, small cat."

Stinging moisture hits my eyes, and I hug him back. "Thanks, big dragon. I'll see you later."

"You will." He draws back with a wide, sparkly grin.

I flip my board down to ride back to the Weeby, enjoying a rush of rainy air. Happy birthday to me!

The lobby is filling with furries waking up, chatting, and heading to panels. It wasn't a total fib to Jade, either. There's plenty of art panels, so I slip into one about anatomy. Notes from Sunspire's panel filled several pages of my sketchbook. I let out a deep breath.

"Okay," I say to no one in particular, and thankfully no one hears me over the chatter in the room.

Mirka is the artist leading the panel, and she's well-known. I think she's even been a guest of honor at this con before. Her stuff is more realistic, and she does a lot of book covers within the fandom. She has a graphic novel coming out soon, and I could sure use some anatomy pointers.

Just as I'm getting sucked into the style, thinking how fun it would be to try some more realistic animals and refining one of my ideas for the art contest, the panel's over. I scoop up my stuff with one destination in mind. It's been a good morning, Jade's weirdness aside. It's my birthday. My mom can't get to me today.

Time to meet Sunspire.

According to the con book, she should be at her table, so I head out of the Aster room and back down the escalators. The lobby is packed with suiters, and it occurs to me it's almost time for the fursuit parade. I hesitate near the windows, watching the dizzying blur of animals move around. I've always wanted to watch a fursuit parade.

But Sunspire is a priority, and a tiny part of me knows I'm stalling.

I weave through the suiters, wary of foam toes and tails and wings, but pause on my way to the Den. I got bumped a lot, and I'm not quite sweaty, but I don't want to smell like I just walked through a bunch of fursuiters, some more recently washed than others.

I detour to the bathroom—immaculate. I'm briefly amazed, considering the number of people, then realize there's a Weeby staffer in there attending, spritzing down surfaces and eyeballing the trashcan when a girl tosses a paper towel in it, to make sure it's not overflowing. It occurs to me what it takes to keep this room smelling like Lysol and tidy and welcoming. I grin at the staff lady, whose shiny name tag reads Brenda. She doesn't grin back, but her expression twitches in amusement at the sight of my ears.

I don't blame her. It's probably stressful. We're weird—I get it. I turn and leave her to her business, plunking my stuff on the sink in front of the long row of mirrors. I pick at my hair, swipe a bit of tissue under my eyes to freshen up, touch up my lip gloss, and consider dabbing a damp paper towel under my arms. I wish I had a scented body spray or something, but—ugh, too much perfume is worse than body odor. I wrinkle my nose at the mirror, then scoop up my satchel, but a sound catches my ear from stalls.

A small whimper.

My head twitches toward the noise. It sounds like someone crying or sniffling heavily. I glance to Brenda and she raises her eyebrows, then nods to confirm the sound for me so I know I'm not imagining. What does one do here? Nothing? Ignore it? I don't think I would want to be ignored.

Haltingly, I step toward the stalls. "Hey? Are you okay?"

The sound ceases with a short intake of breath, and I peer under the row for feet.

My heart thumps. I can't leave it, right? I don't know. I wouldn't want to be alone, I don't think. I think about having my meltdowns in the various Weeby hallways. What would Mauve do?

Love and pixie dust, that's what. Whoever is in the stall can always tell me to buzz off if they want. I find the locked stall and tap once. "Everything okay in there, or do you want to be alone?"

Behind me, a girl with emerald hair and giant fox ears leaves a nearby stall, gives me a surprised up and down look, then frowns in concern at the stall, but I motion her on. She hesitates but moves on.

"Hey?" I tap the stall again.

Sneakers scuff and I step back as the sniffling occupant pushes open the door. I know her. It's my registration line friend. Oh God, what was her name? I don't want to look at her badges because that's so obvious. Instead of a Charizard shirt, she's wearing a shirt from last year's con with Hermes on a tropical safari. Oh God, I know her name I know her name—what is it?

"Mauve?" She presses a wad of tissue to her nose. She's definitely been crying. "Wow, your hair looks amazing." She smiles, blotchy pink cheeks and glassy eyes brightening.

My gaze flicks to her ears. Black cat. Egypt—Nile. "Nira. What happened?" I barely know the girl, but I feel something new, something other than nerves or anxiety stalking forward. I feel protective? Angry? Why should she be crying in a bathroom stall? Did I really just meet her yesterday? It feels like it's been a week.

"Oof," she sighs, tilting her head back. "I'm just, it's just . . . I would like to have one day where nothing happens."

We both stand there for a second in silence because I feel that in my bones. "Do you want to . . . do you need to talk?" I don't know if I have the capacity, to be honest. I want to meet Sunspire. I want this to be a fun day. But I reached out and can't quit now, and I feel horrible because my hesitance might come through in my tone.

But she cracks a bitter smile. "Not really. I don't. It's just everything. It's my dad, and one too many people ignoring me here who I thought were friends, and . . ." She makes a frustrated noise and waves a hand, then meets my eyes decisively. "I'm fine. I really appreciate you asking. That helps." The bitterness creeps out of her smile, and she sniffles. "You look really good."

"Thank you."

We stand there for another second, then Brenda steps in and silently offers a packet of tissues. I take them and nod thanks before handing them to Nira, and Brenda slips away again to wipe down the spotless sinks with determined focus.

Inane small talk questions bubble up and fall away again. I

can't ask *how's your con?* It's obviously not great.

"Listen." Mauve springs forward, and I touch Nira's arm while she presses a tissue to her nose. "Some people suck, okay? I don't know what's going on, but I'm sorry you're sad. It sucks. I think my friends are going to take me out for a birthday dinner later—do you want to go?"

Her eyes go wide with horror. "Oh, I forgot it's your birthday!"

I can't stop my laugh. "Dude, it's fine."

"It's all over Twitter and here I'm just dumping stuff on you." She swipes a clean tissue from the packet and presses it to her eyes with both hands.

I wouldn't call summing up her issues in a sentence *dumping*, but I squeeze her arm. "Look, when I know what's happening tonight, I'll send you a message. Promise."

She looks hopeful but smiles wanly. "You don't have to."

I shrug, then grin. Without dealing with Mom, I find I have a little to give. A little energy, a little something. "The more the merrier, okay?"

She watches my face, brow furrowing. I wouldn't want a pity invite either, but it's not. I'm here to meet people, and she's people, and she was nice to me for no reason at all. "Okay. Sure. Thank you."

"Okay." I meet her eyes, then step back. "I'm headed to the Dealer's Den, if . . ."

She shakes her head firmly once. "Thanks, but no. I think I need to go outside."

"Fursuit parade's starting."

She doesn't look as thrilled as I thought—maybe a suiter broke her heart. Who knows. It's too much for me to dig into.

"Yeah, maybe I'll watch."

"I'll see you later." I'm tempted to do Paige's finger-guns, but it seems too much. Nira only just stopped crying. She nods once, then turns away first toward the sinks.

And I, well, I use the bathroom since I'm there because that chocolate raspberry frozen goodness has gone straight through me, then I head out. Dealer's Den. Sunspire. If I can comfort an acquaintance, I can say hello to my idol. During the parade, the Den should be a little quieter and maybe I'll have her to myself.

Handfuls of people dot the aisles. From the top of the stairs, I get a quick view of the whole room. Sunspire and Piper are at the table eating lunch. Should I interrupt while they're eating? They're probably used to it. After a minute, I realize I'm just standing there again, so I take a good, deep breath and trot down the stairs and over to the table.

I draw myself up straight so that I'm smiling by the time Sunspire sets her salad on the table and stands.

"Morning!" I even manage the first word.

Piper laughs. "Morning."

Slick warmth runs up my face. It's totally not morning anymore. Oh well.

Sunspire grins knowingly. "Happy birthday! Did you have a fun night?"

"Yeah, a really good dinner, your panel, of course, then we gamed in The Reef." I want to say I was up at a decent time this morning, actually, and know it's not morning (as if getting up early is some kind of moral barometer). Sunspire reaches over to touch my arm lightly, apologetically.

"I'm sorry for putting you on the spot yesterday during the panel." She's so earnest but grounded. She must've been thinking about me or noticed my reaction. Neat. But also—ugh. "I know that stuff can be overwhelming."

A clever response comes to mind and drifts right back out again. I slide one hand unconsciously into my pocket but manage to keep meeting her eyes. "It's totally fine."

I try to think of a cool excuse. I try to think what Mauve would say. But I don't really want to be Mauve right now. I just want to be me. I want to fangirl all over this artist and see if she'll have coffee with me or look at some of my work and critique it. Or ask her about the art institute. Or what she's working on now that she's excited about. Or do literally anything but stand there and look at her chin.

And I just can't.

"I understand," she says with a little smile. "I don't mean to put pressure on you. I'm just excited when I see new people who bring good energy to the fandom and who work hard on their art. And you do, Mauve."

My gaze jerks up to her eyes, and I can tell she means that. "Wow." Wow? That's it? That's all I have for that amazing compliment from Sunspire herself? I can do better. "I mean, thank you. That means a lot to me. It really does. I loved your art even before I was in the fandom."

She grins and two things are happening. She's like a normal person, but also it's as if I can see through her to all the art she makes and the way she supports people, and how she tries to be compassionate, even when people are rude. She *is* a lioness, ruling the world and batting away pests, and I'm a little glittery housecat, barely able to scrape two words together for how I feel.

"It means a lot to hear you say that," she says quietly. I glance up incredulously and she laughs. "It's true. Every artist likes to hear that their work is reaching people. Listen, Mauve, I know this is your first con, and if you'd rather not do the panel, I understand."

Dismay freezes my chest tight. Not do the panel? What did I do? How did I screw up? Probably all of my weird disappearances and not answering her on Twitter and standing here like a lump just now.

No, no, no! I scramble for an image of cool Mauve and manage to shift my weight and rest a hand on my hip. "Oh—ah. Sure, maybe I jumped the gun a little." I grin, playing it cool, *no, no, no, no.* Maybe she regrets asking. Is she trying to give me the opportunity to walk away so she doesn't have to ask me to not do the panel?

My gaze drops to Piper, who's just eaten a handful of fried pickles. His eyebrows jump, and he glances from Sunny to me and nods slightly. I don't know what that means.

"Just let me know in the morning, okay? I talked to the other artists who are on it, and either way is totally fine by us."

Totally fine. Like, they could do with or without me, but they're probably better off without. My chest accordions open for a breath then squeezes tight against stupid tears. "Sure thing. I'll let you know."

"Great! Did you get a sticker, by the way?" She motions along the table.

"Hey, I did my job," Piper breaks in and grins at me as if we're in cahoots.

I nod once, but any energy for banter or speaking at all is gone. "Well, I—I'm meeting some people for lunch." I can lie to my idol easier than to my mom, I guess. "So I'll see you later?"

"Definitely." Sunspire smiles gently. I wonder how pathetic and fragile I look. What a mess. I snatch up my tail and swing it as I stride from the table. It's the only thing that keeps me from going to pieces. Maybe I am too stressed to do the panel if I can't even talk to her. She obviously sees something I don't. I'm wasting this precious weekend. In another day and a half, I'll be home—in the house.

My chest tightens, and when I realize I've walked a full circle around the Den without actually looking at anything, I about-face and head out for some fresh air and to watch the parade and try to figure out what I did wrong.

SOMETIMES, THE ONLY WAY OUT is through. So I'm going to keep on bushwhacking through my jungle of emotions until I find the light. Since my attempt at talking on the level with Sunspire turned to disaster (I still haven't decided if I can do the panel), all I can do is watch the fursuit parade until I'm dizzy, then curl up in a corner of the lobby and watch people go by.

After I'm in control of myself again, I find some brain to work on my entry for the art contest, inspired by the big banners and all the enthusiasm around me. I've decided on Hermes the marmot snorkeling with sea otters in some kelp fields. I think I have a chance at winning even if I can't make it next year. I have to try.

People-watching and drawing make me feel slightly better by the evening. Okay, mostly. Sunspire feels concerned for me—and that's okay, right? That's not the end of the world. Maybe I can salvage it. Maybe I could try being honest and say, "You know, I might screw up on the panel," and "Yeah, I am stressed, but I want to do it anyway?"

It probably won't completely ruin my life and reputation, right?

My best friend is taking me out to dinner. If I don't feel

confident enough after that to tell Sunny "yes, definitely, I'm on the panel for sure," then—well, then I guess I'm not ready to talk on a panel. But we'll see. I'll see.

Right?

It's my birthday dinner, so I primp. It turns out I can't style my hair as well as Paige did that first day, but I get a respectable spiky pixie going. It helps that I haven't washed it. (I had to swap out my first pillow since it's now pink, sorry, housekeeping.) Eyeliner, Summer's Eve lipstick, gloss, and a bold, dramatic cat-eye. I want my outfit to be Mauve-y, but nice. Jade hasn't told me the plan, but he's considerate, so I assume if there was a dress code, he would warn me.

I go with semi-casual black, like Sunspire, with purple and pink accents. And my purple Converse, of course. Little butterflies flick around in my chest. I'm supposed to meet Jade and Athen at their room, which seems weird. I half suspect a party, but I don't want to get my hopes up.

My birthday hopes are tempered by reality these days. The feeling of seeing that tablet-shaped box on the table and opening a crappy art kit surfaces, and I suck a quick breath.

Jade isn't Mom. My friends here aren't Mom. I vow to be genuinely happy with whatever does or doesn't happen, even if I get sung to in a restaurant. Ugh. I pause briefly, wrinkling my nose to pixie-me in the mirror. I pluck my cat ears up and position them just so before clipping them in, then my tail. I grab my Totoro sweater, in case it gets chilly, and pause to peer out at the street. It's still light out but rich and gloomy, cooler breezes flickering the leaves on all my pink flower baskets and the dogwoods.

People hustle down the sidewalk toward their dinner destinations.

I grab my skateboard with a grin, looking forward to a stormy night for my birthday. It's spitting rain by the time I roll up to the main hotel and hurry inside—immediately slapped with hundreds of people, a roar of noise, and the dazzle of the lobby. Wow. If I thought the Weeby was cool, the hotel is better.

I halt to process, stooping to grab my board by the front truck. The main lobby sweeps around an escalator and down a hall that seems to lead to a bar and a couple of restaurants. Another direction leads to a pool, based on people coming and going with towels. I don't think you could pay me enough money to swim in a pool during a con. That's too many bodies in the water.

Two mezzanine levels wrap around the lobby and foyer. Guests peer down and wave, and I look up just in time to see someone drop a bat plushie from the third level.

A big, white wolf suiter jostles past me and turns to squeak an apology for bumping me. I take it as a cue to get moving and set out to find an elevator—which has a line of about thirty people. Ugh.

A couple of folks ooze past me toward a plain door at the end of the row of elevators, and I follow them to a stairwell. As much as I don't want to show up breathless, I also don't want to stand there with a million strangers and use up all my giddy energy before I meet the boys.

So it's up—and up and up—for me. The stairwell is plenty full, too. I get a couple of passersby complimenting my ears, but I make it in the time it probably took one elevator to even reach the lobby.

I'm in decent shape, but my heart rate is up by the time I reach Jade's floor. The temptation to drop my board and skate down the hall is high until a group comes around the corner. It's probably against hotel rules anyway. Besides, I'm an adult now. No skateboarding down hallways.

So I saunter, following room numbers until I hit 617, and give an authoritative knock, trying not to be weirded out as usual. I know knocking is protocol, and polite, but it still feels like a weird violation of privacy. Violent. I don't know. Having a nice, quiet evening? Let me bang on the surface that protects you from the outside world.

Or maybe I associate the sound of a knock with Mom asking if she can put Stuff in my room or with people at the door who I can't let in the house.

There's a shuffle, and Jade's voice, slightly strangled as if he's laughing, calls out, "Who is it?"

"Mauve!" I want to laugh. Who else would it be? The memory of Beeper suggesting a party on Twitter suffuses me with anxious glee, but I have to temper it just in case. The lock turns and Jade flings open the door. First of all, he looks dapper in an actual button-down lavender shirt and jeans, but bare feet. I have just enough time to register lots of pink behind him before a dozen people rush into the doorway.

"Happy birthday!" They scream, mostly as one.

A surge of disbelief and surprise (despite my suspicions) swamps me. I take in the details and the people, and decorations behind them.

"Happy birthday!" says Beeper in a pink dress, holding a

bouquet of pink and purple balloons.

"Happy birthday!" Paige says, waving jazz hands. She looks gorgeous in a mauve sundress with a denim jacket thrown on top as if she just strolled off Pinterest.

The smell of pizza hits me. Marlitoo crowds near Paige in full purple toucan glory, flapping happily, and Carico, a toon tiger, is wearing a bright pink—oh my God, is everyone wearing . . . ? Yes, everyone is wearing some variety of pink or purple. Even Athen, who looks pretty snazzy in an off-coral tee. Jade raises clasped hands, his gaze darting over my face to check my reaction.

I suck a breath through my nose as all the anxious glee I tried to suppress leaps up through my body and out my mouth in a happy sob, tears blurring my view. I slap a hand over my mouth, but rather than seem horrified by this show of emotion, everyone claps or throws their head back in triumph.

Yep, they got me.

"Oh," Jade tsks and strides forward to scoop me into a hug, turning neatly to escort me into the room. "Happy birthday," he says quietly, and Paige skips in to hug me. More of my Twitter friends are there, whom I haven't gotten to meet yet, and Tristan. Oh wait, there's someone else to invite.

"One sec!" I squirm in Jade's arm and duck around my phone to send Nira an invite on Twitter, and make sure to tell her to wear pink or purple if she has it.

Inside, I register the suite. It's twice as large as my room at the other hotel. The bedroom is behind another door, and there's a kitchenette, table, two sofas, chairs, and a TV. Paige scurries over to blast the room with Renata. Pink and purple crepe paper festoon the windows and walls. Over the table hangs a handmade poster covered in glitter and pink and purple star stickers declaring "Happy Birthday Mauve," and the balloons, which Beeper releases, float freely around the room. Everyone drifts in, milling or dancing to the music.

Jade squeezes my shoulder, then releases me a half-second before I start to feel like a spectacle. "Want some lemonade?"

"Yes." I sniffle once. "This is beautiful. Thank you so much."

"A lot of it was Beeper." He grins. "I picked the cake."

"Cake?" Like it's a surprise that there's a party *and* cake.

"Uh, yeah." He laughs. "It's not a pixie cat party without cake."

Athen manifests near Jade's elbow and offers me a pink Solo cup filled with pink lemonade. Disbelief and joy bubble up again as I take the cup. Like, that would've been enough. Pink cups. Pink effing cups. It's not hard.

"Happy birthday," Athen says, and I step over to finally give him a hearty squeeze too. He *oofs* dramatically and wraps a big arm around my shoulders. "I think a couple more people might wander in later."

"Birthday girl!" Beeper bops up with Marlitoo behind her and offers me a Kleenex I didn't know I needed, but now I do. I swivel to hug her, then Marli, burrowing into the purple fluff. Then Carico is there, so I admire his shirt and we pose for a picture. Then Paige, and then the other Twitter buds I haven't gotten to meet yet. There are so many hugs. Whatever thing usually makes me not want people to touch me is swirled up in the pink and the care that went into this.

I want it all. I want to be overwhelmed by caring.

Then, pretty much on cue, the spitting rain outside gusts into a full-on downpour. It's as if even the sky is wishing me a happy birthday. I'm submerged in joy. Emotion pulses through my body, and it's so much I just drop into the nearest chair. Jade props the door to the hallway open, and Paige plops down next to me with Beeper on her far side.

"That's my recipe," Paige says, pointing to my cup. "Lemonade and cherry 7UP." She examines her nails, changed from cobalt to cotton candy pink for the occasion.

I laugh and wrap an arm around Paige and squeeze her shoulders, then peer around her to Beeper, who's watching me, proud, as if I've done something great instead of them. "Thank you so much. This is the most amazing—it's amazing. Thank you." Saying it out loud, my throat catches and quivers. I suck down some punch.

Beeper laughs. "Oh my gosh, you're so easy to plan for." She gestures, then splays her hands marquee-style. "My vision was pink. Right?" She grins and I lean over Paige to squeeze her hand.

"Yeah," I whisper. "Easy."

Paige wriggles out from between us and drags me up. "Come see the cake!"

So I do. Athen moves past us to drag the coffee table against a wall, and Marlitoo and Carico fill the space to dance to the music. Beeper's laughing, taking video. Jade strolls over to see my reaction to the cake, which is a perfect shade of lavender, has a cute little stick drawing of a cat on it, and reads "Happiest of Birthdays, Mauve."

"I added the cat," Jade says proudly.

"It's adorable," I say with the utmost gravity. It is.

"Made with love." He grins.

A knock announces more people, and we all turn to see Haute, her girlfriend (I think it's Yorna or Norya—something like that), Sunspire, and Piper.

"Oh geez," I breathe, my heart escalating. Sunspire came to my party. She and Piper are both wearing shades of purple and pink; Piper has a pink Hawaiian shirt. I peer at Jade. "Who else did you invite?"

"All the good people." He grins. "We'll see who all shows up though, right?"

"Right." My nerves give way to another splash of happiness. I let it douse me and trot over with Jade to greet people.

"Helloooooo, happy birthday!" Haute waves and I hug her before ushering them in. "This is Emmie."

Emmie. Wow, I wasn't even close. For a minute, I'm trying to figure out who I was thinking of, then realize I need to greet them. Emmie and Haute are both wearing glorious purple and pink tie-dye dresses, and Emmie presents me solemnly with a gift-wrapped in metallic purple paper.

I take it even though it's a minute before I realize it's for me. "Oh, wow, you didn't have to—"

"I know!" Haute is delighted. "That's the fun part. Oh, Carico!" She pats my shoulder, winks, and whisks into the room, leaving me to greet Sunspire and Piper. I manage a quick breath and am feeling . . . stable. On my turf, with my people. I meet her eyes, managing to draw out a thread of composure and words.

"It means a lot that you came. Thank you."

"Wouldn't miss it." She grins and sort of—checks in? She meets my eyes as if asking if it's okay she's there. I wonder how weird and nervous I'm coming off. Maybe it's because she and Piper are older and I'm still sort of in the kid's crowd. Who knows.

One thing is certain.

"I want to do the panel." The words fly out of my mouth like cucumbers from a salad shooter.

I guess it sounds more confident than it did earlier as she laughs and hangs her head, holding up her hands in surrender. "Great. We'll talk about it. It will mostly be Q and A, and there are two other artists, so it shouldn't be too overwhelming."

"Great." I take a deep breath and find a real smile, letting a bit of triumph out. "Good, thank you."

"Come in!" Jade says from behind me, and I shuffle back from the door. Piper hands me a shiny pink pinwheel with a proud grin, and I nearly melt. Athen cranks the music, and the party's on.

Jade and I join the suiters on the dance floor while the rest cheer us on and sip punch. Athen and Paige end up on the couch talking animatedly, and everything around me is a perfect birthday tableau.

More people trickle in and out, stopping in to say hi or snag a free piece of pizza. I left my phone in my satchel near the table in the kitchen area, and I don't miss it. I can post pictures later.

Rain drums against the windows, and Beeper laughingly reads more birthday tweets from her perch on a stool in the kitchenette.

When enough of the pizza is gone, Jade dials down the music. "Time for presents."

"And singing!" Paige launches from the couch and grabs me

just as I consider getting my phone out for pictures.

Paige escorts me to the cake, and Athen produces a lighter, taking his time to ceremoniously light the two candles 1 and 8 while everyone clusters around. Heat climbs up my neck and cheeks. I expect to start sweating, but I don't. I'm safe. And happy. This isn't nerves, this is . . . overwhelm? There's a tense moment, that awkward hush before Beeper kicks off the singing.

"Happy . . ." Everyone chimes in to sing. Paige's angelic soprano wafts above everyone, and she and Jade harmonize together on the last lines, which just makes me laugh in delight. I hold my breath. Marlitoo and Carico offer jazz paws/wings at the end.

"Make a wish," Jade whispers, grinning.

"Wish we could all be our fursonas," Tristan suggests.

Sunspire laughs. "I think that would end in disaster."

I nod. "Jade would crush everyone."

"Mm," says Athen, and I burst out laughing before sucking a breath.

A wish. Okay.

I want all my birthdays to be like this for the rest of my life.

I blow out the candles and send the wish up with the smoke, and everyone claps because, you know, blowing out two candles is mighty impressive.

"Presents!" Jade declares.

I wrap my arms around myself. "Guys."

"Don't worry," he says airily. "There's only two."

Athen shoulders in, politely herding us away so he can cut the cake. Beeper takes my arm and gets me settled on the couch while others gather around. Jade brings over my two presents—

the shiny one Haute brought and another wrapped in Hello Kitty paper—and drops to sit beside me. Paige perches on the armrest. My gaze darts to Sunspire, standing opposite behind the other sofa. She winks. And rather than disintegrate, I manage a grin.

"Mine first," says Haute, pointing excitedly as she sits on the floor near me, feet tucked under her dress. Marlitoo flops down beside her, cocking her head. I know she's slipped out to cool off once or twice with Carico, but otherwise, she's been in character the whole time. A couple of suiters have joined us—a green wolf I suspect is one of Paige's theater kid friends and a blue jay I know from Twitter—but they hang back.

With all eyes on me, my armpits get damp. The memory of Mom's disappointing gift inches forth from the bottom of my heart, and I shake my head, batting at the curly ribbon before making a show of pulling it loose and tearing the paper. It's a simple clothing box, the kind for a shirt or something. Everyone's eager staring is putting a lot of pressure on this to be awesome. I need to prepare myself to make a reaction if it's not.

To stall, I grin at Haute and pat the box. "It's beautiful. I'll treasure it always—"

"Open it!" she squeals, pointing.

Laughing, terrified I'll have to fake it as I did for Mom, I pry the box open. The entire room is pink, which makes it easy to find pink things to count.

I pick some tissue aside and reveal something fuzzy. Fur that matches my beautiful tail and ears. Emotion lodges in my throat as I pull out a dainty, fingerless glove. Each finger has an individual mitten flap, each hand embroidered with soft lavender paw pads.

My perfect paw glove. I can hold a pencil and draw or flip the tops over and have full cat paws. Custom. Hand sewn. Especially for me. Mauve is complete.

I choke softly, then sniff in sharply and sit up straight. "Haute, I just . . ." I bubble over with a couple of tears. There goes my mascara.

Marlitoo coos softly, and everyone else laughs and claps—yep, they got me again.

"Oh," Haute rolls to her knees and scoots over to pat my thigh like a loving aunt. "Baby, baby. Happy birthday. You bring us a lot of happiness."

I do? That's what I try to do anyway. I sniffle and slip the gloves on slowly, flexing my hand. The material is like something you'd wear to work with a tablet, sport soft and flexible, and the fur is trimmed shorter so it won't get in the way of drawing.

"They're beautiful." I speak softly so as not to break my fragile control. Holding up my hands—paws—I meet Haute's eyes and soak in the happy grins and everyone pointing at my hands. "Thank you."

Jade's hand comes to rest on my back, rubbing softly, and Paige reaches over to pet my hair as if I really am a cat. I love it. I want to keep crying and tell everyone everything because they don't have any idea how much this means. Haute ducks her head with a little smile.

Jade rubs my back once more, then offers the Hello Kitty box. "Now this one."

Piper grins from his seat. "I don't know. Does she need a break first?"

Jade laughs. "Nah."

Paige shifts from the arm to the cushion so that I'm sandwiched between her and Jade again. "Ooh I know what this one is."

I manage a suspicious look and draw a breath. Beeper steps in to offer me a tissue and I laugh and take it, dabbing under my eyes before I turn my attention to the present. A massive pink bow decorates the top, which I pluck off and put on my head.

Okay. It's just a present. Whatever it is, it was chosen with love. A lot of love. So much love. There's so much love in this room; it's pulsing against me like a current. I stare at Kitty's cute little face for a second to regain composure. Jade's hand remains on my back like a life preserver.

I pick a corner free and tear the paper. For a second, I just see another plain, white box. But it's a fancy box. Elegant, firm, matte finish cardboard. Yes, a box can be elegant. And tearing the paper further reveals an image of a slick, silver—

"No way," I whisper. A maelstrom of emotions whips around my chest, circling out of amazement, gratitude, anger (yes, at Mom), and a million other things. Nothing rises or defines itself— just emotion whirling around the sea that is me as I pull the paper in slow motion to reveal a brand-new iPad.

"You guys," I gasp, "this is too much." I look up and can't see a thing but blurry grinning faces. "This is—"

"Everyone gave a little," Jade says, while Beeper drops to crouch in front of me and pats my foot.

"It's just a small one," she murmurs.

Just a small one. I would've been blown away by a twenty-dollar Wacom. I squeeze my eyes shut, touching the crumpled rag of tissue to my nose. Then I realize what Jade said. "Who's everyone?"

Jade laughs, slinging his arm around my shoulders. "Just—a bunch of people."

"Everyone says these are the best," Paige says.

Sunspire lifts her hand. "Can confirm." I glance up at her quickly, and her smile softens. "I was consulted," she explains, mouth twitching against a grin.

Paige touches the box. "When our Fundsy page for it got way more attention than we thought, we figured—"

"Fundsy?" I want to grab Paige and shake her. "You guys crowdfunded me a tablet? A freaking iPad?"

Athen walks over, bearing a pink plate and a slab of cake. "Might as well get the best."

Jade is beaming, and I can practically see his golden aura, shooting happiness everywhere. "There's a pencil around somewhere, I just forgot to wrap it."

I cannot speak.

"It's just the little one," Paige says, echoing Beeper, touching my shoulder.

Just the little one.

"Okay." I cannot go to pieces. The maelstrom still spins, slowly, emotions bobbing up and down. I pet the box with a paw, and from the maelstrom, draw out a thread of joy and a big grin. It's real. I'm feeling it—I'm just feeling fifty other things too. "Thank you, everyone. This is—I can't even tell you what this means. Thank you. I can't wait to try it out. I promise to make beautiful art."

There's a collective murmur of approval.

Jade sees I'm about to drown and stands, perhaps to break the spell of everyone staring at me. "Happy birthday."

He reaches out and Athen deposits a plate to his waiting hand, and he presents me with cake. Paige claps softly and everyone takes that example. Brief applause, laughter, and triumph glow in the room. A few people pause in the hall and peer inside.

Athen continues passing out cake, Piper breaks away for some punch and the spell is broken. End staring-at-Maeve mode, restart party mode.

Sweet frosting and rich chocolate cake iron me out a little. This is good. A good thing. I can be overwhelmed with good. It's good. Rain drums and gusts against the window. It's so good.

Carico hops up, tiger tail swinging, and cranks the music again. My toe taps unconsciously. I should probably take my gloves off to eat, and I see Haute twitching slightly, but I can't take them off now. Or maybe ever. I don't want to. I want to be Mauve forever, in this room, surrounded by rain and pink and people who love me and know me.

Well, most of me. Not the Stuff packed behind that closed door in my heart.

The cake gets heavy in my stomach, and I glance at my satchel. I should probably call Mom. And answer Dad.

Paige nudges me. "You okay, birthday cat?"

"Yeah," I say. I realize it's mostly true and smile at her for real. The maelstrom draws down but is still deep in there. "I am. I'm just going to call my mom."

She nods, no big deal, but she doesn't know what that entails. I finish up the cake, set my tablet on the table, and then head to the corner to grab my satchel and set it on the counter to pull out my phone.

7 Missed Calls

3 New Voicemails

The hair on the back of my neck prickles.

My dad doesn't call obsessively like that. He leaves a message and gets on with his life until I call back. There are his calls, along with five missed calls from a number I don't know, but it's local to Little Tree. Anxiety pricks through the maelstrom of emotion. I stare at the phone, trying to make sense of it.

From the corner of my eye, I see Nira show up in the doorway in an adorable Pinkie Pie t-shirt. Jade glances at me and I motion him to greet her while I gulp a breath. I turn my back to the room, which is starting to pulse. Maybe it's the birthday thing. Maybe Mom freaked him out with the kidnapping thing.

Maybe.

With a sharp sigh, I unblock Mom's number and call her. It doesn't even ring. It goes straight to voicemail like it's off. Scoffing in disbelief, I try again to make sure she doesn't just have it on Do Not Disturb.

Straight to voicemail.

My arm twitches and I consider the missed calls from Dad.

Tingling nausea worms up my stomach. The room shifts around me, pink and happiness and people I love, contorting. It's too much.

A steady droning like fifty hornets starts behind my ears and washes down my arms until my hands start shaking. I don't bother with the unknown number, but my hand is shaking so badly I can barely hit the Play button for Dad's voicemail. The second I do, someone cranks the music. It's one of my favorite songs.

But I can't—

Dad's voice is fast and scratchy. I clamp the phone to my ear, pressing my paw glove over the other.

". . . been an accident at the house. I hope you get this message—"

"Mauve, come dance!"

I wave a hand sharply, squeezing my eyes shut as Dad's voice continues, calm but trembling, ". . . fire—"

"Oh my gosh," Paige calls, but my heart is somewhere in my ears and I can barely hear her or Dad's message. Music pounds around the room, and my face blooms with heat.

I frantically tap for the third and final message.

Dad's voice is dull. "Call me."

That's it? I hit Play again, face scrunched, curling my fingers against my mouth.

"Call me."

I jerk the phone from my ear and, through blurry vision, register that the message is from almost an hour ago.

Call me.

There's a knock at the open door. I look up in time to see uniformed police and Jade trotting over to answer them. Beeper darts up to turn down the music while the police gesture and talk, and Jade points to me.

The maelstrom rages up, sweeping my breath from me—anger, fear, disbelief, injustice—dragging everything up and over, spiraling around me until I can't breathe and I'm sucked down the vortex.

The droning hornets roar, heat swamps me, and one knee

buckles. I grab the counter. I just need to be—not—standing. The other knee buckles and I drop to the floor in relief.

Jade barks in alarm.

I don't hear anything else.

16

WHEN I COME TO. I don't remember anything about what's happening except that it's my birthday party. It's like when I wake up at Dad's house and don't remember where I am for a second.

A circle of people and animal faces stare down at me. I smack a hand to the carpet and try to push up, but Beeper's holding me. She's surprisingly strong. Or maybe I'm surprisingly weak. "It's okay Maeve, chill out a second. You fainted."

She called me Maeve. No one's called me Maeve for two days. So whatever *it* is, it's definitely not okay.

Marlitoo crouches down, staring with unblinking cartoon eyes, then tugs her head off, and I realize I've never seen her face. I'm distracted by her short, sweaty turquoise hair and almost perfectly round face, and dismayed she broke character for me. "Are you okay? Just don't move for a minute. We're calling paramedics."

Beeper pats my shoulder. "Do you need some water?"

No one is talking about the cops in the doorway.

My head pulses and I squint up at Beeper. "Um . . ."

"You fainted," she whispers, her tiny face flushed red with worry, bright green eyes wide behind stylish lenses. I hadn't noticed how cool her glasses are. I'll have to tell her. But first, the police.

"I'm fine." Panic lumps my throat. "Don't call anyone—" but the effing police are here already. Did Mom send them? Why are there police here interrogating my best friend? At my birthday party?

Wait.

Dad's voicemail pounds in my skull. *Call me. Call me.*

"Stop." I think I said it. I can't tell.

Next to Marli, Carico has also removed his tiger head, and he paces and talks rapidly on the phone in Spanish, and then Jade talks over his shoulder to Carico in Spanish, and everybody is talking at the same time.

Voices cut through my fog, arguing with police. Athen. Sunspire.

"Let's just calm down—"

The room is a whirl of people and the smell of pizza—pink everywhere. Someone clicks on the AC as if cooling down the room will help. Maybe it will. I do feel hot.

"Let me up, please." Grunting, I lever myself up to a sitting position with Beeper's help, and the concerned circle of people shuffles back so I have a line of sight to Jade and the police.

"It's fine!" Shouting makes my head spin. Paige shoves a cup of punch at me, and the pink cup, pink punch, and her horrified face make me want to cry. "I'm fine."

The police officer looks at me, her dark eyes appraising, skeptical, as I'm obviously not fine. "We had a call. Maeve Stephens?"

My mouth works and there's a sort of croak. Beeper puts a hand on my back as if I might faint again. I might. Blood rushes my head, and sweat clamps my palms.

I have to fix this.

"Yes. I'm Maeve. Did my mom call you? I'm fine. I'm eighteen. Mom and I had a fight. It's fine. I'm not kidnapped."

"Kidnapped?" The other officer whips out a pencil and pad and starts taking notes.

"Stop that," I plead. "Everything's okay. I want to be here."

"It's not about that," the female officer says. "We received an emergency call."

"What about?" My strength and awareness creep back, and I realize Mom didn't call the police after all. But before anyone can say or do anything else, there's a male voice from the hall. The policewoman steps aside, and my dad comes into the room.

My dad. In the room.

"Dad." He's tan and looks like he hasn't slept in a month.

You'd think seeing me collapsed on the floor, he'd come rushing forward, but he doesn't. Maybe he notices I'm already surrounded, held, well cared for. He's never rushed in before, except when he called Social Services, and he doesn't now.

Also, Athen is in the way, and not many people would try to rush by him.

Dad takes in the room, then me, and he doesn't smile. Not good. "Hi, Kitten."

Everyone is silent.

A piece of crepe paper flutters down from the ceiling.

"Dad?" My voice quivers pathetically. Beeper gives me a tight squeeze. "What's going on?"

"Okay," Beeper says quietly and touches my hand. "Come on."

"I'm okay," I whisper. But I'm not. My dad leans over and

says something to the cops, shows them his ID, and they nod and just . . . leave. They leave, just like that. I guess my dad is the adultiest adult in the room and they listen to him the way they didn't listen to me or Jade or Athen or even Sunspire. My body jerks a step forward. I feel like hot goo. Everyone is staring at me with the looks I never wanted to see—humiliating, nauseating concern and pity.

But I'm not going to cry. No way, not here. I cannot.

Athen pivots from the door and begins to gently but firmly, herd people away from staring at me. Party's over. The crepe paper knew it before we did.

Beeper hands me off to Jade and ducks away to help with whatever needs doing while Jade escorts me to Dad.

"Hey, Kitten," Dad murmurs again, reaching a hand out. Then his gaze lifts to Jade, behind me like a shield, and nods. "Lucas."

I halt so hard Jade bumps into me, then rests a hand on my shoulder while I glance back and forth. "Wait, what?" I flap my hand between them. "How do you know each other?"

"Maeve." Dad reaches out for my hand. He knows physical touch will stop me, startle me into focus. Apparently, how he knows my best friend by his legal name is unimportant at the moment.

I meet his eyes—my eyes, our hazel eyes. I've missed him so much and now he's here, not for my birthday, but because . . .

"There's been a fire," he says quietly, every word calm and punctuated as if he's practiced. Maybe he has. I suck in a sharp breath. Jade squeezes my shoulder, and I recoil from Dad to lean against him.

Dad says it again, so it registers. "There's been a fire. Your mother is in the hospital. She's going to be okay, but it was a lot of smoke and a lot of burns. Maeve?"

"There was a fire," I repeat so he knows I heard. The droning starts up again, and I wave a hand as if it might banish the invisible hornets. "Mom's in the hospital."

He nods, watching me slowly as if he's waiting for something. A fire at the house.

A fire. Did I leave my candle lit? Oh God. My stupid rebellious candle? Did I burn our house down? There's no way there could be a fire. But if there was, it wouldn't take much. Visions of the dust, the balls of paper, the mail bundles near the door—why didn't I just take them to recycle? I could've done that. I wonder if any of my stuff made it. My art. My perfect attendance certificate. My Totoro blanket.

Mom.

My stomach clenches and a knot rolls up my throat and comes out in a sob. "A fire? Where is Mom?"

That's what Dad was waiting for, I guess—for it to hit me. He steps in, gently taking me from Jade—who he apparently knows—and wraps me in his arms.

"She's at the hospital here." I realize he already said she's in the hospital, and I said it, but now I finally hear it. Dad continues. "The one in Little Tree isn't . . ." He doesn't finish. Not equipped for burns, probably.

I can't even hug Dad back. I just rest limply against him. Everything about the party that filled me up is gone. Drained. I have nothing. "Let's go. Let's just go."

"Okay." He kisses the top of my head. "You look beautiful, by the way."

I choke on a laugh and then a sob, tears stabbing my eyes. I don't want to leave my friends. I really don't want to be here and say, *Hey, let's party!* But I don't want to just go. "Jade?"

"Yes." He's still there. Of course he is. "I'll say goodbye for you. I'll catch up, okay? I'll tell them what happened."

"Don't tell them everything," I plead.

He rubs my back, though he hesitates just long enough that I turn in Dad's arm to give him a stern look. Although it's probably just pathetic at this point. "Please, don't."

"Okay," he relents, looking down. "Just the fire." I nudge him and he lifts his face with a weak but earnest grin. "I promise."

Beeper slips up to us and offers my satchel and phone, my Totoro hoodie. Worry wrinkles every centimeter of her face, but she doesn't ask. She doesn't need to because it's my birthday and the cops and my dad showed up, and that tells everyone what they need to know, right?

Right.

I take the bag, then hand it to Dad so I can tug on the hoodie. My rainy day hoodie. I hope it's up to this task. "Thanks."

"Sure." She nods to my dad, but my mom's in the hospital so there's not really time to introduce everyone. Mom's in the hospital with burn wounds. God. Hot, acidic lemonade-flavored bile touches my throat. I swallow hard.

"Let's go," I whisper to Dad.

He nods and wraps an arm around my shoulders to escort me out.

17

"I LIT A CANDLE."

Rain rolls down the car windows, and I stare dully at the lights twinkling over the bay as we drive across the bridge. Normally, the sight of a nighttime body of water, hammered by rain and glowing with reflections of light, would suffuse me with nothing but joy. But tonight, the golden lights just look like fire.

"What?" Dad glances sidelong at me.

I curl tight in the seat. The smell of Dad's car makes me feel like a kid again. "I lit a candle. In my bedroom. I might've left it burning."

He clears his throat. "Maeve. I doubt that was it."

Anger lashes my chest and I squirm, letting out a sharp sigh. "But it might be."

"I doubt it."

I want to slap him and scream, *What do you know?* He hasn't seen the house. But I know I'm not really mad at him. Instead, my voice comes out small and pitiful again. "I'm sorry I didn't answer my phone."

The quiet purr of his engine and the splash of cars passing the opposite way fills the silence for a minute. "I understand."

"Yeah?"

Good. I don't. I rest my head against the window and burrow into my hoodie.

"You have to have boundaries somewhere," he adds, though he sounds exhausted. Dad's boundary was never setting foot in Little Tree after the divorce. Maybe he was afraid he would get sucked back into the house.

"Yeah." I manage a hard laugh. "I really know where to draw the line, huh?" The first bid for freedom I make, and the house burns down.

He's silent again. The bridge passes behind us, and I feel my thin line of support—the con, my friends, my real self—evaporating with the distance.

Mom won.

What a horrible thing to think. Tears pound at my eyes, but don't fall. I'm holding them back with everything I have, even if it will cost me a headache later.

Dad tries again, shifting, driving with both hands neatly on nine and three on the wheel. "You're not on call for her twenty-four seven, Maeve."

"She needs help," I insist. "It's like nobody cares but me. If I lost her the way she lost her mom—" I choke. I almost did, just now. A fire in the house. Mom in the hospital.

That's what did it, we think. Dad thinks watching my grandmother die swiftly and unexpectedly of cancer kicked off Mom's hoarding. The clinging. Keeping everything close. The barriers of Stuff. And now . . .

"She's more than capable of calling a therapist," Dad says

slowly. He's said it before. "She's an adult."

"So am I." Disbelief wells up and crashes over me. I glare at the window. Even Mauve huffs up, back arching in my mind. How dare he question how I handle Mom when he just picked up and left her?

Left *us*.

"I don't think this is the perfect time to support your point. I left for a day and the house literally burned down."

Guilt swarms up from my stomach and snags in my throat.

He huffs out a breath. He sounds like me. Or, I guess, I sound like him when I do that same thing. "It's not your fault."

"Right."

He looks over sharply. I wish he'd slow down. It feels like the car is hydroplaning. "It's not your fault, Maeve."

I offer a flat, "I know."

"Maeve."

I clench the armrest as we surf through a dip in the road and water sprays my window. "Will you slow down?"

"I'm going under the speed—"

The car jerks against another puddle. He corrects, but my heart fractures and pieces lodge in my throat. "Slow down! Please!" I'm shrieking and I don't care. I fling a hand forward, gesturing at the blurry windshield. "Can we not add to the headlines? In a doubly tragic turn of events, a father and daughter speeding to the hospital wrapped around a telephone—"

"Maeve," he snaps but slows, "I've been driving for longer than you've been—"

I smack both hands on the dash. "Oh, you don't like it when I tell you what to do?" I can't shut up now. My rage and sorrow and guilt need a target, and Dad is in range, and I can't throw things in the car. "Maybe you shouldn't tell me how to take care of Mom. Or not take care of her. Or interfere at all!"

He's white-knuckling the wheel. His hands flex, and I feel like my neck muscles are about to snap from the tension. "It's not your job," he says, pointing firmly at me, "to take care of her."

"Someone has to," I cry, then curl over myself, nearly bashing my head on the glove compartment, and squeeze my eyes shut, struggling for a steady breath.

Dad is silent.

We're both silent for the last ten minutes of the drive. My breath shudders and evens out, and I manage not to cry despite my screaming fit. When we arrive at the hospital, I leave my Mauve stuff on. I'm beyond caring. Ears, tail, all of it. I just want to see Mom.

Drizzle mists down and Dad drops me at the entrance, but I wait for him under the overhang. I hover awkwardly near a concrete ashtray and offer it a glare of supreme irony. Smoking? At a hospital? I flip up my hood, working it over my cat ears. Whatever. I wonder if the fire was caused by a cigarette. That just seems so unlikely. I can picture my room and my stupid open flame candle. Stupid. I was so worried about getting out of the house I probably left it lit.

Dad jogs from the parking lot, holding a hand over his head as if it's going to repel anything. I turn to stride in with him, suppressing a shiver. It's a warm, moist drizzle, not freezing like in winter, but I'm still glad for the hoodie.

The doors whisk open and sterile air whooshes over us. Dad

bypasses reception and we head down the hall. Nurses and people waiting in the foyer stop and look at me, and I don't have the heart to acknowledge them or try to be sassy. I'm probably not the first furry they've seen anyway, and I won't be the last. I heard an ambulance headed to the con hotel the very first night.

We loop through a hall and up a floor to the ICU. The giant red lettering on the door tightens my chest. I'm just following Dad like a little pink and black shadow. He stops at the nurse's station to check in. A man with a clipboard double takes at me, and I wave a hand-paw limply and then look down.

"Here." Dad slides a check-in sheet to me, and I write my name, heart rate climbing slowly but surely. Get me out of here.

"This is Maeve?" The man with the clipboard inquires, and I glance up instinctively at my name. I'm grateful he doesn't look pitying, just clinical.

"Yes," I say since Dad doesn't. "I'm—I'm her daughter."

"We know." He seems to note everything about me. Totoro on my hoodie. My paws. My tail. He clears his throat. "You're listed as her primary emergency contact."

At first, the words don't make sense. Then the bile swirls, angry red sparks popping at the edge of my brain. Me? Not Dad? Not her sister? Not an adult? I mean, I'm an adult now, but have I been her emergency contact since I was thirteen? Even worse, I'm her primary contact and I was not there the one time she needed me to be. A breath slides out of my mouth. "Okay. Can we see her now?"

He glances down the hall. "In a few minutes. They're changing her bandages."

"Yeah, I don't want to see." Fidgety, I snatch a random

paperclip from the counter and drift back a step, unmoored. "Dad?"

"She's just down the hall. We can wait here." He motions around the desk to a sitting area where a mom with a little boy sits while a TV blares the weather. Dad looks like he wants to hug me, but I'm back in no-touchy land for the moment, even from Dad.

Jade and Paige and Beeper's hugs fill me up, but I don't think Dad would have the same effect. Right now, my parents are draining all the good things I've built up. I think of Nira, escaping to cons to fill herself up before she goes back to real life. I don't want that. I want to feel full all the time. But maybe that's not a thing that happens. Maybe all you get is two days of happiness here and there, and then you're drowned in Stuff again.

When I realize Dad's waiting for my response about where to wait, I shrug and head toward the tidy sofa with its tight pink cushions. Dad meanders after me, but he seems unmoored, too. Which is irritating because I need someone to be anchored.

He hovers, then glances over his shoulder. "I'm going to find a cup of coffee."

Clipboard Man motions. "It's downstairs in the cafeteria."

Dad hesitates as I plop on the sofa and turn my gaze to the little boy who's flipping through a picture book full of frogs. I think I had it as a kid. *Puddle Muddle* or something. I remember Dad reading me a book that had frogs.

"Want one?"

I look up at Dad from fiddling with my paperclip. "What?"

He frowns—actually we're both already frowning, so it's like every crease in his face just deepens. "Do you want a coffee or anything?"

"Not really, thanks." I fold my arms over my stomach and lean forward, closing my eyes until Dad walks away. Then I start to feel hot and untuck the hood from my ears and sit back.

The clip in my fingers is one of those painted wire contraptions, wire twisted and folded and coiled, designed to the correct tension so it will open and close and hold things but not break. I snap it once, then run a fingertip around the design, wondering how it must feel to be so perfectly made that you perform your function without being too loose or too tight that you're either useless or break.

The people with me in the waiting area come into focus beyond the paperclip.

The boy is staring at me, his big eyes lift to my ears, and he bursts out laughing. His mom, startled, jerks her gaze from the TV and stares at me, trying not to laugh too. I manage a tiny smile.

"Why you wearing that?" The boy points at my ears.

"Because it makes me happy."

He looks unconvinced about me being happy, and I don't blame him. I'm probably not very convincing. "Oh. Why?"

Because I wish I was a cat. "Because it's fun."

"Oh." He picks at the page in his book. "Why?"

I glance to his mom, who motions and shrugs with a fond smile. "Because I like cats."

"Oh. I like dogs, and I like birds. Why do you like cats? We have a dog."

Before we can go further in-depth and I can proselytize the glory of cats, Jade appears around the corner. Still in his lavender shirt, he spies me and heads over. Wow, he was literally right behind us. I feel like I should stand to greet him, but I have nothing left. Clipboard Man calls the mom in the waiting area, and she collects her boy, who waves to me as they head away to visit their person.

Jade helps himself to the spot next to me on the sofa, and I limply lift a paw in greeting.

He glances around at the empty waiting area, then at me. "Can't see her yet?"

"No." I pick at the hem of my shirt. "Did you tell everyone I'm sorry I had to leave the party?"

He offers a crooked smile. "They're not worried about the party. They're worried about *you*."

I sit back, folding my arms over my chest and resisting the urge to bury myself under my hood again. "It's so embarrassing."

He glances up, then watches my face, and there's only concern, not pity, which is nice. "Embarrassing that your house burned?"

Air huffs out my chest and I scrounge for the mental strength to answer. It's Jade, and I can't check out, even though I want to. I have no idea what it will be like to see Mom. I feel like I should be more worried, but I feel angry. Angry and frustrated she landed herself in the hospital the one weekend I was having time for myself.

Which makes me a genuinely awful person.

Jade's watching me, but he doesn't push the question. Instead, he lowers his voice. "Everyone has stuff going on, Mauvy."

I remember Paige saying the same thing, in almost the same way. In that don't-be-afraid way. "I know. I know that. I just don't want everyone dealing with my stuff too. I don't . . ." I gesture vaguely, uselessly, batting away nothing, and toss the paperclip on the table near us. "I don't want to be a burden. I'm the happy one."

Jade's smile slips, and he's not pitying, just sad. "You can still be the happy one. But you don't have to pretend nothing's wrong."

I know he's being my friend, but it feels like a lecture. I know all these things. I know you're supposed to be honest and open up to people and not bottle anything. I know all of it. I had a great therapist. My gaze flicks around, looking for pink, and just settles on Jade's shirt. For a second, we're silent.

Then I remember.

My eyes narrow and I lift my gaze to him. "How do you know my dad?"

For the first time since I met him two days ago, a flush hits his face and he looks down. "I don't think this is a good time to talk about it."

Now is the only time. Anxiety rears its ugly head out of my numbness and irritation. "Okay, but now you have to tell me."

He rests his arms on his thighs, lacing his fingers together. I wonder what he does when he's stressed, the way I count pink things. Or if other people even have to do things like that. I scoop up my tail and stroke the soft fur while he decides how to decide whatever he's going to say.

When he finally speaks, his voice is low in his chest and so quiet I have to lean in. "Your dad didn't call Social Services a couple of years ago." Disbelief then anger smack together in my chest. I know the rest of the sentence even before he says, "I did," and looks over at me with his impossibly earnest and worried dark eyes. "I was so scared you'd hate me. Then the social worker told your dad about me, and he got in touch and . . . I'm sorry. He said he would tell you it was him. And I know how messed up that is now, and I'm so sorry."

I stare at him for a second. That knock on the door. The people failing to keep their looks of amazement and pity to themselves. My screaming match with Mom and Dad about me moving or not moving out of the house. Thinking it might mean there would be change, some help, but there was nothing.

The neighbors peering out their windows and stopping on the street. Dragging things out of the doorway in prep for our visits from the city. The endless, exhausting months begging Mom to put things in totes, to pick up a piece of trash, to take a bag for recycling, to actually open eBay to sell something, even offering to package it and take it to the post office for her. Sneaking trash to the neighbor's dumpster at night as if I was stealing precious jewels.

If there's anything worse than living with a hoarder, it's living with a hoarder and having the authorities know. They knock on the door without a moment's notice, and you pretend not to be home so you have time to clean. And you watch your hoarder struggle against the change and the help with every last fiber of her being because she needs the Stuff to cope and can't see that it's destroying her. She needs the Stuff to fill the empty and sad places in her heart. And people know that and still tell you to just leave as if that will fix it, her, and you.

Heat swarms my throat and I recoil, finally, as my brain whirls back to this moment, with Jade staring at me as if I'm a hundred miles away.

I shove some words out. "You what?"

He doesn't repeat himself because he knows that's not really what I'm asking. "I was trying to help," he whispers. The word slices to my bones. "You were so stressed out all the time. I'm sorry. I wanted you to see that you could leave the whole situation. I thought it would help." He swipes a hand through his curls and gestures upward, then drops his hand. "I didn't know it would make it worse. I'm sorry."

Something else, something warm, an uncomfortable realization prickles at the back of my neck, similar to the one before I passed out. I curl forward, head between my knees, gulping breaths.

That's the year he got me my Totoro hoodie. My rainy day hoodie. The hoodie I'm wearing, my favorite thing. He got it because he felt guilty.

My favorite thing from Jade is a guilt present, just like this whole weekend is from Dad. Guilt and pity. He knew I blamed Dad. And he let me be angry at my dad this whole time—this whole time.

I surge to my feet and pull the hoodie off, tangling arms and cat ears and probably exposing my stomach to the whole floor before I manage to wrestle it off, bringing some pink hairs along with it.

Jade's face crumples and his eyes brighten, and he shoves to his feet. "Mauve—"

Breath shudders into my chest in pathetic whimpers and he reaches to me as I thrust the hoodie at him, keeping him at bay with my outstretched hands. "I can't—I can't do this right now. You don't even know . . ."

"I do," Jade says quietly. He looks panicked now, and Clipboard Man peers at us over the nurse's station counter. Jade's fingers close around the hoodie. I can actually see his heart breaking when I shove it forward and let go. "I do know, please—"

"I—cannot." I grasp my head, fingers closing in my hair, and hold up my other hand between us. "I can't make you feel better right now."

"I'm not asking you to." He steps in and I step back, waving a hand to maintain my personal bubble. He holds the hoodie to his chest, and my gaze fixates on the corner of Totoro's grin amongst the folds. "I just want to explain—"

"You did. No more. Not right now." I know I asked. I knew it would be bad, that's my life, but I can't hear more right now. My hands clench to fists, holding myself together, and I finally close my eyes to have less stimuli going on. "Leave me alone. Please." My whole body is rigid, holding everything in, and I fight the ramping impulse to stamp a foot or throw something. He doesn't move. "Please, *Lucas*, leave me alone. I can't right now. I can't help you. I don't want any more help. I don't want anything."

He doesn't answer. I open my eyes, head down, but don't look up at his face, just his feet. They're still in flip flops, but not cheap ones like I get from the drugstore; nice, solid, ergonomically shaped gray ones. He's wearing a silver toe ring that looks like a dragon coiled around his toe, and I stare at it until he moves. One foot finally scuffs back, then the other, and he doesn't say anything else.

Steps approach down the hall and I know it's Dad. I whirl around to find him, leaving Jade in the waiting area. Dad has two cups.

"Hey, I got you some tea just in case—"

"Thanks." I snatch the steaming paper cup, and a nurse comes out of a room down the hall, thank goodness, to save us all from dealing with each other anymore.

"Mr. Stephens?" Her gaze flicks to me and twitches, trying not to be amused by my attire. That's fine. I'm glad someone's happy. "You can see her now."

I about-face and head down the hall without a word.

18

MOM DOESN'T HAVE THE ROOM to herself. There are three beds, and she's right in the middle, curtained off.

The nurse pauses Dad and me at the door, speaking in a firm, gentle tone that eases through the shock in my brain.

"We've done all we can do for now. She'll be just fine, maybe a little scarring, but we're going to hold her for at least two days and keep her on some medication because pain is intense with these kinds of burns."

I watch her eyes, nodding once to show I comprehend (though I don't), and appreciate her honesty. "But she'll be okay?"

The nurse considers me and keeps her hands to herself. I can tell she wants to offer a comforting touch, but I'm glad she doesn't. She keeps it simple and clear, perhaps perceiving that beneath my furriness there is just a shocked daughter. "She will. She'll be fine. She just needs to rest. There's nothing else we can do right now."

"Thank you," Dad says, and we move into the room.

She's awake, which is disconcerting. I wanted a minute to take this in—to sit at her bedside and feel bad and tell her I'm sorry without her hearing or responding. But she's awake as my gaze lingers on the bandages around her arms and neck, the IV, and the little tube to her nose running better oxygen, and my brain helpfully compiles a reel of cinematic scenarios of what might have happened.

She had to have been asleep, right? Or she would've gotten out before getting hurt. Or maybe she tried to put the fire out. Or maybe she was trapped by Stuff. Maybe she just sat in her chair clicking surveys while the house burned, and she couldn't smell it until it was too late.

I could have lost her. I could have lost her instantly and without warning, almost the way she lost her own mom so fast.

My hands tighten around the paper cup until it almost buckles, and I force myself to relax my grip. Dad stands behind me.

Mom's mouth spasms in a smile and then fades. "Do I look that bad?" Her voice is hoarse, squeaky, and rough like someone with pneumonia.

"Yeah." My body twitches, instinctively wanting to go to her, but I've never seen her look or sound this fragile. The oxygen machine makes a little *k-tss* every few seconds. I wish I'd kept my hoodie on, honestly, even though its fleece is a betrayal.

Then she moves one hand, just barely, fingers lifting and settling again, to invite me to sit with her. For two seconds, I'm six again and shuffle forward, but I just can't sit on the bed. There's too much stuff that could be disturbed. Dad pulls a chair closer and I sink down, taking a heartbeat too long to reach out and touch her bandaged hand.

"I'm so sorry, Mom," I whisper.

She frowns, then closes her eyes and breathes slowly through the oxygen tubes. Maybe it makes her throat feel better. "It's not your fault."

"I know." I force myself to leave my hand in hers, though what I really need is to curl up and cry. But Mom's at the center of this, not me. You don't sit at someone's bedside in the hospital and get them to make you feel better. You just don't.

"Your hair looks good," she offers, and I manage a hard laugh, nodding once.

"Thanks. Paige is amazing." I sound listless even to myself. Not exactly how I pictured my hair reveal to Mom.

"Mm."

We were fighting about all that and the con, and she doesn't add anything else. Guilt splashes across my heart. If I'd just gone home—if I'd been there, this wouldn't have happened. It just wouldn't have. I know it.

I wonder if she's thinking the same thing.

We remain quiet. I know Mom's looking at my ears, outfit, and runny makeup. Finally, Dad can't handle the silence and clears his throat.

"The fire department got back to me."

Mom and I both look up at him slowly, Mom not quite comprehending, as if he's speaking another language. In a way, he is. She answers in her own. "I'm not doing this right now."

He shifts, sliding a hand into his pocket, where I know he's fiddling with his change. Maybe I stroke my tail and count things, and he fiddles with change. "They think it was a cigarette. They just don't know how it got so severe so fast." His tone is sharper than it needs to be, but at the same time, a small part of me fractures in relief. A cigarette. Not my stupid candle. "I'm just telling you."

Mom shifts, moving her hand and looking at the ceiling.

"I know what you're doing."

"They just said if you have any information, it's really important—"

"Oh?" Mom says. "It's important? Thank you for the clarification, Mark. I wouldn't have known."

"Please stop," I plead dully. Dad looks at me and his face pinches to a disapproving sulk.

I know he's not trying to get information. He's trying to figure out how to blame Mom for this while she's lying there in a hospital bed. And it's not like I'm not trying to do the same thing, but at least I'm waiting until she's upright and has the lung capacity to shout back or the strength to throw something. I don't kick her when she's down.

I'm used to intervening because their fights stress me out. But what I do next takes even Mom by surprise.

"Dad, could you just give us a minute? Alone?" I can handle one or the other of them, but not both at the same time. Not together. They're just not nice to each other. I wish Jade was there, with his hand on my back. But I also don't want him here because he's been lying to me for years and pretending to be on my side.

Dad sighs. He shuffles aside, slides a few coins together in his pocket, then steps forward to touch my shoulder and kiss my hair, and leaves without speaking to Mom again, as if she wasn't the reason we're both here—as if she's not right there. He probably wishes she wasn't.

Mom and I sit there, listening to the oxygen machine, rain on the window, and, intermittently, someone snoring from the next curtained-off bed over. I wonder what happened to them.

When I look over, Mom's closed her eyes. I suppose the pain medication will just put her right to sleep? But I can't let her go just yet. Even though I don't want to blame her for the fire, she has to see, right? She has to know this is it.

This is her sign to get things together, her rock bottom. Her moment of clarity.

In a bizarre way, I'm hopeful. I try not to think about the few precious things I had in the house. They're gone. They're just stuff. And they're gone, and I won't be her, clinging to them, even if I mourn a little.

They think it was a cigarette, Dad had said.

I want to ask if she was smoking. But I don't.

"Were you asleep?"

"Yes." There's a soft pause, and she chuckles wryly. "The alarm in the kitchen was still working, so once that went off, I woke up and was able to get out." She makes a noise, clearing her throat, lowering her voice. Maybe it's painful to talk. I don't tell her not to. I need to hear. "I got out through the front."

Two-foot entryway, I think, *you're welcome.* A little relief cools my chest. Maybe I helped, did something right, at least. But she doesn't thank me for maintaining the path, so I just nod. Then she closes her eyes.

I wonder what's happening at my party, then feel bad for wondering and resist checking my phone. I've ruined everyone's evening with all this worry, and the party is probably over.

Mom exhales roughly and her eyes snap open to glare at the ceiling. "I swear, if this has something to do with that stove—"

"The stove?" I blank for a second. Then I hear Dad again.

They think it was a cigarette. They just don't know how it got so severe so fast.

All I can picture is smoke. A tiny fire, maybe, crawling from the overflowing ashtray in her office, consuming paper, boxes, crumpled tissues, devouring the hallway and lampshades, then the kitchen. If she tried that stove earlier in the day, turned on the gas and couldn't smell it, and left it on . . .

My pulse pounds my neck, revving for a fight. "Mom, did you try to use that stove?"

"No." She turns her head to look at me, her face scrunching with brief pain. "It wouldn't even turn on, for one. Or that's what I thought." Her squeaking, hoarse voice loses some impact and yet is more threatening at the same time. Then she shakes her head bitterly and glowers at the ceiling, lips moving for a second before she speaks. "If this was gas, I'm going to wring someone's neck at the gas company."

My pity drops to the floor, my belly hardens to a block of ice, and I slide to my feet. "Are you serious?" Disbelief crowds out my anguish at seeing her hurting and pitiful. "Oh my God. Mom? Are you *serious*? You're going to blame—"

"What?" She looks over.

My mouth is open, but I can't bring anything out for a second. But only for a second. "Mom, do you think . . . do you think maybe if there was less, um, stuff, in the house, there would've been less of a danger? Or maybe, if you hadn't smoked inside?"

She closes her eyes. "Please don't do this right now, Maeve. I'm tired and I'm hurting. I can't be lectured to right now. It was an accident. Fire is fire."

"I'm not lecturing. I'm—I'm . . . I . . ." Heat washes from my head to my feet and that buzzing starts again. I force myself to flex my knees a little. I cannot pass out again tonight (even though this would be the ideal place, I guess). Mauve circles, intent. She isn't scared, the way I am.

Mom doesn't answer.

"Mom!" I need her to look at me. The next patient over snorts in their sleep and I lower my voice, "Seriously?" I'm all but hissing, flinging my hand out as if to point to whatever smoldering wreckage is left of my home. The whiplash from fear and pity back to desperate anger almost makes me nauseous. "I'm begging," I whisper, pressing a hand to my chest. "Mom, I'm *begging* you. This is it, okay? This is where it has to change. It has to."

I know I shouldn't lay into her right now, but I can't stop. I can't believe she's still trying to ignore the root of all this, to stay adamant and stubborn, even laying there in a hospital bed.

She closes her eyes again, to shut me out. "Maeve, please."

"It has to change, Mom. Look at yourself. And, and . . . look at *me*." I clench my hands together near my chest, literally begging toward her, warm tears breaking down my cheeks because if something doesn't give, I'll shatter. "Do you know all the crap I've had to do? How ridiculous it is not to shower in your own house? How people avoid me at school because I smell like mold? How I crawl through the window some days?" I suck a breath, the little control I have over my voice beginning to fracture. "Do you know it's actually weird to never eat at home, not really? It's normal for us, but I don't think it's normal to not cook or make a sandwich because I'm afraid it'll kill me. Mom—"

"Then you should have left," she snaps, stabbing me right in the gut with her brittle, sharp voice. She's not appreciative, sympathetic, or surprised at my confession, or grateful I stayed and tried. Just defensive and angry as if my suffering is a direct attack on her. "Like everyone else."

Like everyone else? Me, who stayed the longest and tried the hardest? It takes me a minute to gather my skewered soul off the floor and respond. How dare she. Hurt and anger wrestle each other in my heart, but anger claws its way toward the top. "I—I stayed to *help*. I couldn't leave you alone."

That pauses her, at least. Another sigh, but she turns her face away. "I am sorry, Maeve. I know you did. I'm sorry. I want to change." She laughs weakly. Impervious to my emotions. "I guess this is one way to empty the house?"

"Yeah." My heart pounds. I'm sweating, fighting this battle again, trying to see what landscape we're even in now.

"I'll try," she whispers. "I know you're right."

I would be hopeful, except I've heard that before—a lot—especially after the first visit from Social Services and the city. We put things in totes and took out the trash. We organized (some). We got rid of a few things. But it always came crawling back. Little packages from Amazon. eBay. A visit to the thrift store or the Dollar Store. A piece of junk mail she wouldn't throw away. A sale somewhere.

The thought of living in that again—watching her *not* change, and spiral, and defend herself—makes me want to scream, but I don't have the strength.

"I just need you to understand," she adds quietly, and my last hope fizzles. I do understand; it's just never mattered.

I've understood, and listened, and helped, and failed. And the second she says that, I know where we're headed. I know the landscape now, the weather pattern. The teeny part of me who was hopeful is gone, and it's just me and Mauve, shaking our head slowly.

I stand there shuddering under the dim fluorescent light and realize it doesn't matter that the house burned. All her stuff. Possibly all of my stuff. My Totoro bedspread, my tapestry that was a gift from Jade. All my artwork, years of sketchbooks, and my clothes. But I don't even have space to grieve *my* loss, because Mom takes up all the space. Mom and her stuff.

And even if there's nothing left, it doesn't matter.

Because the Stuff wasn't inside the house.

It's inside her.

It will always be inside her and it'll always find its way back until she figures out how to deal with it. It'll be back, in the form of junk, furniture she doesn't need, magazines she doesn't read, clothes she doesn't wear, and trash she won't throw away. I know because I can feel the Stuff trying to take hold of me, too. It's too late for Mom.

My throat clasps around the truth. I stand there and suck breaths through my mouth and stare at my Mom as if she's a mile away.

And I realize this isn't her moment of clarity. It's mine.

"Mom," I whisper.

"I can't, Maeve," she cuts me off. "I can't, right now."

Of course not. She's covered in burns and breathing from a tank and exhausted and in pain. I'm a horrible daughter for trying, for doing the thing I kicked Dad out for trying to do. But she won't talk about it tomorrow, either. Or when she's healed. Or when she has a new place to live. Or when the Stuff starts to pile up again.

Now I feel something. Warmth and sorrow swarm my throat and face. I swallow again, hard. My hands close to fists. I don't think I can save her. And I don't think I can try anymore. And if I'm there, I'll be buried—sucked in, dragged under—for the rest of my life.

If I don't let go, it won't matter if I'm in Olympia or Portland. Maybe Dad, my aunts, the friends—maybe they didn't abandon her. Maybe she abandoned us by choosing her stuff. Maybe they saved themselves before the stuff could devour them as it has me.

I know this road. I'm staring at all the familiar turns, pauses—it's horrible scenery. The only thing different, suddenly, is recognizing we're about to turn onto it.

And I don't think I want to again.

The nurse's summation floats back to my weary head. *There's nothing more we can do right now.* I swallow back a sob. There's nothing more I can do. But I don't know what that means. I don't know a road that doesn't lead back to the house. I don't know what that looks like. I don't know how to care without caring—how to sit at the edge of the abyss and love her without falling in.

Mom's eyes are closed.

I force out a whisper. "I'm . . . I'll be right back, okay?"

She nods but doesn't open her eyes. I hope it's the pain medication and not her blocking me out. I jerk my stiff limbs around, leave the room, and nearly bump into Dad, who puts out an instinctive arm. I curl into it and loose a sob against his chest.

"Oh," he murmurs and tightens his arm around me, then the

other one. I try to remember what happened to the tea he brought me or where I put it down. "Oh, Maeve. She'll be okay."

I shake my head. "No, she won't."

He pulls back, eyes narrowing in confusion, then his expression clears when he realizes I'm not talking about her injuries. He looks—almost hopeful? As if I've finally seen the light. "Maeve—"

"I know why you left." I drop my gaze from his. I'm upset and tired and guilty that I've been angry at him for years about a thing he didn't do. "And I know you didn't call Social Services on her, but I wish you would have told me. And I just . . . need you to understand why I stayed." My voice sounds limp even to me.

"I understand," he says softly. And instead of speaking more, explaining, apologizing, or doing anything else to dredge through the past, he just pulls me back into the hug—and it breaks me.

I crack open and everything I held back in the room pours out. Everything. The emotions I don't let Mom see because they don't work, they don't matter. The emotions I don't let everyone else see because I don't want to scare them away. Resentment, fear, frustration spiral up my core, and my tight braid of emotion whips loose and unravels, releasing in a hard sob.

"Dad—" My voice chokes out and the tears I've feared all my life come. I grip his shirt and sob into his chest, sniffing as my whole body wracks itself to get rid of the Stuff. Something has been lanced, and the awful puss of anger streams out at last.

"Sh, sh. That's right. That's right. Oh, Maeve." He doesn't tell me to stop crying. He's breathing hard, holding himself together, absorbing it, and patting my back, but not telling me to stop.

He doesn't tell me to stop crying, and I don't think I could if I tried.

Our nurse peers over the desk at us, and Dad waves a hand. All fine here, thanks.

When most of the tears are done, and I'm breathing somewhat normally, he brings me back over to a chair and my lukewarm tea on the table. Vaguely, I hear the weatherman talk about thunderstorms tomorrow. I curl up in the chair and force down a sip of something chamomile-ish while Dad sits by me and folds his hands in his lap.

For a minute, we're quiet. I'm empty. Raked clean but hurting, emotionally bruised and sore.

The news transitions from weather to sports, and Dad speaks quietly. "The firemen said some of your room was okay because the door was closed and the hallway was . . . dense. With stuff. I'll help you see what's salvageable, okay? And we can replace anything that can be replaced. Clothes. Those things." He gestures, drops his hand back to his lap.

"Thanks." My whisper doesn't sound much better than Mom's. "Okay."

Anything that can be replaced. Clothes. My lamp. My cheery Christmas lights. Closing my eyes, I try to form a clear, hopeful image of my totes of sketchbooks and artwork and other things that *can't* be replaced.

Dad leaves it at that, and I feel a little clearer even though I'm exhausted. I feel like I've been throwing up. But the bad stuff is mostly out for now. Maybe I should've had a good cleansing cry before the con. I draw a slow breath through my nose and look at the tight weave of the pink upholstery.

"So, is there a place to sleep here? If Mom's staying overnight . . ." I eye the tidy sofa.

Dad clears his throat, as he does when he's got something to say. "Maeve, I think you should go back to your convention."

My head turns like a satellite to improve my reception. "What? I can't just leave my mom alone in the hospital."

"She's fine," he says quietly, firmly, in a manner I haven't heard since he still lived with us. "That is"—he gestures, weakly— "not *fine*, but she will be fine. She's in excellent hands. She'll probably sleep straight through the night with the medicine, and you will sleep here, miserable and worried and waking up every ten minutes. Come back tomorrow and see her, but there's nothing you can do right now. There's no point in suffering overnight and being uncomfortable, especially after I already paid for your hotel room."

He grins, halfhearted. I know he wants to be firm and fatherly, but by the end, he's more pleading as if to help me see. I do, a little. I see. I see myself falling back into my pattern: What do I do for Mom? What do I do to maintain control over her and the house and make sure everything's okay? I can't. I know he's right. I can't do it again, but it's hard to comprehend what that really means. That to change I have to actually, you know, *change*.

"Just go back?" I swallow more tea, thirst burning my raw throat now, and gesture toward the middle distance. "Just, oh hey guys, what's that? No, my house just burned down and Mom's lying in the hospital, but hey let's hit up that vintage toon panel?"

Dad smiles. Gently, not pitying, but in that unrelenting way. His battles-of-wills are different than Mom's. Mom gets angry. Dad plants his heels and maintains kindly until I relent, just as he did for the con. "Yes. I think you should do that, exactly. I think you should go and be with your friends, buy some fuzzy stuff, try to smile, and take care of yourself. Your house burned too, Maeve. Not just hers."

Take care of myself. I just raise my eyebrows.

"What a concept, right?" he murmurs. I shake my head and sip my tea. I'm not gonna lie—the thought of going back is better than the thought of trying to sleep on this small sofa or a cot in Mom's room, even though it'll be awkward and stressful to explain to people. It's better than waking up in the hospital and starting the battle with Mom again.

But I wonder if it has to be a battle. Or if I can just go. Maybe me going will be Mom's rock bottom. Maybe she'll never have one. Maybe it's not my responsibility to wonder.

I've sure hit mine, and I have to get out even if she doesn't. That's the thing—the thing I finally understand about Dad and Mom's family and all the rest. They got out.

Relief, guilt, and frustration prickle my scoured heart. Dad just watches me, and I scoot to face him more.

"I'm a horrible person for wanting to go," I say casually. And yeah, I am fishing for him to say I'm not. I can't be. I don't want to be the horrible daughter in this situation.

"You're not," he says quietly. "You're normal."

"Ha." I grin at him weakly, Cheshire, in my pink cat ears. "Right."

"You're normal for being tired and done," he clarifies, without smiling, when I deflect. I look down. "It's normal. And it's okay. Actually, you're better than normal and it's better than okay.

You've tried so hard. You've done more than you should have and I . . . well, I'm sorry." He pats his own knees, rallying. "But we can't go back. We can't change the beginning, but we can change the ending, okay, Kitten? I'm here, and I'm going to stay so you can go back. I'm going to take care of everything. All right?"

I thought I didn't have tears left, but that brings a trickle. A bubble of relief pops in my chest. That's what I need from him—to be here. To be the primary contact. To be the adult so I can escape. To take care of Mom, so I can take care of myself. I draw another shuddering breath and whisper, "Thank you."

He nods and rests an arm across the back of my chair. I mostly finish my tea, then we silently agree it's time to go back in before she passes out for the night.

We come around her partition, and her eyes open. I stop at the foot of her bed and gently touch her ankle under the blanket. We used to give each other foot rubs and pedicures when there was room in our house and our hearts for it.

She doesn't look at Dad, who stops behind me and rests both hands on my shoulders as if to keep me from drifting away.

"Hey, Mom. Um. They said you're probably going to sleep from the medication soon, and I'm . . ." Dad squeezes my shoulders. Mom moves her foot a little, acknowledging the touch with a tiny smile. A lump solidifies in my throat, but I can't surrender. I can't. "I'm going back to my hotel for the last day of the con. I have a panel with the artist I love, and I—I'm going to go."

Her tiny smile fades and her gaze lifts to Dad, who relaxes his hands so he doesn't look like he's forcing me to say this, probably.

"I'll come visit tomorrow," I continue, drawing Mom's gaze

back to me before she can assume he's making my decisions. "I promise."

Her jaw tightens. Mentally, I brace for a fight. For the argument, then resentment, the *oh yes, leave just like everyone else*, the standoff. Our little tradition.

But she doesn't say anything.

We stare at each other across a vast and widening space, and when I don't cave to the silence, I feel one link from the chain that anchors me to her and the house start to loosen. Her gaze lifts to Dad again, and they have a moment of silent staring until Mom looks at me again. Maybe it's the pain medication or the fire or exhaustion, but she doesn't look angry. She looks defeated, hurt. Her jaw muscle twitches. All I want is to run to her and touch her face and ask if she needs something, promise to help, and slide back into the Stuff with her and fight the battle.

But I don't.

I don't cave.

The link loosens a fraction more, giving me space for a breath that feels almost free.

"I understand," she says softly, at last. If she's angry or bitter, she's keeping it in. Another silence hangs over us until she adds, "Send some pictures, okay? But to your father's phone. Mine is . . ."

I nod. Hers is, literally, toast.

"I will." I glance up to Dad, closing my hands again as they start to quiver. Oh, God, it's relief. I don't want to feel relief. I don't want to be a horrible, uncaring person, but I'm relieved she said that. I can't remember the last time she did anything to show me she wants me to be happy. Dad squeezes my shoulders and lets go, stepping back.

I stroke Mom's foot gently, then walk to the head of the bed to touch her hand and lean over to be close, without hugging. She's injured and it's just us. We don't hug that much. There's never room. But maybe there will be, eventually.

"Sleep well, okay? I'll see you tomorrow."

"Have fun." She takes a scratchy breath. "I love you, sweetie."

I shut my eyes and lean in close because I believe her. "I love you too," I whisper. It's true, and I love her for letting me go. Not physically, but here, in my heart—letting me go without making me feel guilty.

Her eyes close, and Dad and I slip out.

"Um." We pause at the hall that leads out. "Can you give me a ride back?"

He laughs. I think he's even more relieved than I am that I decided to go. "Of course. I think she's all settled in there."

"Thanks." I'm not sure I want to ride with Dad, honestly. There's a lot of scramble in my head, and he's not necessarily going to want to talk about it without telling me what to do. But there's no way I'm taking an Uber. That's a bigger step than I can take tonight.

He collects my satchel from the waiting area and steers me out. At this point, I have no idea what way we came in. The signs might as well be hieroglyphs for all I can interpret letters right now.

When we reach the exit and the overhang, there's Jade.

I stop. He's on the phone, pauses when he sees me, says something and lowers the phone, then tucks it away, watching us. My hoodie is neatly folded under his arm, and he gestures slightly, a silent *can we talk?*

Dad pauses behind me. "Or . . ."

The decision is easy, even though seeing Jade raises a jumble. It feels like I was angry at him a year ago. I've felt so many emotions since then, and seeing him standing with a backdrop of rain in his pretty shirt he wore for my birthday, watching me with concern, is like a healing balm. "Yeah. Yeah, I'll get a ride from him. Thanks, Dad." I turn to hug him, and he wraps me up in a quick, firm embrace, then steps back.

"Go on before you change your mind."

I step back, force a Cheshire grin, and finger-gun him, a la Paige. "I'll send pictures." Then I add, "I won't change my mind."

Dad chuckles wearily, gaze traveling over my whole attire, and nods once. "Good. Good night, Kitten."

"Night, Dad." I look at him, and the approval radiating off him gives me a glimmer of strength. I whirl around, letting my tail flick, and stride toward Jade. Dad doesn't watch us, but heads back inside because he trusts Jade. He trusts *me*.

"Hey." His arm twitches out, offering the hoodie, watching my face. He looks calm and attentive, not dramatic. Just him—normal and grown-up and calm. The thing happened and we're dealing with it now. Is this being adults? Is this having a fight without yelling and throwing things? I want to collapse in for a hug.

Instead, I take the hoodie and put it on, which makes him smile. I duck my head. "I'm sorry I freaked out."

He exhales roughly. "Nah, it was worth freaking out over." His eyes travel up the architecture around us. "Is everything okay?"

"No." I slip my hands into the warm, familiar, fleece-lined raggedy pockets, suddenly grateful I brought this with me.

I think of the house. Even if everything didn't burn, I imagine irreparable damage from smoke. There are no tears left in me, but I know I'll cry again at least once, for the house, for my stuff, before I let it go. Jade looks down to meet my eyes with concern, and I offer him a teeny smile. "But it will be."

We stand there as rain sluices off the roof at the corner, a waterfall of silver lit by the parking lot lamps.

Finally, I offer, "I understand why you did it."

He slides his hands into his pockets, searching my face. "Thank you."

I pick at the strings on my hoodie. "I know you did it because you care, and maybe because I always joked about you rescuing Mauve, and you wanted to rescue me."

His expression crinkles again and he extends an arm. I hesitate, but I'm so ready for the hug that I step in. He closes his arm around my shoulders and tilts his head down to speak against my hair. "I did. But I should have asked if you wanted rescuing."

"Thank you," I whisper and squeeze my eyes shut. "I secretly did. I wish it had worked, but it just didn't." When I confess, he makes a soft noise and gives me a squeeze. "I wanted someone to see me, you know? And you did. But I didn't know how invasive they would be and how much I wasn't ready to leave her alone. I thought if someone came in who wasn't me, it would magically fix it all."

"I understand," he says. His voice is so soft it's mostly just breath on my hair. He doesn't add more and I appreciate it. He doesn't bury me in what he was feeling, all the times I must've jokingly complained about the hoarding, secretly wanting someone to swoop in and fix everything, how hard it had to be for him to watch, how much he wanted to see me break free—break free the way I wish Mom could. He knows I've already felt a lot tonight and can't handle more feelings. We'll talk about it later. We will.

At length, his arm relaxes around me but keeps me there. "Why don't you want people to know about your mom and everything?"

A sigh huffs from my chest, which tightens threateningly. "It's embarrassing."

"Oh Mauvy, everyone has—"

"I know." I don't quite snap, but it stops him. He looks at me, eyebrows up. "I know everyone has stuff. My problems aren't special."

"I didn't mean it like that." His voice sours. "I meant people understand. You know why I left home, Mauvy—people will understand. You have to trust people sometimes. I know it's hard, really hard, but I promise it's worth it."

"I know." I draw a quick breath, amazed that the crying has stabilized me. I'm not trying to hold it back. "I just—I'm the happy one. You know? I'm the one who cheers people up. I don't want to be a burden, I don't—"

"You're not." He cuts me off firmly and moves around, taking both my shoulders and staring me in the face. "You are not a burden. You're allowed to have problems. You're allowed to tell people, and I promise you'll still be our little glitter pixie cat."

Emotions I can't distinguish well up, and my lip quivers, but I draw myself up and nod once, whispering, "Thank you."

That's what I needed to hear and all I need to say. It'll take practice, but maybe it will be less exhausting than pretending every-thing's okay. Maybe it will give someone else permission to not be okay, too. He pulls me tight again with a playful growl, and I hug him back, squeezing until he fake-grunts.

Once our hug and confessions settle out, he draws back, glancing to the hospital, then me. "Do you want me to bring you anything?"

My turn for a surprise. My mouth twitches, but I don't have the strength to smile yet. "Oh. I'm actually not staying." I swipe some pink hair from my eyes. "Can I have a ride instead?"

For two tense heartbeats, I'm afraid he's going to think I'm horrible for leaving. But then he breaks into a full-on dazzling dragon grin. "Wait here, I'll bring the car."

"No. I'm coming."

He laughs, turns neatly, and all but drags me through the rain toward Athen's car. We break into a sprint and race, but we're still soaked by the time we get there. He fumbles with the keys before we finally haul ourselves into the car and smack the doors shut, dripping onto Athen's beautiful upholstery.

"He's going to kill me." Jade laughs, teeth chattering, and starts the car.

"I doubt that." Then I remember his reaction to me spilling twenty grains of sugar in the car, consider the soaking seats, and lean forward to make sure my pink head doesn't drip on anything. "Okay, maybe just a slight maiming." I huddle in the front, safe in my Totoro hoodie. My foot nudges something and I grab it. An umbrella. Which I raise and shake at Jade. "Really?"

"Yeah," he says, cranking the heat. "That's there."

I laugh, giddy, letting some relief lay across my raw heart. "What's wrong with you?"

"Uh." He turns on the stereo. "I was distracted?"

"The Story of Tonight" from *Hamilton* floats from the speaker, and I whip a suspicious glare at him. It's too fitting. It's as if he's sending me a message. He lifts both hands, palms out. "It was already on."

"Hm." I huddle into my seat and shake the rain from my tail. Hopefully Athen's seats will dry. It feels strangely satisfying to worry about someone other than Mom.

Jade steers us away from the hospital. I force myself not to look back and focus on the windshield wipers. The rhythm is soothing, distracting, though at odds with the music. His fingers tap on the wheel, and he hums lightly along with the song.

My mouth twitches in spite of me, and I murmur, in my very best/worst French accent for Lafayette, "Let's have another round tonight."

That's all he needs. As if he was restrained by the weakest leash, he bursts out singing.

And I join him, harmonizing so badly he peers at me and grins around his lyrics, but he doesn't stop me from singing. He would never. Music is his way of getting through things, and I don't have one yet except throwing things and crying, so I'll borrow his. Fortunately, he has a playlist of cathartic Broadway ready to go.

We sing all the way back to my hotel.

19

JADE BRINGS ME TO THE doors, idling in the check-in parking spot. The rain has diminished to a misty drizzle, diffusing the street lamps and turning the distant bay into an indistinct impressionist painting.

"You'll be okay?" Jade leans over as I climb out, brow creasing deeply, and I know exactly how he's going to look when he's fifty.

"Yeah. I'm just going to take a shower and try to get some sleep."

"Sure." He reaches out to touch my arm as if to ground me. "If you change your mind, we're going to The Reef to game again."

It's tempting, but I'm just starting to stabilize and I need to recalibrate. "I might. Thank you." He ducks his head with a smile, and I lean back into the car and squeeze his shoulder. "Really, thank you."

He reaches up to lay his hand over mine, then grins and leans back, shooing me away. "Go on. I'll see you later."

I slip back, tugging up my hoodie, and he waits until I'm inside before pulling away. There's a surprising number of people in the lobby, I realize I don't even know what time it is, and I shuffle through to the elevator, even though stairs would probably be good to get rid of nervous energy. I keep my head down and gaze at the floor. A couple of other people step onto the elevator with me. Judging by the shoes (yes), I think they're furries, but I just can't bring myself to interact.

They get off at the third floor, sparing me from them noticing my tail or anything else. At last, my floor. My room. I left the AC on, so it's chilly. Without turning on the lights, I drift across the room to look down at the wet street, at the people hustling to and from bistros, hotels, and toward the Weeby. Cars trundle by, tires splashing through puddles. I leave my satchel on the table and don't look at my phone. I don't have it in me yet.

My little Sunspot sticker is still sitting on the table, and I pick it up slowly, holding it to the amber light of the street lamp.

Wisdom. I think of the other snails, Serenity and Courage.

"The Serenity Prayer." Chance's graduation speech soars back to me, having apparently tucked away in my subconscious.

May we have the serenity to accept the things we can't change, the courage to change what we can, and the wisdom to know the difference.

A breath huffs out of my chest. Maybe I got the right snail after all.

Time for that glorious shower.

In the water, in the steam, with all the fun soaps, I scrub the whole mess of emotions down the drain, imagining that scalding water can give me a fresh start. My limbs quiver with relief that I'm not sitting in the hospital right now. I brush aside a flicker of guilt. Dad's there. He's doing it for me. He's adulting so I can have this. If nothing else, I will enjoy it so it's worth it for him.

Vigorously touseling a towel through my short hair is

satisfying. Then I burrito myself in that fluffy robe and nestle into my pillows, switching on a lamp and tilting my head back to breathe, alone.

Raindrops remain on the window even though it's stopped raining, picking out points of light from the street below. Laughter floats from the hall, then feet stomp past my door. I close my eyes. I could just fall asleep. Nobody would care.

Well, they would care. But they wouldn't blame me; I wouldn't blame me. It's so cozy right here. I can find a movie or start blocking in colors for my contest entry—*nope*, my brain reports back. There's not enough capacity to draw right now. Tomorrow. My gaze drifts back to the window, the streetlights. I could just sleep right now.

But then I think of Jade and Athen, maybe Paige, Beeper, or new people I haven't met, sitting around one of those big tables in The Reef. Or huddled around a movie or game on one of the TVs. My body twitches and I glance toward my phone.

I did say I wasn't going to sleep during the con—ever.

Restlessness squirms in my chest. I'll have plenty to deal with after the con. Plenty of time to be alone and reflect and get myself together. I will not have plenty of my people surrounding me or chances to make stupid puns in person with Jade or keep getting to know Paige. I think of how I felt, trying to comfort Nira. Did I think less of her because she had a rotten day and a crummy family life? Not really. Not at all.

Maybe I can face everyone after all. Maybe I should.

I shove from the bed and grab my phone. It's not even ten o'clock! It's still my birthday. While I'm looking at the time, a text buzzes through.

DeeBee: *Thinking of you.*

She follows the words with a frowny face and a pink heart, so I answer her.

Thanks DeeBee. Heading to The Reef if you want to meet up.

Deebee: *Yaaaaaay!*

Followed by a barrage of hearts and flowers that makes me grin. I hop on Twitter. There are more birthday messages, but I don't have time to wade through them right now. I just enjoy the glow in my chest, the soft rekindling of energy.

Finally, I compose a simple tweet:

Purrrrlympian Pixie @MauveCat

Heading to The Reef if anyone wants to wish me happy birthday!

I yank open the dresser and throw together a new outfit. I can't wear the same thing out as what I wore to see my mom in the hospital. Maybe the same shoes. My makeup needs a complete do-over, and you bet I do it so I can feel more Mauve and fresh and fun. A quick tousle of my pink hair is good enough. Ears, tail, and now *paws*.

I leave my drawing stuff and just take my phone. No skateboarding this time; I don't need wheel splash on my leggings or tail when they're still wet from running in the rain with Jade. Haute would never speak to me again. But I clip the tail so it sways as I trot down the sidewalk toward the Weeby. Paige was right, by the way, it's exactly six minutes. Well, five when you're trotting.

It's still packed when I arrive, a circus of people and fursuits that swamps me in happy chaos and floods out any lingering regret or doubt over leaving the hospital. Mom's okay. She's cared for. I'm okay. We're okay—still good.

Suiters pose near the fountain. Clusters of people hang on benches, or in corners, talking. Lulluella's concert is happening upstairs, bass pounding in the walls, and I orient myself toward the ballrooms downstairs.

A couple of people wave at me, and I show off my paws with a wave back. It strikes me that I left my new iPad when I left the party, but I know Jade has it safe somewhere.

When I hit the top of the stairs down to The Reef, I pause again to find my people. And there's Jade, as promised, though he's changed to a sweater, and so has Athen. Actually, there's Beeper, Nira, and Haute . . . it looks like my party drifted here to The Reef because almost everyone who was there is here now. They've changed out of pink party mode since it's chilly, but that's okay.

I'm here to bring the pink.

Giddiness rushes up from my toes and out my mouth. "Hey!"

Jade jerks around and grins, throwing both arms triumphantly into the air with a grin. I twirl my tail. "Any cake left?"

The others look over and I strike a pose, complete with jazz paws, and they cheer in welcome as I trot down to join the group. Paige surges up from her chair, along with Jade, and they both scoop me into a hug.

"Momo!" She sounds worried and relieved, and the whole thing—passing out, police, my dad appearing—comes back, and I realize that the last time they saw me I was leaving in a daze with Dad.

Athen comes over and offers a cup of punch from the party, which he apparently saved. I look at it, then him, with a lopsided grin.

"Waste not, want not," he intones, then cracks a smile. "Glad you're okay."

Paige draws back, swiping hair from her face, and looks me over with a frown. "What happened?"

I glance to Jade, who tilts his head down, eyes lifted encouragingly, then back to Paige. "Let's sit down." I take the punch from Athen with a quick smile and suck a quick breath. "And I'll tell you guys everything."

And they do.

And I do.

And after a little while, the questions are worn out and I soldier through the surprise and pity, but mostly concern. But I'm not an outcast. They just know now. We ease away from the topic, and then we're laughing again and having fun. I cluster people together for some pictures with me to send to Mom and Dad.

After a couple of games, a few of us break off to see the last hour of Luluella's concert so we can dance and say we were there. Someone starts a conga line that snakes around the perimeter of the room. I've got Jade ahead of me and Paige behind, with Marlitoo shaking her purple tail feathers in the rear. It feels like my head will fall off from laughing. I'm only feeling *this*. There's nothing under it—nothing to hide. I told them everything. The door is open and they're inside. Yeah, it's a little messy, but they still love me and here we are.

I get pictures in full-Mauve glory, dancing in Lulu's signature cobalt blue and lime green light, and surrounded by the weird and wonderful that is the furry fandom. Mom will have a barrage of photos to scroll through in the morning.

She needs to see this. I want her to see me happy because I don't think she remembers what that actually looks like. Maybe if she sees what it looks like, she'll understand, and maybe that's what she'll want for me.

And if she sees it's possible for me, maybe she'll believe it's possible for her, too.

I don't know anyone who really likes public speaking, except maybe Paige. It's not a phobia, but it's definitely not something I've done a lot. Or ever, really, unless you count the occasional presentation for class.

I arrive a whole half hour early for my panel with Sunspire and the other artists, Mauve to the nines and shaking like a blender on high.

Also, bleary. I'm pretty sure I went to sleep an hour ago, but that's what coffee's for. My girl at Tidewater hooked me up with a hot version of the raspberry chocolate miracle because it's still raining. Sugar and caffeine infuse strength and goodness into my soul while I press against the wall and wait for the current panel (on drawing perspective, which I couldn't drag myself to; too much thinking and straight lines in the morning) to end.

"Good morning, Mauve!"

I jerk to attention as Sunspire glides down the hall. Yes, glides. Strident and purposeful. My breath drains, so I take another one and lift my venti coffee cup but fail to make words happen, which makes her laugh. Thank God.

She stops near me and hooks her thumbs into her pockets, rolling her shoulders. Her energy is like half prophet, half gym teacher. "Did everything turn out okay last night?"

My lips purse. Right. She was there when the police and Dad arrived, but she was not at The Reef for the explanation.

"Yes. Some things . . . I have some things going on at home. There was a fire—it's okay. I'll tell you about it sometime if you want to know, but it's okay right now. Thanks for asking." I force my voice smooth. I'm glad I told my friends everything last night, or I might have lost it this morning. But this morning, I'm a little stronger. And it must show because Sunspire accepts my answer with a nod and looks to the door.

"Ready to do this? Sorry we didn't get a chance to chat, but I think it will be mostly discussion and audience questions, so we can bounce off each other with Mirka and Soniah like a round table."

It all sounds like something she would say to a fellow professional artist, not a trembling pile of goo in the vague shape of me. Then apologizing that we haven't talked, as if it's her fault, not mine, for being a complete helicopter crash all weekend.

"Yes." I jerk my head in a nod. "Yes. Sounds good." Pathetic. I try to channel some Mauve or Paige energy and lift my chin, picking a few of the words my brain is babbling at me. "I'm really excited. Just um, nervous. I really . . ." My eyes drop to my coffee lid, and I force them up, meeting her sparkling eyes. "Your art means a lot to me. This means a lot to me, and I'm—I'm really honored. I'll try not to mess up." I stop before I can babble, and her whole face lifts and relaxes into a gentle smile.

"You won't mess up. It'll be fine. I think we need more cute, happy art in the world, so I try to encourage it when I see it. I got help and encouragement, and I pass it on. You work hard, and you've got something really special. I think you'll inspire the other young artists." She lifts a hand as if to touch but checks in. I nod from my daze, accepting her compliment, although I'm sure if she touches or hugs me, I'll burst into flames.

But I don't. She squeezes my shoulder and gives me a playful little shake with big-sister energy. "Better wake up! The panel attendees can fall asleep, but we can't."

Her gentle shake dislodges the terror from my stomach, and I manage a nervous laugh. "Don't worry. This will kick in any second." I lift the coffee and she nods, wisely. "Then you won't be able to shut me up."

"Good." She grins, then watches me sternly. "Make sure you speak up when you think of things, okay?"

"Oh sure. I'll just interrupt the guest of honor and two other professionals while people are all, *who are you again?*" I give a firm thumbs-up, sip my coffee by way of a rim shot, and she actually laughs.

Happy bubbles float up in my chest. I did it. I sort of talked to my idol like a normal person. And by the time I get to the bottom of this raspberry potion, I may even banter. Or transform into an actual pixie cat and pinball around the room.

We'll see.

"Oh, and think of an answer for 'where do you get ideas,' because someone will ask you."

"Me?" I laugh.

She nudges me companionably with an elbow. "Yeah, you. Think of the things that inspire you."

I turn a look at her and she's smiling at me, normal, mortal, and warm. Inspiring. "Okay," I manage.

Sunspire turns and leans back next to me, hiking up a foot to rest on the wall, thumbs sliding to hook into her pockets again. I look at her hands, which create all the art I've admired since ever. My gaze draws to her fingernails, and for the first time, I notice every last one is gnawed to the quick. I close my eyes and settle against the wall.

We've all got stuff.

It's an easy quiet, and I count a couple of dots on the carpet, then clear my throat. Maybe it's seeing that, her fingernails, or the way she's so relaxed, that gives me the courage to speak up again. "Um."

Without moving her body, like a big cat, she tips her head my way to listen, and my thumb fidgets against my coffee lid.

"I know this is forward, and maybe a lot, and you don't have to answer right now, but I wanted to see if you might look at my portfolio sometime. When you have time."

She's looking at me now with a growing smile.

"I really want to attend the art institute in Portland. Like, I know a lot of self-taught artists don't go to college, but you've mentioned their illustration program is so good"—the coffee is kicking in—"and the connections are good, and I'm planning to go and get my residency, then apply. So—"

"I would be happy to look at your stuff," Sunspire says, stopping me gracefully before I can blather more. I shut my mouth, sip my coffee, and try to refrain from exploding into pink glitter or happy tears. "And you should apply for the scholarship. If you have any questions about what they like, or if you want a letter, let me know."

The urge to spring into the air like a cat and sprint down the hall is halted only by the sight of people headed our way for the next panel. Our panel. My panel with Sunspire.

Instead, it's a deep breath for me, and I meet the eyes of this artist, this woman, who's just a person like me, trying to help, trying to show me the way. Maybe I'll be in her place someday.

"Thank you. Thank you so, so much."

She grins that wide, fierce, lioness grin. "You're welcome, Mauve."

Then her gaze lifts past me to the people coming, and I look too. All casual and cool, you know. Just another day in the life.

Leading the cluster of people headed our way are Paige, bright-eyed and waving wildly as if I'm a celebrity, and Jade, less bright-eyed but bearing a massive coffee and grinning proudly at me. Athen flanks them and gives me a thumbs up. They came even though it's early. Even though none of them are artists. They're here just for me.

I spot my Angel Dragon fan from Friday, who gives a little wave, and Tristan, who shrugs with a smile, just coming to support. Nira, carrying a sketchbook, grins enthusiastically when she catches my eye, and I grin back. This one will be packed. Oh boy.

The door near us swings open and I jump, then move a few steps away as people stream out, chattering about triple point perspective.

Sunny pushes her weight from the wall and plants her foot, looking at me with a soft grin. "Ready?"

I think about it, taking a breath, checking in. There's a surprising emptiness in my chest where a weight usually is, the tug, the chain. I fear it'll come back tomorrow, there will be things to handle, plans to make, things Mom and I still need to say.

But for now, those are just thoughts, not weight. The emptiness isn't bad. It's space. There's some space, finally, around my heart. Right now, there is the glorious sense that there's only this—this moment that's going to be way too short. But it's the only thing I need to worry about for the next hour.

I roll my shoulders as she did and nod once. I think I am ready. "Let's do this."

20

EPILOGUE

THE LIVING ROOM IN DAD'S apartment is all sunshine.

The great big windows take up a full wall, and the sofa is prime napping territory. This main room is open concept: living room, kitchen, foyer all in one. Not big, but open. Clean. With a normal-person amount of things like potted plants and books and a stray sock here and there. Perfect for a single man and a temporary daughter-roommate.

I check a text from Mom and am glad to see she found a computer to replace the old one, but I don't answer just yet. It's a thing now. I take a little time to answer. It's only been two weeks since Furlympia, and honestly, the dust is still settling. We're all learning new patterns. Mom's burns aren't fully healed, but one of my aunts came to help her get into a new apartment in Little Tree, so I know she's safe and leave a little space. My new therapist reminds me to consider my pain too, not just my mom's.

I am no longer the emergency contact.

When I fall into my old habit of defending Mom or minimizing everything, protecting her and our secrets and the house, my therapist stops me. She reminds me I wasn't hit, but I was *hurt*, it's much the same, and I don't have to protect the person who hurt me. On an airplane they tell you, in the event of an emergency, to secure your own oxygen mask before helping others. So I'm trying to do that.

It's not bad, but it is weird. I feel like she's still super close, like when someone loses a limb and they feel like it's still there. Phantom limb. Only it's a phantom parent, and I'm surprised when I remember she's not in the next room somewhere or in the house. Then I remember there's no house. I definitely have a phantom house, too.

Of course, it couldn't just burn cleanly to ash. There were smoldering filthy walls and melted Stuff and junk, the poor neighbors watching workmen haul everything away. Dad said the lot is clear now, and there wasn't much worth salvaging. I wish I could feel more emotions about it, but the only thing I feel is relief and an occasional sting of bitterness I'm trying to let go of. No one let Mom go see the rubble because they thought it might be painful—but I know what would happen. She would pick through to find stuff. I know it. I know it like I know there are bones in my wrist.

I, however, got to salvage what I could of my things. Quite a few of my artworks survived, and Dad assured me it was not hoarding to keep them. Honestly, when I saw the charred wreckage of the house, it was nauseating to think of saving anything. Like Mom saves things.

But the firemen had thoughtfully taken my things to safety, and I got to pick through to rescue my art bins, a few clothing items not singed or destroyed by smoke, and a couple of books. Jade's tapestry didn't quite survive, and I thought of keeping the little bit of it that wasn't singed, but I let it go. I have Jade. I don't need the thing. I'm not going to keep my soul preserved in things.

Capturing myself in thoughts about Mom and the house, I take a breath, relax, breathe, and look out the window for a second instead to put myself here. In Tacoma. In Dad's living room, in this moment.

Because this is a good moment. I'm closing in on finishing a little sticker commission on my iPad, which definitely has a learning curve, but I love it.

Later, Dad, Paige, and I are heading to Portland to scope out the art institute and investigate living options while I get residency. And of course the bookstore and the art store. After the con, Paige and I vowed to hang out as much as possible this summer before she goes off to her theatre school in Seattle and I go to Portland. It feels like she brings out the best in me. The me I want to be, like the empty space where the house was now has a special, warm spot just for Paige, so I'm going to fill it while I can. Whatever that means for us later, I'm excited to find out.

For now, it means summer road trip! There's a fur-meet while we'll be in Portland and Jade's entering a karaoke contest, so I get to see him sing in front of people for the first time ever. He told me his sisters and his little brother have been watching and commenting on his TikTok, which is amazing. Maybe even if his parents don't approve of art education as a career, he still has family rooting for him. It feels like everything is right. Like the world is opening up all possibilities.

Dad bursts in the front door, fresh from a jog, and slaps a bundle of mail on the counter, huffing and puffing dramatically because he chose to jog on a moist summer morning.

"You got something," he gasps, waving a hand at the mail, and heads off to shower.

With a squeal of glee, I place the iPad carefully on the coffee table like a holy relic, then spring from the sofa because I know what's coming.

Among Dad's bills and a *Forbes* magazine blazes a crisp, cyan envelope with a return address sticker bearing the Furlympia logo.

I hug the envelope and hop onto one of the stools at the counter to open it. First is a letter, boring, and I skip to the certificate officially declaring me the winner of the ninth annual Furlympia art contest. Honestly, I think that incorporating all the notes from Sunspire's color panel tipped me up to a new level. I can't wait to show Dad, just for that, just to show him the whole weekend was worth it.

Now I read the letter, which congratulates me and informs me the piece was successfully auctioned online and all the proceeds sent to the con's chosen charity, Joint Animal Services. I knew I won because they announced it everywhere—Twitter, Facebook (well, I don't have Facebook, but Beeper told me), and the con website. But I might frame this certificate and put it up on my own someday-wall. It can go right next to my perfect attendance award, which stubbornly survived the fire, or maybe above it. Right above it.

Most importantly, it includes my registration code for a super sponsor membership for next year. The theme is "somewhere over the rainbow," and the letter looks hand-signed by Monaghan with a little scrawled, *see you next year!*

Happy pink bubbles rush up my chest. *Yes, you will see me.*

I read the letter again, trace the fancy Furlympian lettering, and then release a slow breath. Armored in my happiness, I send Mom a way-to-go text about her computer, bursting with hearts and flowers, along with a picture of the certificate. It's a little easier.

There's still an invisible cord that binds me to her. She's my *mom*, but every day it's less of a chain. Every day my breath is a little calmer, and the texts from her are less needy and more informative. Every ask, every decision, I give myself space to think it over. The thing binding me to her is less like iron links and more like the thin, silver, un-severable line of love. Love for her and love for myself.

I glance out the window to see a neighbor cat walking the fence between yards across the street. That's all this is, really, a balancing act. On one side, I could fall back into the Stuff. On the other, it's cutting Mom out, which I'm not ready to do as long as she's trying—as long as I can balance. And I think I can. I can walk that line. I'm sure I'll fall once or twice, but that's okay.

Cats always land on their feet.

THE END

ACKNOWLEDGMENTS

IT TAKES A VILLAGE TO make a book. At the top of the list of those to thank will always be those who have always been there: my family. My parents, who steadfastly believed that "writer" was a viable career choice, my favorite sister Jennifer Owen, in whom I am fortunate to have a fellow writer and built-in, lifelong critique partner, and my husband Dax, for his passionate support of my work and for understanding when the writing comes first.

This book was my first dive into traditional publishing, so I will heartily thank my excellent agent Cortney Radocaj, whose unbridled enthusiasm for the book, professionalism, and encouragement have continued to keep me on track and excited for this journey. She has truly been a wonderful match for me and for this project (and hopefully many more).

I am so grateful to my editor, Tamara Grasty of Page Street, not only for connecting with the book and believing in it and me, but for her sharp insights, her sensitivity and thoughtful nurturing of the characters, and for appreciating my corny in-story jokes. Thank you for insisting that we push it to be the best book it can possibly be.

I have several first readers for this story, whose commentary helped me whip it into shape from idea to story. As always, Kate Millward, my dear friend, whose constructive critique of any genre is unparalleled, and for her cheerleading and all the gold stars. Fellow writer and wildlife artist L.V. Adams, whose comments on the manuscript and the query itself helped me to solidify what the actual conflict of the story was. Mason Brubaker, for observations on the con life, furry culture, and the emotional arc of the characters. My friend Annie Rottenbiller, for reading and lending her special expertise on social work, family dynamic, and her own questions and emotional journey through the story. And my "birthday twin" Lauren Head for reading and connecting emotionally to the story and the character, and her unending support and puns through the years.

Thanks also to Dennis Foley of Authors of the Flathead for his inspiring dedication and service to the writing community. His classes and talks have inspired me to improve my craft daily while also making this writing life seem imminently doable. He is an inspiration in more ways than one.

Finally, I want to thank the furry community for just being themselves. I wrote and published an indie fantasy series that brought me into their world, and they welcomed me into the community with open arms (and paws and wings, etc). To my friends and colleagues in the Furry Writers Guild, thank you for your support. To the suiters, artists, authors, fans, con-organizers and volunteers, musicians, patrons, and the rest of the absolutely bonkers tapestry of people who make up what "Furry" is—here's to you.

ABOUT THE AUTHOR

JESSICA KARA IS A PROFESSIONAL author and artist. With a BFA in technical theater, she worked as a stage manager for eight years in regional theaters and on several national tours. Eventually, she left the business to focus on writing, which has always called. She has served as President of her local writing organization, Authors of the Flathead, and is a member of the Society for Children's Book Writers & Illustrators. She frequently speaks at local conferences, schools, and college classes, striving to inspire a new generation of writers to pursue their passions.

Jess has indie published a young adult fantasy series featuring gryfon characters and is excited to dive into the pool of contemporary young adult fiction. She currently resides in northwest Montana with her husband, spends her time staring at the mountains, drinking a lot of coffee, dreaming up things and people, and chirping back at birds.

Her stories, whether fantastic or contemporary, are noblebright at their core, woven with a spirit of determined hope, belief in the power of kindness, and the faith that good will overcome.